CRYSTAL CLEAR

A NOVEL BY BARBARA COMBS WILLIAMS

ISBN: 978-1-7336352-1-9
2020 A REMEMBER TOO DESIGN

A REMEMBER TOO DESIGN©2010

Thank You!

I want to thank so many people for helping me make this second novel of the Mattock family saga, *Crystal Clear,* possible. There is of course my wonderful husband Heyward, who without his influence this past forty years, I never would have even started writing. He's my muse, my confidant and the shining light that directs me forwards.

Thanks to our lovely daughter Nicole who gave me so much help with understanding millennials and what makes them tick. She guided me through the world of emoji's, texting and 21st century nomenclature.

Thank you Candice, my editor. Without her help, none of this would be happening. You got me to put it to paper and to never stop. You cheered me on despite my reluctance. You told me to share my writing with the world, so here it is.

And last, but never least is Mrs. Evelyn S. Combs, my mother who transcended this world October 2019. Her love and guidance gave me all the inspiration to go above and beyond. A mother's love is eternal.

Thank you all from the bottom of my heart!
Barbara @ www.BarbaraCombsWilliams.com

Foreword

This book is for every woman, no matter the age, race or creed, who mistakenly believes she no longer matters to the people in her life and the world. Never doubt the positive influence you have on others. Without you in their lives, they will never become the people they are meant to be.

Remember, everyone has a story to tell. Be brave enough to tell yours.

Chapter One

Chrystal Marie Mattock stood up from the floral-patterned sofa and walked over to the glass front door. She looked out onto the perfectly manicured yard surrounding her grandmother's house. Dusk was settling, but she could still see the lush green lawn and the multi-hued flowers blooming in the late afternoon sunshine if she so chose.

Chrystal ignored the vibrant blues, reds, and yellows. They could have been suspended a hundred feet in the air doing cartwheels, and she would still have given them no notice. There were beautiful magnolia trees and meticulously trimmed shrubs everywhere one cared to look, but she took no interest in any of it. She only saw inward, and any beauty there was smothered with distrust, dishonesty, and self-loathing.

1

She was twenty-three years old with three children. The oldest, Jewell, was almost five. Her middle child, Oro, was three, and the youngest, Jade, was sixteen months. Chrystal started on this path early, and to date, she was still treading stubbornly along it.

She loved her babies, all three of them. Yet, she was little more than a child herself. Sometimes it was so hard to show them love and care for them as she imagined a good mother should. Maybe if she had a better example, or maybe if her parents hadn't divorced when she was twelve, then she wouldn't suck so badly at parenting. Maybe if she hadn't been so hell-bent on showing her mother, Jackie, that she didn't care, then maybe she wouldn't have been a single mom with three different baby daddies.

If things had been different, then maybe at least one of the daddies would take some responsibility. *Yeah right, like when blazing hot hell froze over.* Even Chrystal knew that was a hell of a lot of maybes. She was at the point where she hated just about everyone and everything. Most of all she hated herself for what she had let herself become.

Chrystal spoke aloud to the silent room, thinking of her mother. "I didn't want to keep secrets from Mama. So many times, I wanted to tell her the truth. I tried to talk about my feelings, and I even tried to bring up the subject of Daddy, but she didn't want to hear it. So I thought maybe if I had something to use . . . to bargain with. If I knew something she didn't, something she didn't want anyone else to know . . ." She hesitated for a moment and continued in a sing-song voice.

"I thought, you know, Mama would do what I wanted. I thought she might try to love me. I don't know. It's been so hard for me. I just wanted something that was only mine.

2

Something special. To make me feel special." Chrystal took a deep breath and absent-mindedly wiped at the tears on her cheeks. She stood eerily still, poised in the frame of the door, a tragically lovely silhouette.

"She only had time for Royce. She didn't love me. Sometimes I felt like she didn't even see me. She loved only him. He could do no wrong. But everything I did was wrong."

She looked around at the faces of her family. There was her father, Jimmy. His significant other, Bryan. Her grandmother, Ms. Sylvi who sat huddled into herself beside her daughter and Chrystal's aunt, Nancy. Chrystal's mother Jackie and Jackie's lover Eric escaped into the kitchen. She couldn't blame her mother for that. She desperately wanted to escape from the awful truth herself.

Someone in the room made a noise as if they wanted to interrupt, but hurriedly said, "Excuse me," and the silence resumed from the listeners.

Chrystal continued, as if she had to get the words out or else she would explode. "He . . . Royce was the baby boy, the do-gooder. Whatever he wanted, he got. I even tried to do what he did, but Mama still didn't notice me. I wasn't smart like him. I didn't make all As, talk geek talk, or speak a foreign language. It was like I didn't even exist in her eyes." Everything was so clear now, but back then, she couldn't see. All she did was feel.

She continued her sad soliloquy. No one interrupted. There was no throat clearing and not even a sigh was heard. She stood amid her family. Her grandmother, Ms. Sylvi, silently rocked back and forth, as if doing so would banish all the hurt from her granddaughter.

3

Her mother's only sibling, Nancy, gave her a look that somehow questioned Chrystal's honesty in what she was saying. And finally, her father and Bryan, stared at Chrystal as if she was a tiny little alien blob under a microscope.

Crystal gave a huge sigh. "You know, Royce and I could have done the same bad thing, but it was me who was punished. He was the golden child. The explanation was always the same. 'He couldn't have possibly done that. He's not that kind of boy.'" Silver tears rained down her soft cheeks. "That's what she, Mama, would always . . . always . . . say. I guess she meant I was that kind of bad girl."

She finally turned from the door and looked at her father, Jimmy, sitting on the sofa. She scrubbed at her face as if there was some foreign matter there. There were big liquid drops of pain in her hazel eyes. Chrystal still wore the beautiful jade green dress she had worn to her brother's wedding. It fit her like a glove. The only adjustment was to her stiletto heels; she had kicked them off as she put the children down for their naps.

"Nobody loved me but Daddy, and then he went away, when Mama made him go away. I felt like a big useless nothing and I knew it was all her fault." She fingered a gold, heart-shaped necklace around her slender neck. She held on to it as if it were her lifeline. Chrystal broke down and cried like her baby girl Jade. There was nothing street or hood about her now.

Her father got up from the sofa and went to Chrystal and hugged her tight.

Nancy confronted Chrystal with steel in her voice. "How could you speak of your mother like this?"

4

Chrystal finally sat down on the empty sofa, but it was obvious she was distressed and didn't quite know what she was saying or doing. Her head snapped back with every word her aunt uttered.

"I saw her fight hard to do everything she could for you and Royce," Nancy said. "She has given her soul and paid the devil with her very lifeblood to take care of you two. And yes, Jimmy you are the devil. How could you think she was the only problem behind your parents' breakup? I don't have time for this mess. I'm going to check on the babies." Nancy stood up from her hard chair and turned to go out of the room.

Chrystal twisted her hands together and shook almost as if she had a chill. She jumped up again as Nancy started to leave. Nancy stopped in her tracks and turned back to look at Chrystal as Chrystal shouted, "Aunt Nancy, you just don't understand! You weren't in the house with us. You don't know what it was like for me. I know you never cared about me anyway. But Daddy loved me. Me, his only daughter. It seemed Mama didn't want us to be together. It was like she was jealous of the relationship we had. I don't know. I tried so hard to be good like Royce and no matter what I did, it didn't matter. You don't know what I went through. Nobody cared how I felt. How many times do I have to say I'm sorry? Okay!"

Jimmy came over to Chrystal where she stood, still breathless and crying. "That's enough, Nancy! Stop trying to make Chrystal into your whipping post. She is no more guilty of hurting her mother than Royce is, but you've always held Chrystal up as the bratty poster child. I will not allow you and Jackie to continue to harass my child."

Jimmy gave Nancy a look that could melt concrete and Nancy returned the look tenfold. There was definitely no love between the two. Jimmy took Chrystal's small hand into his large ones and pulled her close.

"Your mother and I loved you from day one. In fact before you were even born. But, I guess I didn't help any by filling your head with my anger at her for leaving me like she did. She has never done anything to hurt you or Royce. It was always about what was best for you."

"But, Daddy, I saw and I heard how she treated you. I wanted to run away so many times. She never had a nice word to say about you. She didn't even want me to say your name in her house. I hated being with her and Royce." Chrystal wiped at her eyes. They shone golden with tears.

"Yes, I can imagine that's how you felt. But some of it was how I made it look also. It was what I wanted you to believe. I didn't think about much back then except what I wanted. I didn't care how I hurt your mother, as long as I got what I wanted."

Bryan stepped up to Jimmy and stood on the other side of Chrystal and hugged her.

Jimmy said, "This isn't easy for me to admit, but your mother put up with a lot. I didn't treat her right from the beginning. I did some very mean and childish things to her. I wasn't true to myself." He looked at Bryan over Chrystal's head and smiled.

"I loved you all the best way that I could. But when things went bad, I only wanted to hurt your mother for what I felt was her betrayal. Like I said I have done some terrible things to her. We don't need to go into it now, but I played a huge part in your mother's and my breakup."

Jimmy stood back from Chrystal but continued to hold her in his long arms. "I never thought things would deteriorate to this degree between the two of you. For that, I will always be sorry. Please forgive me."

"I want to. I want to more than anything. I want to love Mama like a true daughter should. But I've made too many mistakes, I've done too many things that I'm so ashamed of. I've said things to her that I can't take back. I don't know if she can forgive me." *Really, I don't know if I can forgive myself.*

Later, Chrystal sat quietly in a corner while the rest of her family moved silently around her. She thought about what her aunt and father said. She wondered if she'd only seen what she wanted to see, blaming her mother for things way out of her control.

She scrolled through the years, recalling all the boys and men she'd let use her. All the times she looked for love in all the wrong places. All the substitute daddies, and even mamas, she searched out. Each time, she convinced herself they would love her, and only her, for always. She would be worth something more by being seen through their eyes.

She remembered Jewell's daddy, Jason Bailey. Although none of the males she had been with deserved that term of respect. They all were the furthest thing imaginable from being a true father. They were only sperm donors.

She was only sixteen, but she knew Jason was sent from heaven to rescue her. Her prayers had finally been answered. She poured all her childish fantasies of love and marriage into

7

that relationship. He would take her away and treat her like the princess she knew she deserved to be. She would show her mother she was worth loving, that someone cared about her.

Jason was so very handsome with his black curly hair, which he twisted into dreadlocks, and the most beautiful almond-shaped eyes. He had that smooth burnt-honey skin, miraculously free from pimples. All the girls ran behind him. He was a senior, and she didn't want to lose him to another girl, so she had given him the gift of her virginity.

She knew something just didn't feel right though, and she definitely didn't like the sex, but if that was what he wanted, then she was in it for the long run. Chrystal knew he was special to her, and she thought she was the same to him. There was nothing she wouldn't have done for Jason. She met him when and where he said. She gave him everything she had, physically and emotionally.

Sometimes the little voice would whisper, *Why do you let him disrespect you like this? You know you're too young to be doing these things. And besides, you don't even like doing it.* But she did it anyway and told the little voice to shut the hell up. It didn't know Jason like she did.

The word no wasn't in her vocabulary when it came to him. She thought the sun rose and set on his perfect smile and the only thing she asked for in return was his love. No one could make her see that he was only using her.

He told her she was beautiful and smart. He said he couldn't believe she'd picked him out of all the boys at school. He convinced her she was the only one he cared about. But he never said he loved her. Besides, what does a teenage boy know about love? His hormones ruled his feelings, but she felt so special with all the attention and praise Jason showered her with.

She didn't question why he didn't want to be seen with her at school. She thought he wanted to keep what they had private. If his treatment of her was less than gentlemanly, she didn't mind. She liked his macho act, and his bad-boy attitude thrilled her in a way that only a sixteen-year-old girl could appreciate.

And she bought it all and strutted around with her head held high, secure in her knowledge that she was loved by the most popular boy in school.

It didn't matter how many other girls were envious of her. She wanted them to be. *See what I have and you don't.* Her one and only girlfriend, Chantrelle, cautioned her to take it slow, not to believe everything Jason told her.

Chrystal made it clear that, if she wanted Chantrelle's advice, she would ask for it, and since she hadn't, just shut the hell up. Her friend dropped the subject. Chrystal didn't make and keep girlfriends easily, if at all.

She didn't realize she was just bragging rights for Jason. He joked with his football buddies how he had turned out the little sophomore girl. She was ready and eager to do whatever he wanted. "Man, she is some kind of freak for sure," Jason told his friends.

She didn't question why his friends whispered and rudely called her name every time she passed them in the hallway. She was young and naive and so in love. She didn't know the first thing about true love or sex, but she quickly found out. Like most kids her age who wanted to grow up too fast, she met a dismal fate head on. For as soon as she found herself pregnant, he disappeared. She was another statistic, an anonymous name to add to the list of similarly, foolishly, unfortunate girls.

Chrystal remembered the day and the time she told him she was going to have his baby. It was a Wednesday, and the bell had rung for third period. She managed to catch him before he went into the boy's bathroom. She wanted a more romantic spot, but he'd been distant lately and they hadn't met like they used to.

"Jason," she yelled out. "I have the most wonderful news. I've been waiting to tell you." She could barely get the words out; she was so nervous. Quieter she said, "you're going to be so happy. You're going to be a daddy. I'm pregnant."

He looked at her as if she was a stranger with three heads. Then he did the worst thing imaginable; he actually laughed in her face. "You might be having a baby, but it sure ain't mine," he said. "I got five friends who'll swear they had sex with you too. Everybody knows you just a little football ho."

She was devastated. She couldn't believe he would do this to her. She couldn't have been more surprised if he'd spit on her and then rub it into her face.

He gave her a look as if she was smelly, discarded trash left at the curb, and then he practically ran into the restroom, all the while roughhousing with some of his friends. She could hear them through the door, laughing at her. She was a joke to them.

The man of her dreams had become the tormentor of her worst nightmares. She silently escaped to the girl's restroom, to stall number thirteen, where she let the tears fall. She didn't make it to her next class. She cut school and went home, where her mother, Jackie, found her later. She was still crying off and on, but she told her mother it was bad cramps.

Her mother took that answer and didn't question further.

Jackie didn't really want to look any further for the truth. Her own life was a misery, and in many ways, she believed Chrystal didn't deserve any better. They had never communicated well, so Chrystal's behavior didn't surprise her.

But Jason was the first in a long line of males who would do this to her and break her heart into tiny little fragments until she had none left. It never occurred to her that she sought out this kind of person, as if she wanted to be punished and made miserable. She withdrew even more into herself, believing she deserved this and much more.

Chrystal had no one to turn to. Her cousin Nikki had been the cheerleader, telling her how to get a senior boy. "Girl, you know you got to put out to hold on to a senior. You can't expect him to stay with you just on some kissing. Go on and put it on your man before some other hoochie be getting all up in his face."

But when she ran to Nikki, telling her she missed her period, Nikki laughed, "I told you to put it on him, not to go raw dog. Girl, you so stupid!"

They went to the drugstore, pooling all their money to buy a pregnancy kit. Of course, she was pregnant, and her cousin Nikki hissed at her. "You better tell your mama cause there ain't nothing I can do for you now. You just so stupid."

Of course, she was ignorant and naive, but no one deserved this punishment for being young and in love.

Her girlfriend, Chantrelle, looked on with pity in her eyes. She wanted to help, but she knew to keep her mouth shut. Nothing she said would change what was anyway.

Chrystal couldn't go to her mother. She was too ashamed. Her mother would never understand. They didn't have that kind of relationship. She could barely talk with her mother about schoolwork. They never had that chummy mother-daughter relationship some families had. Even Nikki and her mom got along better than she and hers. Her mother didn't care about Chrystal's broken heart. Chrystal believed her mother only cared about herself.

She wanted to go to her daddy, but she knew it would be worse than with her mother. She didn't want her daddy to know she'd been so careless and stupid. He wouldn't love her anymore. She wouldn't be his little princess ever again. She felt like used dirty rags.

She was so heartbroken she couldn't talk about Jason or what she'd been through. She stopped going to school. Months passed, and no one was the wiser or even seemed to care. Letters and phone calls came to the house about her absences, but she intercepted them before her mother suspected. She left for school as normal but doubled back home after her mother left. Later she hung out at the mall, the library or fast food restaurants. She wasn't missed and nobody made a big issue out of it.

She tried to hide her pregnancy for as long as she could. Jackie was so preoccupied with her sad life that she didn't even notice the weight gain or the big shirts her daughter wore. Chrystal was eight months pregnant when she had no choice but to come out with it. She wouldn't answer when her mother pleaded with her to tell her who. They became even more distant.

Chrystal kept to her room as much as possible. She avoided her younger brother, Royce, as if he had the plague. But Royce would come and sit quietly in her room anyway. She threw him out, over and over, because she couldn't stand the pity in his eyes.

Even after she delivered a healthy, beautiful baby girl, while suffering through the pains of five hells, she still wouldn't tell them who the father was. Silence was all that was heard when the hospital clerk asked for the father's name for the birth record. She would only say she wanted to name the baby Jewell.

She loved the name because it reminded her of her favorite singer. Chrystal thought, if her daughter started out with a unique and beautiful name, she would be ahead of the game for the life Chrystal wanted her to have. She wanted more love for her baby than she had, and she was determined that Jewell would get it.

She couldn't go back to school afterwards. Everyone would know what happened and laugh at her. She could never face Jason or his friends again anyway. So she let Jason go and wouldn't even whisper his name to herself. She would see him at a distance, sometimes, at the mall, but she always turned away before he noticed her and the baby. Why did the people you thought loved you always treat you the worst and abandon you when you needed them most?

And now here she stood, years later, smarter than when she was seventeen, but her life was still no better.

Chrystal's brother, Royce, and his wife, Jessica, had left to go on their honeymoon, out of the fray that he'd instigated by inviting an old lover of their mother's to the wedding. Royce wasn't concerned about her anyway, she thought. And the Miss Thang, Jessica, that he married had never been a friend of hers.

So she sat on the sofa alone, the only one in the house under the age of twenty-five, besides her babies.

She wished the floor would open up and swallow her whole, sending her straight to hell. There's where she belonged, although it felt like she was in hell here on earth. She was so very tired of everything. There had to be somebody, someone who would understand and not condemn her.

No one ever really cared about what happened to her. She felt like a throwaway that nobody needed or wanted. And now it seemed her father had been using her as well. She was a means to get back at her mother, a tool to be used, and when broken beyond repair, discarded. She wasn't worthy of being loved, respected, and cherished.

She looked over at her father and his Bryan. They were sitting on the sofa, fuming still about the tell-all that had been going on since Royce and Jessica's wedding reception.

And what do you even call a fifty-something homosexual partner of your father? She didn't think boyfriend fit. She didn't think they'd gotten married either. As liberal-minded as she thought herself to be, that idea was still kind of hard to take. Which one was the husband, or were both husbands?

When her father told her about Bryan, she didn't really let it sink in. She was still so angry with her mother that anything her father did was just great. He could have told her he just got back from visiting Neptune with Donald Duck and she wouldn't have blinked an eye. She didn't question any of it.

It wasn't until today that she found out that Bryan and her father had been together since before her parents were married, since college in fact. She had thought her crazy mother had driven Jimmy into a man's arms.

When she was younger she thought she had seen something on the internet about that being possible for a man to change like that. But now she knew he'd been gay all along. It was hard for her to believe anything he said now. Was he just using her to torture her mother. Some of the things he had done to help her, now didn't sound so caring and giving as when they happened. Who was telling the truth, and did she really want to hear any more of it?

Still, it was supposed to be a beautiful, romantic wedding for Royce and Jessica. It was held at a small chapel with blush roses adorning the altar and sparkling champagne for the reception. Royce and Jessica had even written their own vows, and when they recited them, it brought tears of joy to every eye.

But unbeknownst to everyone but Royce and Jessica, Royce had invited an old friend of their mother as a surprise. It was such a surprise that their mother, Jackie, fainted when she locked eyes with her old friend Eric.

Now she was in the kitchen with him, Eric, the man Crystal used to call uncle. And it seemed Eric was actually her mother's lover and Royce's biological father. What a hellish day it had been. Her brother was really her half-brother. If it wasn't so serious, she would laugh at all the craziness that had been revealed.

And to add to the confusion and her misery, every lowlife person she knew had also shown up at the wedding. Her double-crossing cousin, Nikki, and that no good wanna-be pimp, Calvin, aka Smoke, had shown up and marched down the aisle like royalty. She'd had enough trouble with them the night before. She thought back to Friday night.

Friday night, the Bluff - Chrystal

Chrystal found it hard to believe this shit was really happening to her. This had to be a joke Nikki and Smoke were playing on her. But nobody was laughing. She was being accused of taking some of the money from the drug people she was to deliver the money to. She didn't have their ten thousand dollars, and she sure as hell didn't have the stuff. In fact, she wasn't even sure what was going on. *This has got to be some Nikki mess, trying to set me up.*

Duck, the so-called leader of the group, thumped Chrystal on her head with his fist and said, "This couple of dollars don't even come close to what we agreed to with Smoke. You know, baby girl, ain't no free rides. You always got to pay somehow, some way."

For the first time in her short life, Chrystal understood real fear. She looked at the people Nikki had sent her to in the Bluff and wanted to strangle that bitch. This guy, Duck, was involved in for-real gangster shit, and she couldn't talk her way out of this.

Duck looked like the worst evil villain she'd ever seen. He had a bald head and a full, thick beard streaked with orange. He wore a greasy, tight tee-shirt emblazoned with a black laughing skull across the front. His look mirrored the tee-shirt's crazy smile.

Another one of the gang members wore nasty pants that were sagged so low he was gonna trip every time he took a step. The smell in the room, coming from him, was enough to gag flies around a dump truck.

Finally, the used-up trick they had with them was old enough to be Chrystal's mother and didn't have five good teeth in her mouth. Duck called her Cutie Doll. She had on a dirty wrap dress that was four sizes too small. There was no way in hell that dress could close. Cutie Doll left it gaping, showing off way too much skin and torn lace panties.

Chrystal knew she had to come up with something quick, something to take their attention off her. "Wait a minute, y'all. I think I can get in touch with Smoke. Just give me a second to find out what's going on. My girl, Nikki, told me y'all were cool with everything."

Duck laughed crazily and said, "We ain't cool with this. Bitch, you and Nik is crazy." He fingered the tattoo of a serrated dagger running up and down his thick arm. His message was very clear.

Chrystal frantically hit Nikki on her cell. Her fingers shook so badly she could barely hold the phone. *That skank better answer*, she thought, and to her overwhelming relief, Nikki finally did.

"Girl, where Smoke? These people keep asking about where the rest of their money is. They say there's not enough here."

Nikki popped her gum and answered, "Chrystal, what you calling me for?"

Frantically, Chrystal yelled into the phone, "Is Smoke there with you? I need to talk to him real quick."

Nikki, much too calmly replied, "Yeah, and what about it? Bitch, you supposed to be handling our business not calling me. But hold on, here Smoke."

"What?" was all Smoke said as he took the phone from Nikki.

"Hey, Smoke, Duck say the count ain't right. I told him I didn't know anything about that. You need to tell him yourself."

Chrystal was so afraid she didn't wait for Smoke to answer. She handed the phone to Duck.

Duck gave her a nasty look and said, "Yo man, this ain't even the right count. You know what I mean. Yeah, well, you better get your black ass down here, or honey gonna be swimming in the Chattahoochee."

Duck looked at Chrystal and laughed. "You know you one pretty bitch, but we want our money, so I would hate to see you not looking as pretty as you were when you came in here. Fat ass Smoke better get up off his monkey ass and get here quick. I'll give him twenty minutes before I start hitting."

A silent crystal tear rolled from the corner of her eye. *These crazy people are for real. I hope and pray Smoke get here quick. Please Lord, please! What a shitty-ass way to make a living and I fell like a fool right into the trap.*

Duck cracked his knuckles, Saggy Jeans belched loudly, and Cutie Doll, the crackhead ho, looked at Chrystal like she was her next meal.

Nikki and that stank-ass Smoke came to the wedding like they had no knowledge of the night before. They tried to act like it hadn't even happened. Chrystal had to tell them off, right there at her brother's reception. As she thought back to the events that happened at the wedding, she remembered the look on their faces when she cussed them out, and she almost smiled.

Chrystal had looked at Nikki and Smoke as if she couldn't believe they actually had the nerve to show up. And to top the whole thing off they couldn't look more ghetto if they tried. Smoke looked like a clown in his big, sloppy suit. And it looked grimy and smelled worse. She didn't know they still made mess like that. In fact she was sure he probably got it from a run-down thrift store somewhere.

The tight, short shit Nikki wore looked like it came straight from the dollar store. And every seam was stretched so tight, she looked like a rubber banded watermelon about to pop. Her fat titties were pushed up so high they bounced against her chin with every step she took. If she bent over half an inch, all her fat ass would be hanging out and her breasts would fall out the top.

"I would have thought you were recuperating after last night Calvin," said Chrystal in a sugary sweet voice, calling him by his real name just to irritate him. "Oh, my bad! I'm the one who should be recuperating, considering I was beat up by your no-good friends."

"Chrystal, you're always the drama queen," said Nikki as she gave Chrystal the side eye. "I don't see a scratch on you. You're just making shit up as usual. Boo-hooing about nothing."

Calvin tried to jump in the conversation as if he were an invited guest. "Yeah, what I tell you? You always talk too damn much. You ain't that smart, bitch. I told you to respect grown folks. Now get your ass out of our way so we can congratulate the happy couple."

Smoke and Nikki tried to push past Chrystal, but she didn't budge.

"Look here, bitches. Don't make me get ugly here at my brother's wedding. You and Smoke know damn well what happened last night. Sending me over there with those crazy ass thugs. You knew some of that damn money wasn't there when you sent me. Now you both got the nerve to show up here and act like I did something stupid. You both come here like somebody want you here and got the audacity to call me names. Nikki, you family too."

Nikki popped her gum and mumbled, "Yeah, whatever. Your Mama invited me and Calvin is my escort, so there."

Chrystal shook her head at both of them. "I never thought you would stoop this low, but I got too much respect for my real family to get into some mess with y'all. I'm not going to play games with you, Nikki, and certainly not you, Smoke."

Chrystal continued to tell them both off. "I am through with you both, and I mean what I say, and I'm ready to back it up.

Don't be causing no shit up in here. Get your little feed on—
like either one of you need more food—then you both get the
hell out of here and out of my life. All I want to see is the back
of both of y'all fat asses as you walk out that door."

Chrystal couldn't help but be discouraged about her life. She
was so tired of the street life, and she had to finally admit she
wasn't the least bit street and didn't want to be. Really, she
wanted to curl up beside her babies and sleep until it was all
forgotten. Although that might take a thousand years.

She was cried out, worried out, just plain put out. If this
wasn't some Jerry Springer kind of shit, then nothing was. Her
whole family was dysfunctional as hell and seemed to be
trying to outdo each other for the title of most screwed up.

She sat quietly on the sofa hoping to draw less attention to
herself, but her grandmother, who everyone called Ms. Sylvi
out of respect, came and put her arm around Chrystal. Jimmy
and Bryan had gone into a back bedroom for a quiet moment
together. So had Nancy escaped to the back to check on the
small children.

Ms. Sylvi was the matriarch of the Stinson family, Jackie's
mother. Chrystal was a firm believer that her grandmother
hated her. Maybe hate was too strong; dislike was probably a
better word. Chrystal had let everyone down so many times
over the years that the only expectations her grandmother had
of her was she would only do worse. Chrystal was the older of
the two grandchildren and should have set a better example
for her brother. But here she was with three children,

unmarried and not even a baby daddy in the picture. That was a serious problem. In the Bible days, she guessed, she would have been stoned to death.

Her grandmother had disliked her, so the story went, since she was a baby, but she loved Chrystal's father, Jimmy. He could do no wrong in Ms. Sylvi's eyes. It seemed she preferred him over her own daughter, Jackie. At least, that was, until today. Today, everybody heard all about how Jimmy had been having an affair with Bryan since before he even married her mother. Chrystal had no idea her father had done those things. He didn't deny it, so it must be the truth. All these years she'd wrongly blamed her mother for the breakup, when in reality, her father started it all with his lies and double life.

Homosexuality was a sin that would send someone straight to hell, according to Ms. Sylvi. Jimmy had definitely lost some of his shine as far as she was concerned. It was probably even too late to repent and change his evil ways. But it didn't look like he would anyway since he had been comfy as hell on the sofa with Bryan. So maybe now Chrystal wasn't the highest on the list of ungodly people in her grandmother's eyes. Maybe now Ms. Sylvi could actually come to love her just like she loved her brother Royce.

Her father's family was a totally different matter. They were as different from her mother's people as night was from day. Something was just off about them. They didn't seem to like her mother or even their own son, Jimmy. Chrystal had only seen them a couple of times in her life. She remembered when they came to town from Denver when she was around ten. In fact, it was right before her parents' divorce. Even through a child's eyes, it topped the list as the most awkward interview she ever endured.

That day, her grandfather looked them over as if she and her brother were something that needed to be fixed. Not a single smile crossed his face. He hit them with question after question about their school life until she gave up trying to answer. Chrystal thought he had to be the meanest Scrooge she'd ever seen. He didn't seem very impressed with her anyway.

But her brother, Royce, was treated totally differently. Their grandfather couldn't get enough of him. Chrystal finally went into the kitchen with her mother to hide out. Later, she found out from Royce that their grandfather wanted them to call him Grandfather James and his wife was to be called Grandmother MaryBeth.

They never did seem like grandparents to her. It didn't feel genuine even when Grandmother MaryBeth came into the kitchen and tried to hold a conversation with her and her mother. MaryBeth was a beautiful lady, but she held herself back as if she would take flight at any moment. They all tried, but it was so obvious that none of them had anything remotely in common. Her grandmother gripped her hands so tightly that they turned red and showed the prints of her nails on her palms.

No one could find a topic to discuss. After the weather came "how's everyone doing" and then silence. It was as if she was afraid her husband would come in the kitchen and catch her doing something sinful, like having fun. Everything about them was uncomfortable and felt so phony that neither Chrystal nor Royce ever accepted their invitations to come visit. They did pity their grandmother, but not even pity could change their minds.

Chrystal's grandparents on her mother's side were like a breath of fresh air in comparison. Ms. Sylvi was a petite, seventy-six-year-old, silver-haired woman. She still had a wrinkle-free, light-brown complexion with light-brown eyes. She appeared to be frail and helpless, but she had the strength of ten women double her size. She also possessed a wit that could heal or cut clean as a scalpel.

Ms. Sylvi lived alone now in a rambling, mid-century ranch home in Atlanta. Chrystal's grandfather, Buddy, had added room after room onto the house as the years went by. It now looked and felt like a maze, but they had been so proud of the house. Chrystal had loved to run through the house as a child. Her grandfather had treated her like a little princess with the time he spent with her.

Their home was their first and only property purchase. They'd loved and lived there for more than fifty years, raising their family as they thought a good Christian family should. Her grandfather had been gone for more than two years. He had been the one calming element that kept the family together. Chrystal really missed him and the gentle way he always showed he cared.

Ms. Sylvi leaned into Chrystal and said, "I think I hear the babies. They're probably about ready to wake up. I don't know how they could have slept through all that carrying on, but they did. Nancy went back there to check on them. I feel so tired myself. I don't think I can take any more news today. How about you? Are you all right?"

"Yeah, Grandma, I'm tired too. I think I'm going to gather up the kids and go home."

Chrystal gave her grandmother a real hug, and Ms. Sylvi held on to her even tighter.

24

"You don't have to go home. You know I got plenty of room here for all of y'all. I can cook us all a little something and we can watch some television. What's that movie the little ones like to watch so much?" asked Ms. Sylvi as she moved to take her seat.

"You mean *Frozen*? They do like that movie. I don't know why. I must have seen it ten thousand times since it came out. And Jade doesn't even understand what's going on. She just laughs with the others."

Ms. Sylvi stood up to go in the kitchen. "Well, let's do that. I could use the company if you don't mind. In fact I feel like I really need y'all company. Too many secrets been revealed, and I'm aching something terrible for your mother. Imagine, Jimmy deceiving me about his real self for so long and your mama is the true victim. I got to make it up to her somehow."

Ms. Sylvi stood still for a moment. She looked lost in thought before she finally said, "For too long I put all the blame on Jackie as to why their marriage failed. I understand now. No woman could have put up with that. I can't blame your mama for looking elsewhere for love. I'm gonna see if Jackie and Eric are still in the kitchen. Why don't you let your housemate know you and the kids are staying the night? We don't want her worrying about you all."

"Okay, just let me call Chantrelle and then I'll meet you in the kitchen." Chrystal looked at her grandmother as she leaned on her chair for support. She knew her grandmother was a strong woman, especially since her grandfather was killed in a terrible car accident. But even Ms. Sylvi now seemed so lonely. She was jumping at any chance to keep her great grandchildren around her. And Chrystal thought, *she's so lonely she even wants me here too.*

25

Before Ms. Sylvi turned around, Jackie's older sister, Nancy, came out of the back. She was the second in command if anybody was. She'd never been married and had no children, but she knew how to gather everybody together and likewise how to shut them down and put them in their place.

Nancy looked a lot like her late father in that she was very statuesque. She was also several shades darker than her mother, but she had the same facial features and curly silver hair as Ms. Sylvi. She also had the same wit and used it at every opportunity that presented itself. That wit could cut large men down to size in a heartbeat. But there was always something hovering around her smile that belied the mellow, jovial persona she presented. If you looked deeper, you could see pain deep in her chocolate eyes.

"Jackie just called me," Nancy said. "She and Eric slipped out the kitchen door while everybody was still out here crying and telling all. She said Eric was taking her home and not to worry. She's all right. And the kids are just waking up and starting to play a little. I heard Jimmy and Bryan whispering back there in the bedroom next to the kids. They're a real mess. I can't blame Jackie and Eric for wanting to get away from their ass."

"Well, I can understand Jackie and Eric not wanting to come back this way too. I still can't believe some of the things I heard today. I know it's the truth because I can see it in the children's faces. And Jimmy and Bryan, that is just more than my poor Christian soul can take." Ms. Sylvi's steps faltered as she again leaned heavily upon Chrystal.

Chrystal hugged her again and Ms. Sylvi seemed to stand a little straighter and shake off the melancholy threatening to overcome her. "Chrystal and the kids are going to stay the night. Why don't you stay too? You know I got plenty of room. I could use the company. We can have a pajama party," said Ms. Sylvi as she walked Chrystal towards the kitchen, winking at her granddaughter.

"I got plenty of nightgowns and pajamas I can lend you both. And you know I keep stuff for the babies, diapers and little rompers and all that. I even got some of that little tyke's food if they want it. We can cook us something and have a real good time." Ms. Sylvi smiled brightly at her daughter.

"Okay, Mama. I'll stay. You must know I don't have anything else to do on a Saturday night. Besides, I don't think I could drive home myself." Nancy lived on the other side of Decatur in a cute little bungalow, closer to Jackie's house than her mother's.

"I am just plain worn out," said Nancy. "Today has been a little bit too much. You know they say the truth hurts, and right about now, I truly believe they are absolutely correct. I'm hurting all over. I feel like a Marta bus has run me over."

Nancy turned around and went into the kitchen. "Well, let's see what we can find to cook. Mama, you got any chicken? I feel like fried chicken, especially after that food at the wedding. Not that I got much of that."

"That's probably a good thing. I got some kind of food I couldn't even make out. But you know I got chicken here. Just look in the freezer and set it in the microwave on thaw or defrost. It'll be ready to do something with in a little while."

Chrystal called her roommate as Nancy went about getting the chicken out of the freezer. Ms. Sylvi sized them both up. "Let's see what I can find for you ladies to wear. I know I ain't got none of them panties you probably wear Chrystal, them

27

thongs, so you'll just have to put up with some of my granny kind or go without. You probably do that anyway. Now Nancy, I can't see her not having an extra pair somewhere. She always seems to be prepared."

"Grandma, you too much. I know you kidding me, right? I do wear panties, thank you very much, but I don't want to wear none of your granny panties. I'll keep on what I got." Chrystal couldn't help but laugh at her grandmother.

"And why do you think I got extra panties everywhere?" asked Nancy as she got the chicken ready to put in the microwave. She mumbled to herself as she shook her head at her mother.

"Well, don't you?" Ms. Sylvi was picking and picking. "I was trying to give you a compliment. I ain't ever seen you unprepared for anything. That's good organizational skills. You probably got another outfit in your bag too. You never know what you might need sometimes." Ms. Sylvi winked at Chrystal and Chrystal winked back.

"Well, you're correct about another outfit, but I don't have it in my bag. I left a comfy change of clothes out in the van. And you are absolutely correct about me. I always try to be well prepared for anything and everything," said a serious-looking Nancy. "But today has been a hell of a day. Even I didn't anticipate all this commotion."

They laughed so freely that Jimmy and Bryan heard them as they were coming down the hallway. They came in the kitchen and asked what was going on.

Ms. Sylvi told them, "This here is woman talk. You wouldn't be interested, but then again you might. Ain't that right, Chrystal?"

"You right, Grandma, you sure are right."

They were all in the kitchen. Some standing, some sitting, but everyone was enjoying a delicious fried-chicken dinner.

"I don't care what anybody says. This has got to be the best fried chicken in Atlanta. Ms. Sylvi, you need to go into business. It's that good," said a beaming Bryan with a mouth full of chicken. "And this macaroni and cheese is to die for."

"You're right, but my favorite has always been the pot roast with new potatoes and green beans. Now, that is one good meal." Jimmy said. "And that sweet potato pie Ms. Sylvi cooks just melts in your mouth." He and Bryan ate standing near the stove.

"Thank you both for your compliments on the cooking. I can't claim the macaroni and cheese though. Nancy made that. And your baby girl threw down on some green beans."

"Nancy made the macaroni and cheese? I didn't know you could cook up anything besides a mess, but everything is so good. Thank all you ladies," said Jimmy. He continued to smile as he picked up another piece of chicken and put it on his plate.

"I'm too tired to play with you, but I do know nobody makes bigger messes than you and your boyfriend. You two give messy a new meaning. Today's revelations have certainly confirmed that," said Nancy as she gave Jimmy a look that could melt rocks. Chrystal looked back and forth between the two but didn't say anything.

"Jimmy, that wasn't called for, and you know it. Can't you give a compliment and let it go? You and Nancy have been fighting for years now. Let it go. One day before I die, I would like to see everybody get along for at least one day," said Ms. Sylvi as she held Jade in her lap.

Jimmy had the nerve to look contrite for a moment, but it didn't last. "You know that was some terrible food at the wedding. Who picked that menu?" he asked as he licked his fingers and finally put down his plate.

Nancy was trying to "let it go" as her mother said. She answered Jimmy in a civil manner.

"That was Natalie's menu, Jessica's mother. She planned the whole thing right down to which champagne went best with the prime rib. I don't know what some of that stuff was. I think she said stuffed Brussels sprouts, goat cheese with pears, or something like that." Nancy's mouth turned up in a grimace of distaste. "By the way, Jimmy, did Chrystal ever tell you what the children's names mean?"

"What the children's names mean? No, and why would Chrystal have special meaning to their names? I mean they are beautiful names for beautiful babies, but I thought that was as far as it went." Jimmy looked to Chrystal for clarification as he glanced at Jewell, Oro and Jade.

Chrystal looked at her aunt and squeezed her eyes closed. *What's she trying to do now?* But she answered, "Well, I named the kids something precious and meaningful because I always thought my name was something fragile, easily broken, and worthless. You know, just plain old glass."

Bryan gasped and Jimmy shook his head sadly. "Jackie sure has messed up your head with her foolishness. That was never my intention baby. We named you for your beautiful dazzling eyes that sparkled like cut crystal. There's nothing worthless about you. I love you and your mother does too."

"Well, for one thing, Mama didn't mess up my head, but she said that same thing too, but I know how I felt, and I wanted more for my kids. I believe there's power in a name, and I wanted them to feel proud of what I could give them."

Everyone was quiet for a moment letting Chrystal's words sink in. She had again made her family pause and Jimmy shook his head as if he couldn't believe his daughter could entertain such radical thoughts.

Ms. Sylvi slowly got up from the table with Jade in her arms and went over to the window. They looked out at the peaceful night sky. "It's a beautiful night. We're going to have us a good time." She asked the children, "You like *Frozen*?"

Jewell and Oro answered loudly, "We love *Frozen*, that's our favorite." And little Jade echoed, "Frozhens."

Ms. Sylvi laughed outright, and Chrystal finally cheered up.

"Once we get you all washed up, then we're going to sit right down and watch it again. Right, Chrystal?"

"Yes, Grandma, we will." Chrystal got up and took her plate over to the counter. She had barely touched her meal.

"Baby why are you still so quiet?" her father asked. "And you hardly ate anything. You could use some weight. You're almost skin and bones."

"I ate. I'm not that hungry, that's all." Chrystal made a move to leave and turned away. *Why is he always trying to get in my business? Acting like he care, when he just wants to use me some more.*

"What's that? Is that a bruise on your cheek?" Jimmy asked, as he turned her back around to him. "It looks like a handprint. Did somebody hit you?"

Chrystal tried to pull out of her father's grasp, but he held on. She'd forgotten about the bruise she'd covered earlier with makeup, but she guessed with all the crying and wiping at her face, it must have come off. With everything else that had gone on today, she didn't want to talk about any of this now, but her father was waiting, determined to get an answer.

She finally answered in a hushed voice. "I told Grandma earlier that I'd fallen against the refrigerator last night. That's all." Jimmy let go of Chrystal, and she moved over to the table to pick up Oro. "It's nothing. I was just clumsy, that's all."

"That doesn't look like a fall against the refrigerator. A refrigerator can't produce a handprint. I can almost see fingerprints on your skin. Who did this to you?" Bryan tried to hold Jimmy back, but Jimmy held barely contained fury in his eyes.

Nancy and Ms. Sylvi turned questioning eyes Jimmy's way. Nancy calmly said, "Chrystal why don't you take the kids on back, and I'll come help you give them a bath. You can put them all in together, but it's probably going to be a little harder, since you don't have all your things here."

"Thanks, Aunt Nancy. I'll do just that, and yes, I could use some help."

"Wait a minute, Chrystal. You didn't answer me. Who hit you? From the looks of it, I would add that a lot of force and anger was behind it. Did some man hit you?"

32

"Daddy, I don't want to talk about it right now. Okay? Besides, you're scaring the kids with all the loud talk about hitting. They'll never calm down if you keep shouting about it." At that moment, as if on cue, Jade whimpered in her great grandmother's arms.

Jimmy asked, "Does this have anything to do with your mother?"

Everyone gave Jimmy a horrified look, especially Ms. Sylvi as she tried to quiet Jade.

"That's enough," said Ms. Sylvi in a voice like sharpened steel. "Whatever in the world would make you say something like that? I think we all have heard enough today, especially from you. Why don't you and Bryan go on home and we'll talk later?"

"I'm sorry Ms. Sylvi. I didn't mean—I don't know what I mean. It's just that obviously someone hit her. But you're right. That's enough for tonight. We'll call you in the morning. Good night, everybody."

No one said a word as Jimmy and Bryan left through the kitchen door, but both older women turned to give Chrystal one last pityingly look.

Chrystal looked at her grandmother still holding little Jade, but she thought about her father. *He is such a pain. Sometimes I wish mama had never met him. God only knows what mess he's going to start now.*

Nancy glanced over to Chrystal who was trying hard not to look guilty. After Jimmy and Bryan left, she said, "I don't know what's going on, but I sure as hell know we're going to find out, one way or another."

Chapter Two

Saturday Night - Jimmy and Bryan

Jimmy was driving home to Alpharetta, a suburb outside of Atlanta. He and Bryan had moved years ago from the renovated Victorian in Midtown Atlanta. He had loved that house, but after the battle he and his ex-wife had in it, it wasn't the same. In fact, it almost felt tainted.

He used to love to walk through the house, marveling at the woodwork on the grand staircase. More money had been spent on renovating the kitchen and bathrooms than he paid for the house itself. It spoke to him in a way the new house never could. He'd tried to rid his home of Jackie's hateful essence by having the entire house repainted, but nothing he did to it could dispel the feeling of wrongness.

Crazy ghosts seemed to hover in every nook and cranny. The final showdown, when he'd let Jackie catch him and Bryan in bed, left a bitterness in his mouth; no amount of rinsing could ever erase the foul taste. He hadn't meant for it to backfire on him as it did, but once it was over, it was finally over. Jackie had left him and never looked back. She had gone on with her life as if he had never been in it. It sadden him somewhat to know how little he really meant to her.

He'd sold the renovated Victorian at a big profit and had taken only his personal items—his clothes and his extensive art collection—and started over in a brand-new house. He left all the furniture with the old house, especially the king-size Regency bed that had been his greatest joy. Jackie hadn't wanted any of the furniture or other household items after the divorce. She didn't even ask for alimony. She only wanted child support for Chrystal and Royce through their college years. At the time, he wouldn't have given her a penny of alimony anyway, but now, knowing what he knew, he wondered if that was the right decision. If he had, he could have kept tabs on her better and made her feel beholden to him by accepting alimony.

He and Bryan had furnished the new house with every convenience and toy on the market, even going so far as hiring a Feng Shui consultant. He poured every dream wish into the new house, but it still felt wrong, empty somehow.

They'd been quiet for most of the ride home. Each was lost in his own thoughts, but it was very hard to ignore the big white elephant in the small car.

Finally, Jimmy broke the silence as he expertly handled the Jaguar. "I know something bad is going on with Chrystal. She's always running around with that hood-rat cousin of hers."

"What cousin? Do you mean that girl she was talking to who was with the nasty dreadlocked guy at the wedding?"

"Yes, that's Nikki."

Bryan looked incredulous. "They were a mess. The guy looked like he had on a bad suit from the big-hair eighties. And the girl, poor thing was so worn-out looking. I almost felt sorry for them."

"Well, save your pity because neither one deserves that much compassion. Nikki has always twisted Chrystal around her finger, and that guy she was with is a piece of shit," mumbled Jimmy as he blew his horn at a car swerving into his lane.

Bryan leaned over and placed his hand on Jimmy's leg and patted. "Don't get too agitated about it. You know how young people are. If there was really something wrong going on, I think Chrystal would tell you."

"I don't know about that. We haven't always had the best relationship, and now that she found out about you and me being together for so long, I just don't know. I wish I did."

"Is the cousin from Jackie's side of the family? Do you know anything about her?"

"Unfortunately, I know way too much about her, and that loser, who calls himself Smoke, she was with too. I've regrettably had some run-ins with him, here and there. Nikki has always been in the life, you know. Fast money, fast cars, fast men. That kind of life can only be found in the most unsavory places. She's Jackie's cousin, Shelia's daughter. Remember way back when Jackie tried to set you up? Shelia was another little whore if I remember correctly."

Jimmy shifted his eyes nervously from the rearview mirror to the side mirrors as he thought back to the wedding.

"Oh my God, yes, I remember now," said Bryan. "She actually was a lot of fun. We did have a good time. I remember she asked me was I gay about five minutes after we met. I said why, and she said she could always tell, so she guessed a little nookie was out of the question. I must have missed her at the wedding. We could have gone over old times." Bryan laughed uproariously.

"You never told me that," said Jimmy with an edge to his voice as he exited the interstate.

"Well, you were trying so desperately to keep us on the down low, and you know how I felt about that. You're not the only one who can keep a secret. That's just one of mine." Bryan gave Jimmy a tight little smile and turned to look out the window at the passing lights.

"I won't forget what you said, but we'll have to talk about that later. Anyway, I remember Nikki when they were younger. She would get Chrystal into all kinds of trouble and then sit back and let Chrystal take the blame. It was like a game to her. I felt something evil from that little girl even then."

"What do you mean? Children aren't evil by nature. That's not even possible."

"Have you ever had any children?"

"Well, no, you know that, but I was a child once. I'm just saying that you have to teach them how to be that way," said a clearly agitated Bryan.

Jimmy gave Bryan an incredulous look. "I believe blood will always tell. She and her mother are a special kind of sleazy. I guess that's where Jackie gets it from also. Whoring runs through their family. I guess you could say whores of a feather fuck together." Only Jimmy laughed at his ugly joke. He gripped the steering wheel tighter as he unconsciously sped up.

Bryan closed his eyes and gave a big sigh. "Jim, you have got to let it go. It's been way too many years to even keep thinking that way. If you paint Jackie with that dreadful brush, then Chrystal is the same color. Are you saying there's no hope for Chrystal? I don't believe that."

"You must be joking. You don't know the first thing about children, or women for that matter. Jackie is one ungrateful bitch," said Jimmy with clear loathing in his voice.

"Not that I'm a big fan of Jackie's. She cut me so badly today I might faint from blood loss. But I will give old girl one up because that Eric is one tall, good-looking piece of masculinity. Did you see the muscles on him?" Bryan was clearly taken with Eric as he continued to smile at the memory.

"So what? Now, you're sniffing around Jackie's used goods?" Jimmy gave Bryan a disgusted look.

"I guess the same could be said about us. You're not exactly fresh off the vine. If I remember correctly, you spent a lot of time with Jackie yourself."

"Look, I'm not trying to fight with you. What Jackie and I had was in the past, and you know how I felt about that. I did what I had to do. You know the stipulations my father put on me. At the time, I was too young to fight him. I agree she wasn't that nice to you, but she saved her poisoned claws for my jugular."

"Speaking of your father, did you at least tell them Royce was getting married? And before you say it, I know how you feel about them."

"Then why are you even asking me that? My devil-spawn of a father hasn't even returned my call from a year ago. At this point, I don't care if I ever hear from him again. I guess he keeps my mother tied up and bound somewhere. I know she would have wanted to come, but . . . anyway. And I don't even know where my sister, Teresa, is. The last I heard from her was about five months ago. I think she was in Paris at some art exhibit she held."

"And you have the nerve to talk about Jackie's family tree. I love you, but I will never understand you."

"You don't have to understand. You just need to believe what I tell you because I'm always right." Jimmy gave Bryan a long sideways glance as he waited at a red light.

"Whatever, I know what I know." Bryan moved to open the glove compartment. "Jim, we forgot to give Royce and Jessica the gift! I thought I left it in here, and now they'll think we didn't bring anything. I don't want them to think that." Bryan was so flustered he heated up and started fanning himself.

"Calm down. I talked with Royce after that silly fake scene with Jackie. I told him we would get with them after they came back from their honeymoon. I didn't want to cause any more disruptions than necessary."

"You could have told me. I tried my best to anticipate what they needed and give them a thoughtful gift." Bryan sighed loudly. "You always seem to forget that I'm your equal partner. I want to know what's going on. Especially now that you know for sure that Eric is Royce's biological father, I don't want them to think you feel differently towards Royce."

"Eric may be Royce's biological father, but Royce is my son, like Chrystal is my daughter. I've known Royce didn't share my genes for years now, but I don't feel any differently about Royce or Chrystal. I need to make sure Jackie and Eric understand that."

"Well, okay, but I still want my say in things. You are way too controlling. I've told you before that people don't respond well to a dictatorship. At least, I know I don't. You keep too many things held back. You're too secretive. It doesn't do anybody any good. And you are not always right!"

Jimmy didn't respond to Bryan's last statement. He was too busy thinking up ways to mess with Jackie and Eric. He wanted nothing more than to make them look as bad as possible. He wanted everyone to think of Jackie as a whore, in fact he just might have more ways to help it along. He just needed more time to mull over his thoughts without Bryan intruding into his mind with all his foolish talk.

They had ridden silently for a while until Bryan couldn't take it anymore. "Jim, did you hear what I said?" Bryan turned sideways to look at Jimmy as he drove. Bryan could tell that he had zoned out on him again.

"I heard what you said, but I need to concentrate on this traffic. It's Saturday night, after all, and everybody's out and about. You know how foolishly people drive after they have a drink or two."

"Yeah, right," said Bryan as he turned back in his seat. "I said you take me for granted too much. I try to help, and you ignore my advice. One day, you'll have to listen to me. I just hope it won't be too late."

Bryan decided to stay quiet for the rest of the ride home. He knew once Jimmy got something in his head there was no moving him unless he had his own reason to change his mind. Bryan didn't like it, but what could he do? He wished Jimmy wasn't so hell-bent on destroying his ex-wife.

It'd been too many years to still carry a grudge. Besides, it wasn't like Jim was an innocent in all this. He'd been fornicating with Bryan all the while, so why get so mad because Jackie went somewhere else to get hers? He should be thankful that at least one of the children was his and count his blessings that he didn't have to still sneak around.

Bryan could never understand why Jim was the way he was. Based on his family history, Jim should have been all the more compassionate towards others, more understanding. Instead, he'd become a manipulative, cold-blooded, egotistical chauvinist.

He remembered when he first met Jim. It was imprinted on his mind forever. It was the spring of 1980 in Atlanta. The dogwood trees were blossoming all over campus and the sun was shining bright. Bryan loved the outdoors. He had a free period and was out enjoying the nice weather and not paying attention to what was directly in front of him. They literally ran into each other in the student quad. Jimmy had been in a hurry to get to his next class, and Bryan had been strolling along.

Jimmy dropped everything he'd been carrying when he collided with Bryan. "I'm sorry man. I didn't see you there."

"No problem. I wasn't watching where I was going," said a clearly flustered Bryan.

"Here, let me help you gather up your papers." Jimmy had hit Bryan so hard that the contents of the loose-leaf binder

Bryan was holding went flying every which a way. Jimmy wasn't particularly graceful in his movements and hitting someone head-on upset him in more ways than one.

They bent down to gather up the papers and their heads banged together. They both went down hard. Bryan had tears in his eyes from the impact. His ears were ringing, and he felt a bad headache coming on.

"I'm sorry. I don't know what my problem is today. Are you all right? You look a little funny." Jimmy tried to help Bryan up, but his knees were so wobbly that he kept falling back down.

"I think I need to go to the infirmary. I don't feel so good."

"Yeah, you do look a little green. I didn't know a black guy could turn colors like that. But you have really light skin with that funny-colored hair."

Bryan was a petite young man. He only stood about five-four, and that was with heels. He was slim and always dressed in the latest fashions. That day, he had on forest green pants and a yellow shirt. His hair was a flame-red afro that was unnaturally enhanced. He thought the colors of his outfit complemented his skin tone and his hair. He did look very stylish in a flamboyant sort of way. But Bryan didn't know whether to be insulted or take what Jimmy said as a compliment. *This guy is really cute.* He thought he knew all the good-looking guys, and he wondered where this one had been hiding. Of course, it was too much to ask if he was gay too, but he sure did hope so.

Bryan did know that he needed medical attention. Apparently, when they hit each other, Jimmy's book bag had swung around and caught Bryan in the midsection. Not only did his head hurt, but his stomach was doing flip flops and everything he had for breakfast threatened to come up.

"If you can help me to the infirmary, I would really appreciate it," said Bryan as he sat up on the ground. He was starting to feel better just having Jimmy's hands on him, but he still felt dizzy.

It turned out that Jimmy not only helped him to the infirmary but stayed around to help him back to his dorm room when he found out Bryan had a mild concussion. That day had been the turning point in Bryan's life. To have run into each like this on their Atlanta college campus was more than luck; to Bryan, it was fate.

It wasn't until they made it back to Bryan's dorm room that they were able to really introduce themselves. Jimmy was young, but Bryan could tell he had a lot of potential. He came across as being shy and bookish, but he also seemed very sure of himself. He was tall and so slim that he looked in need of several good meals. Jimmy had black wavy hair that seemed to shine brightly in the dim dorm room. But his eyes were the most striking thing to Bryan. They were a dark brown color, with a black ring around the iris.

Bryan wondered what kind of family Jimmy came from and if he even knew he was gay. *This one would take a little wooing,* he thought, but he felt up to the challenge. He was never wrong about a person's sexual orientation. Even if the person wasn't aware of it yet, Bryan could always tell. He'd come across many a boy and girl who didn't know they were gay or who didn't know how to get involved in activities where they would be accepted.

But he never dreamed the path his life would take from that day forward. He thought he would be the one to guide Jimmy

43

to the truth of who he was, but instead Jimmy taught him a thing or two. James Mattock was not as innocent of the world as he appeared. He was a quick learner, and once he accepted, to a degree, who he was, he wasn't satisfied until he mastered it and anyone he considered his.

That day, they talked about everything in their lives, on campus and off. Bryan was from a little parish in Louisiana, while Jimmy was from the mile-high city of Denver. Both were a long way from home, but they hit it off so well Bryan didn't want the day to end.

Bryan was older than Jimmy and had been on campus for a while. He was a rising senior and a biology/pre-med student, but really, he was way out of his comfort zone. It wasn't that he wasn't smart enough, but his passions lay in the theater, not a laboratory. His desires were to be on the Broadway stage, not spying on lab rats in their little cages.

Jimmy, on the other hand, was a freshman, just out of high school. It wasn't until much later that Bryan found out Jimmy was only sixteen when they first met. Jimmy was high on engineering and anything analytical that went with it. He loved math, science, and physics. His people skills were deplorable though. He didn't seem to make many friends, nor did he try.

While Bryan was openly gay and knew most of the gay people on campus, he hadn't settled down with any one person. He was more like a social butterfly, fluttering around from person to person, experiencing all that life had to offer. He was one of the beautiful and fun people and fit in any social setting. He enjoyed dipping his nose into every available flower to sample the goods. He had the exotic good looks and a personality that made him an instant hit in any setting.

Bryan Denveue was from an old Creole family who loved to entertain but were somewhat impoverished socialites in their small parish. They were a happy family, nevertheless, and Bryan grew up loved and protected from the harsh realities of life. He was the baby of the family and came out at the age of fourteen. His mother, father, and three siblings stood firmly behind him, one hundred percent.

Bryan seldom met a person he didn't like or who didn't like him. He was outgoing and loved a good time. His one fatal flaw was that he was too trusting. He chose to come to Atlanta for all the variety it offered in lifestyles, and he was not disappointed. Atlanta gave him everything he craved and more. However, Bryan had no idea about the things he would do and be asked to do for Jimmy's love, the lies he would tell, the people he would betray. He hadn't known that he would have to sneak around, portray himself as something else, and become the other man.

If he had known, would he have so readily agreed to be Jimmy's lover? Probably not, but it was too late now. No one had that kind of future insight, and even if he had, he would never have believed he was capable of so much dishonesty and deception. For almost forty years, he'd let Jimmy control, manipulate, and finally destroy who he really was.

He was in too deep and barely recognized himself these days. It had been too many years and much too much conditioning that made him into the man he was now. He loved Jim, faults and all. But was it really love Jim felt for him? Besides, Jimmy never willingly gave up easily what he considered his. Bryan wondered was he just another of Jim's possessions.

Jimmy continued driving, lost in his own thoughts. He had returned to a time when he was unsure of himself. He remembered feeling lost as he first stepped into the college scene. He felt alienated from the rest of the students there as he couldn't identify with any of them. Until Bryan came along and made him see his life through another's eyes. Even his father couldn't hurt him as badly with Bryan by his side.

In college, Jimmy was an obvious contrast to Bryan. He was awkward and standoffish. He was tall, but too thin to fit in with the jocks. He still had the gawkiness of youth clinging to his frame. Girls flocked to him, but he was too shy to do anything with the attention. Besides, he was never that interested in girls. He'd needed confirmation and recognition from his male peers at the science fairs, museums, and exhibits he frequented while growing up in Denver. He transferred that same interest to Atlanta. He was seen frequently at the High Museum, Fernbank Science Center, and similar venues.

Jimmy never asked himself which gender he identified with or, for that matter, was sexually interested in. He didn't have the strong sex drive most teenagers had. He sometimes touched himself when he was alone, but it wasn't something he frequently indulged in. Jimmy's curiosity did not lie in that direction, so he accepted himself as he was and didn't dig any further.

The Mattock family was privileged and had many political connections in Denver. His father especially, was a man's man who smoked huge cigars and always had a bourbon or Scotch in his hand. James Sr. was big in stature and voice. He had a reddish-brown complexion and coal-black curly hair. He'd made a lucrative business out of nothing, or so he said, when he opened a shop that catered to the skiers who came to conquer the Colorado slopes. He was a self-made millionaire.

"Son, one day all this will be yours." He loved to call Jimmy son, never his actual name. "But you have to get your goddamn head out of your ass and get some real experience in this world! Science and technology are good, but politics is where the real men work and play. You'll always be working for somebody else if you stay in that lane."

Jimmy's mother, Marybeth, and only sister, Teresa, were mere shadows in their bustling household. They had help who cooked and cleaned, help who tutored, and help who drove them around. They never had to lift a finger to do any chore, but he never knew if his mother preferred this or not. She never said much in his presence. He didn't let it bother him though. Like his father, Jimmy put females in a very small compartment in his mind, and after he used them for his purposes, he tended to ignore them.

Marybeth came from a wealthy St. Louis family. When she met James, she was a beautiful, outgoing woman. She had long black hair, creamy skin, and dark brown eyes. Her family could trace their origins back to the aristocratic Creole families of New Orleans. What she was doing with his father, Jimmy never knew or cared to understand. He did wonder sometimes why few relatives visited, and when they did, why they never stayed very long.

His sister, Teresa, was a year younger and was prim, proper, and quite beautiful. She was a tall girl and grew into a long, lithe, model-thin woman. Her long, lustrous black hair was similar to her mother's, and her hazel eyes were inherited from some long-dead ancestor. There wasn't much below the surface though. And if she ever had yearnings of her own, Jimmy knew nothing of them. They were not close as children, and that relationship did not blossom further as they became adults.

Jimmy had no fond childhood memories of little league or summer camp. He had no memories of Christmas toys or Thanksgiving dinners. He never remembered playing with his sister on the lawn of the family estate. No picnics, no visits to grandma's house, no anything that normal families, black or white, took for granted. In fact, Jimmy found it very difficult to remember much that made him happy as a child. His only escape was into math, science, and an occasional biographical account of some long-dead scientist.

Jimmy was to do all the things his father didn't get to accomplish with his limited education. The Mattock legacy rested on Jimmy's back. James Sr. expected Jimmy to go to Harvard and that was that. He was willing to entertain Jimmy's little hobbies only to a certain point. If he wasn't doing what he was destined to by twenty-one, then all financial support would disappear. He made sure Jimmy understood this.

Jimmy had no respect for his family and certainly no love. He tolerated his abused mother, who could not save herself and certainly not her children and who slowly blended into the very furniture, a mother who rarely spoke to him. She may have had a better relationship with his sister, but he never bothered to know. She had never been a touchy-feely sort of mother, and middle age certainly did not make her more so. He didn't inconvenience himself to wonder why she disappeared to her room more often than not. Sometimes she stayed there for days, unnoticed. When she emerged, she always smelled of some sweet liqueur.

Then there was his sister, who had no self-esteem and lived only to please a father who never noticed her. She could disappear tomorrow, and only a tentative search would ensue. She was taught early on to be as quiet as the proverbial mouse, and she succeeded quite well at it.

And finally, there was his father, who Jimmy despised most of all. He was a tyrant and a bully who forced his wants and desires onto a hostage-held family. There would never be enough ransom to satisfy him. He was a father who considered himself justified in doing anything within his power to make his son succeed as he directed. He believed wholeheartedly that the end justified his means.

Late Saturday Night - Jimmy

Jimmy and Bryan made it home safely. It had been a fairly comfortable drive with only a minimum of traffic backups. Bryan had gone into the bedroom to settle down for the night. Jimmy made his way to the family room.

Jimmy was still thinking of his father and the horrid childhood he endured. He finally had to admit that he was afraid of his father. It wasn't that he feared physical violence, but rather the psychological warfare that was inflicted upon him, and he assumed, his mother and sister.

The senior Mattock had many weapons available and was always eager to test their effectiveness upon his family. If

Jimmy was told to devise the worst possible torture for the most heinous criminal imaginable, having to endure his family, especially his father, for a year, would be it.

It was a miracle he wasn't more damaged than he was.

As Jimmy sat in his comfy chair sipping cognac, he still had difficulty digesting the knowledge that Jackie and Eric had outsmarted him. His stomach was churning with the information. He'd guessed something wasn't right from the beginning with Royce's paternity, but he'd never thought Jackie had the balls to do what she did. Royce always had a look about him that didn't quite fit in with the Mattock looks. Not that it was that far different, but together with his looks was the doting Jackie tended to lavish on him.

And that big doofus, Eric, just the thought of him and Jackie together made Jimmy want to stab somebody. They'd managed to make him look like a fool, and that was one thing he couldn't and wouldn't tolerate.

Royce had invited that idiot to the wedding. What was he thinking? Royce was a lot smarter than he had given him credit for though, and even more devious than he'd ever imagined. That had taken some good detective work on Royce's part. All he had to go on was a name from some childhood memories. But he'd managed to track Eric down. For what reason? Did he somehow guess Eric was his father?

He did all this because Jackie had been a little depressed lately and he wanted to do something special for her. At least that's what he said. So he thought this old friend would cheer her up. He wanted to thank his mother for all the love and encouragement she'd given him over the years. That was a bunch of bullshit.

Jackie hadn't done anything for him. That was Jimmy's money that had kept him clothed and fed and a roof over his head. His dollars sent Royce to the best engineering school in Atlanta. Granted Royce had a full scholarship, but Jimmy supplied the rest. Royce should have been thanking him, not his damn mother. Jimmy didn't even get a real invitation to the wedding, just a phone call. It was like he was a last-minute thought while precious Eric was tracked down and personally invited. And that fool had come and upstaged the hell out of Jimmy.

To say he was embarrassed was an understatement. Jimmy was furious. He could barely contain himself when that buffoon told them all he was in love with Jackie and always had been. Eric was so conceited that he actually thought both Chrystal and Royce were his offspring.

The fucking nerve of them both! Jimmy was getting madder and madder as he thought about the two. His cognac only added fuel to his blazing fury. They had been doing the nasty right under his nose and he never smelled it coming. Sure, he'd had an inkling that their relationship wasn't as platonic as they proclaimed, but he never thought Jackie could set him up like this.

He would have never believed she was that intelligent. That was one of the reasons he picked her to be his wife. He thought he was the master manipulator, but that bitch outsmarted him. She passed off a baby as his and made him take care of him, provide for him, and love him.

It never entered his mind that he caused his own downfall or that he was the one who was unfaithful to begin with. None of that mattered. He didn't want Jackie to be happy. She didn't deserve happiness. She'd made a mess of all his carefully laid plans and then she had the nerve to walk out on him like she was a queen. He couldn't live that down. His father taught him better than that.

Jackie had never done for his daughter, Chrystal, like a good mother should either. She let the child get into all kinds of crazy situations with that skeezer cousin of hers. Jackie was the one responsible for all the missteps Chrystal had taken, and he was going to make sure she paid for it.

Even though Chrystal had been dealing with him while she continued to get pregnant and her run-ins with law enforcement and the court system all occurred partially on his watch, he discounted his part in that neglectful child rearing. Jimmy still put all the blame on Jackie's bad parenting. In his mind, he might not have been able to stop what Chrystal had done in the past, but he was determined Jackie would pay for it all now.

His baby girl was hurting. Any fool could tell that. Who had been beating up on his baby? *Somebody has been mistreating her and I know where to start asking questions,* he thought.

That thug they called Smoke was the first name on his list. It was laughable that fool thought he was anything besides fat. Jimmy had wanted to choke that fat clown when he saw him sitting in the chapel. And then Nikki had the nerve to introduce that felon as her fiancé. That was just too funny to ignore. How in the world had Chrystal managed to get involved with that felon? It was probably more of Jackie's lack of parental control.

And where was Jackie now that Chrystal needed consoling? She and Eric were probably somewhere humping like the deranged animals they were. Just the thought of the two of them in bed somewhere made his stomach turn over and bile rise in his throat. It wasn't jealousy, was it? It couldn't be. He didn't want Jackie, did he? The thought that he would be jealous of Eric was laughable, wasn't it?

It didn't matter that he'd been living a secret life since the beginning. It didn't matter that he used every opportunity to be with Bryan. Or that he lavished expensive clothes, cars, and even a condo on him. It didn't matter that he lied to Jackie from the start and married her under false pretenses. None of that mattered because he was a man, and he had been taught by his father how a man should be. The end always justified his means.

And most of all, it didn't matter that he was gay. Bryan, Jackie, Chrystal, and Royce were his, and he jealously guarded and controlled what was his. Anybody who thought differently would soon find out that he was a man who called all the shots.

Chapter Three

Saturday Night – Chrystal

C hrystal had finally gotten the kids to settle down and go to sleep after giving them a bath and finishing the movie. The kids may not have been tired, but she was worn out. She couldn't count how many times she'd seen *Frozen*, but the kids absolutely loved that stupid movie.

She had to hand it to her Aunt Nancy; she knew how to get a plan going. If it hadn't been for Nancy's quick thinking at dinner, Chrystal didn't know how she would have gotten out of her father's questioning. But Aunt Nancy also brought up the name thing again. Why couldn't she let it be? What did Nancy want from her?

Her father was acting like an idiot and being a major pain, as if he all of a sudden wanted to be concerned about her safety. He didn't seem to care so much when she asked him for a loan to help her out. In fact, he turned her down when she wasn't forthcoming with why she needed it. Instead, he put her on a budget and doled out an allowance based on what he considered necessary. Sometimes, she wondered how much was for real love and how much was just for show.

Chrystal's phone rang shrilly. She turned back into one of the spare bedrooms to take the call. In her agitated state she didn't notice the name. "Hello, who's this?"

"Hi Chrystal. It's Tyler. How are you?"

"Okay, so now you want to call. Why did it take you so long to call back?" Chrystal moved over to the window to stare blankly into the dark outside.

"Baby, I got hung up at the Paris airport. I tried to call you earlier, but your phone kept going to voice mail."

"Well, the wedding is over now, and I don't need you. Since you were out of the country, you can just stay your ass out of the country. You know damn well a wedding don't go on all night."

Tyler tried to answer in between Chrystal's rapid-fire questions and insults. "Chrystal, will you please listen to what I have to say? I'm here now and can come over. Where are you? What's the address? You know I want to see you and Jade and the rest of the kids."

"What? You must be crazy. I don't care anymore. I gave you a chance, and as usual, you messed it up, so I guess you won't get to see her then. Like you really care! I was ready for you to finally meet my family, but you have never kept your word and I don't know why I believed you would this time. It's always the same with you. You're apparently more concerned with your music career than your own daughter. I guess I made the same old mistake of thinking somebody really cared about me. I am so tired of your same old shit. Goodbye, Tyler."

Chrystal put her head against the wall. She wanted so badly to cry, but the tears wouldn't come anymore. For some reason, she thought Tyler was different, a real man for a change, but she had given him everything she had left and apparently it still wasn't enough. One minute, he was as warm and cozy as fresh baked bread, and next moment, he switched up. She felt as if he doused her with ice cold water.

She didn't know why she kept letting herself be played by these so-called men. If there was one thing she had to agree with her aunt on, it was to never trust a man. All they did was lie and hurt you and then tell you it was your fault they had to act like they did. She gave a heavy sigh and turned to join her grandmother in the living room.

"Wow! I'm really beat. I think I'm going to sit right down here on this comfy sofa, and if you don't mind grandma, I'm gonna put my feet up for a minute and relax."

"Go ahead. It's just us here in the family room, and we all family. Is your auntie still back there cleaning up? I thought I would fall out when Oro threw his washcloth right in her face. That little boy is a mess. He reminds me of you at that age. I couldn't do nothing with you either."

"Now, I know I wasn't that bad. Besides, y'all spoiled that boy. I told you to stop carrying on about his pretty hair and eyelashes. That child thinks he's a runway model or something. You should see him at home. He likes to run around butt naked with a towel around his neck, acting like he's an avenger." Chrystal giggled like a little girl. She seemed relaxed for the first time in hours.

Ms. Sylvi chuckled and shook her head. "I still don't know where that boy got all that pretty hair from. He must look just like his daddy." She knew she'd hit a nerve when Chrystal stopped smiling and dropped her head.

Chrystal had never given up any information on the children's fathers. It was painfully obvious that no two children had the same father. Jackie told Ms. Sylvi she begged Chrystal for information about each baby's daddy, but she wouldn't budge. The second child, Oro, was the same as the first; Chrystal gave no indications she was even pregnant. She stayed hidden for most of the pregnancy and no man or boy ever showed up to claim any of the children.

Ms. Sylvi wondered if Chrystal had been forced into something. It made her shiver to think what might be happening to her granddaughter. "You know you can talk to me, don't you? You don't have to be afraid of anything or anybody. I want to help you anyway I can."

She looked at Chrystal, who was slumped down in the sofa with her feet on the coffee table. It was a heartbreaking look of sadness and defeat. *She's such a beautiful young woman, but her heart is so full of sorrow.*

Ms. Sylvi couldn't understand why the good Lord gave Chrystal such a heavy burden to carry. Even as a baby, she had been troubled, and now, Ms. Sylvi just didn't know.

Chrystal looked her grandmother in the eye and lied. "I'm fine. I don't need any help. I can take care of myself. It's not like I neglect my children or anything. They all are doing fine with just me. Besides, Daddy helps out and Mama too. If it means I'm a single mother with no help from the fathers, then so be it." Chrystal picked at the flowers on the old-fashioned nightgown her grandmother had loaned her but didn't say more.

"I know they're fine. I'm not trying to say you're doing anything wrong with them, but everybody needs help now and then. That's all I'm saying. I know you young people think about things differently nowadays, but what's right is still right. These children need a man in the house, especially Oro. A woman can't raise a boy to a man. That's all I'm saying."

Chrystal rolled her eyes and picked up a magazine from the table. Ms. Sylvi shook her head again. She knew she had to reach her granddaughter somehow. She wasn't going to give up, especially now that so much had been revealed. Finally, she understood there was much more to Chrystal than she let on. Just knowing was the first step to helping and healing.

Ms. Sylvi tried to lighten the mood by ganging up on Nancy as she came out of the back. "Nancy, you still wet? That little boy got a good aim." She figured Nancy could take it. She wanted to pick at her about the too-short pajamas but held back, one thing at a time.

"I think you enjoyed that way too much. Instead of laughing, you could have given us a hand." Nancy was still styling her hair as she looked at her mother.

"Well, I was helping all I could. I didn't want to get in your way. That would've made it too crowded in there."

"All you were doing was standing in the doorway. I'm the one who got down on my achy knees to wash three little wriggly, giggly bodies. And then Oro hauled off and slapped me upside my head with that soapy wet washcloth. You're right. He does have a good aim. It's a good thing I was going to wash my hair anyway."

"I'm sorry, Aunt Nancy. I didn't know your knees were hurting. You didn't have to get down like that on the floor. I told you I could've done that."

"It's all right. I wanted to help," Nancy said, "and it sure did make the girls happy to see Auntie all wet. I'm good. Like I said, I needed to wash my hair anyway. It's natural, so it can take a little water, and these new hair products can fix anything."

"Now that it's just us grown folks and it's only ten o'clock, what are we getting ready to do?" asked Ms. Sylvi as she straightened up in her comfy chair. "I wouldn't mind an adult movie. How about y'all?" She picked up the remote to the big flat screen television her children had given them a few years ago.

"Mama, you want to watch an X-rated movie? I didn't know you were into that sort of thing. You ought to be ashamed." Nancy looked over at Chrystal, laid out on the sofa, and winked at her.

"What? Don't you be sassy, Nancy. You know I mean something for adults, not that kiddy stuff. I mean something like one of The Rock's movies. I like him. You know, action and adventure." Ms. Sylvi had to fan herself, she was blushing so badly.

Chrystal and Nancy both tried to hold back a laugh. They knew what Ms. Sylvi meant, but they wanted to prolong her agony.

"But that might be too much excitement for you at your age, and it's getting late. You probably won't sleep with all that stimulus." Nancy looked over Chrystal's way, nodding her head. "Isn't that right, Chrystal? A woman her age can't take too much excitement like that. That man has so many muscles that you have to cross your eyes to see them all."

"Well, I don't know about you two, but I know I can handle it. I've seen plenty muscles in my lifetime, and a few more with a good-looking head on top is just the thing I need to get me to sleep and have wonderful dreams."

"I know she didn't say that! Grandma, you are too much. I would never have thought my grandma would be interested in some man's muscles. You know you too old to even care." Chrystal couldn't hold back the laughter any longer. "I think I need something to drink on that one," she said as she laughed her way to the kitchen. "Aunt Nancy, you want anything?"

"Let me come with you and see what we can find. I think I saw some spirits and juice in there somewhere. I could use a strong something-something, right about now. You want anything, Mama?"

"It depends on if I get to see The Rock. The Rock is worthy of some spirits." Ms. Sylvi was channel surfing and finally found the movie she was looking for. "All right, here it is. I knew one of his movies was on tonight. I like this one especially because he hardly ever has a shirt on and those little shorts he wears—Lord have mercy! Let me have some of that Moscato in the refrigerator, please. I know I'm going to enjoy this one."

"Yes, ma'am," said Nancy. "I'll be right back. I wouldn't mind watching The Rock either. He has the best body around."

Nancy and Chrystal went into the kitchen to look for the wine and spirits.

"How're you feeling about everything that happened today? I know I was confused there for a while." Nancy went to the sink to clean her hands and then to the refrigerator and got out the wine. "Hand me a couple of wine glasses there, Chrystal."

I knew that heifer was up to something. Now she just trying to get in my business, thought Chrystal as she handed over the wine glasses. *I'll turn this shit around right now.*

"Here you go. Well, for one thing I wasn't as surprised as you, probably. I remember Uncle Eric being around some when I was little. Mama always was a little too happy when he came to town, if you know what I mean." She went to the refrigerator and rummaged around. "Even then, I think I thought something was going on between them. They seemed to always be holed up in the kitchen, whispering. I guess I put it out of my mind when I had so much of my own going on." Chrystal moved from the refrigerator to the pantry where she found a bottle of whiskey on the shelf. She opened the bottle and took a big whiff. "Wow, this is some strong, nasty-smelling stuff. I might need to stick with the wine, like Grandma."

"Hand that right over here. I can handle that. It's been one of those kinds of days." Nancy ignored the digs about Jackie, hunched her shoulders, and continued with her questioning. "You don't believe in true love? I understand it can be magical, especially when it's meant to be?" She fixed herself a tumbler of whiskey on the rocks and took a small sip.

Chrystal turned to her aunt and gave a disbelieving laugh. "Yeah, right. Like when pigs fly. I doubt there's much true love involved with what they were doing." As she gave the word "love" air quotes, she continued to laugh. *You the last one who probably know anything about true love. You old as dirt and I ain't never seen you with a man.*

Nancy continued on as if Chrystal hadn't spoken. "But I think it's not such a shock as it is the timing, you know. God has a plan for all of us, and to think this one took more than twenty years to come full circle is amazing."

Chrystal grunted and continued on into the pantry.

"A little chip and dip would go great with our drinks. I'm just about ready to get my Rock on." Nancy swirled her drink around, clinking the ice cubes.

"I found a bag of nacho chips in here. And you're right. The Rock is pretty easy to look at. You know, for an old dude." Chrystal giggled like a kid as she came out of the pantry.

Nancy laughed out loud at what Chrystal considered old. "Hey, here's something I've been meaning to ask you. Have you ever wanted to get married. You know, like Royce? Your mom thinks he and Jessica are too young, but there's something there that goes beyond age. So what do you think about marriage? Maybe with Jade's dad for instance? Weren't you in love with him?"

Chrystal got out a bowl and heated a jar of cheese dip in the microwave and mixed it with some salsa. *I wish she would stop with all the questions.* But something buried deep inside her psyche made her want to answer.

"This cheese dip should go with the chips pretty well." She still hesitated, but finally answered "You know, a long time ago, I guess before Jewell was born, I really believed my prince would come. But now, I know better. I know not to believe the lies everybody tells. I know there's nothing true about love."

Nancy stopped arranging everything on a tray and looked at Chrystal. She had finally gotten through to her and wanted to really hear what she had to say.

With Chrystal's very light brown coloring, it was easy to see a clear red imprint of a hand on the entire right side of her face. It was also swollen when you compared both cheeks. Still, it didn't take away from the beauty of her face with her large dark amber eyes and long eyelashes. Her face was flushed, and she started to perspire.

Nancy, like Jackie, often wondered why Chrystal chose to put that burgundy weave in her hair when she had long, thick, lustrous, dark-brown hair. It was almost as if she wanted to disguise the real Chrystal. Even after three children, her figure was as trim and perfect as a fashion model's.

Chrystal looked up, but it was obvious she was lost in her own thoughts. "Yeah, now I know better. It's been a hard lesson to learn, but I know there are no princes, no pink cotton candy castles, no one to rescue me from the evil stepmother. Or I guess stepfather in this case. Sometimes, I think I'm in the wrong body, you know. Or I guess it's like out of body. Like I'm watching this other person be me and she's totally fu— oops. Sorry."

"No, it's okay. Go ahead with what you were saying," said Nancy as she carefully watched what Chrystal was doing.

Chrystal looked down at the dip she was mixing in the bowl. "But she's totally messing everything up. I want to yell at her. Stop it, bitch! This is ridiculous. Don't you know any better? Nobody's gonna love you if you keep acting like this. What you're doing is just so crazy. Why won't somebody stop her? I really hate this bitch."

Nancy felt such compassion for her niece. For longer than she could remember, she'd only seen Chrystal as a thorn in Jackie's side. She was only now seeing a side of Chrystal that went beyond the bluster, selfishness, and irresponsibility.

Nancy had always felt badly for her sister, Jackie, and placed the most blame on Chrystal for their strained relationship. Now, she was close to tears as she talked to Chrystal. "What about your mother? Did you ever tell her how you really felt? Or Royce, are you close to your brother?"

Chrystal hesitated for a long moment before she finally whispered, "She didn't want to hear anything from me. I was invisible in her eyes. Sometimes I wished, just once, she would say, 'I love you Chrystal.' Hold me in her arms and let me cry over my skinned knee. I wanted to tell her about the boy in school I had a crush on and who didn't like me back. I wanted to hear her say, 'It'll be all right baby. Mama understands.'" *I don't know why I'm telling her all this. I've never told a soul how I really feel, but so what? She's probably gonna turn it around on me again. So what the hell.*

Now that she'd started, it was as if she had to get the words out or choke on them. She continued on with a long string of remorsefulness. "You know me and Royce were never close. Because all she ever saw was Royce. I couldn't get in their conversations even if my hair was on fire. I guess I was just too jealous of him. I didn't want anything to do with him."

Chrystal stopped as if to gather her thoughts or, worse yet, as if the memory was still too painful. She continued on in a shaky voice. "She would say, 'Royce got As again, of course. Let me see. Oh you got Cs and Ds. You're not trying at all. Get your head out of the clouds or boys or whatever. How do you expect to graduate with these grades? And a college education is shot to hell. Royce was elected class president, but you want to be a cheerleader? Okay then. But don't be out there acting up, and I don't have time to come to the game to see a bunch of skinny girls showing their panties.'" Chrystal made a noise somewhere between a sob and a strangled laugh.

Nancy looked on and could only shake her head in disbelief. She'd never once thought to look at things through Chrystal's eyes.

"'Royce is about to graduate early at sixteen, and you, you can't even finish high school. And Jewell, that poor baby, you have got to do a better job with her.' She'd say these things almost as if she hated me, her only daughter. I could never understand why. I knew I had to get out of there, or else I was going to go crazy."

"Did you try to talk to your dad? I know he would pick you and Royce up for the weekends when you guys were kids."

Chrystal shuddered and one perfectly formed sapphire tear fell from her eye and splattered on the countertop. In the stillness and quiet of the kitchen, it reverberated like a drumbeat.

"I thought he loved me and Mama was keeping us apart because she was just being evil. I blamed her for tearing us all apart, but later I tried to reach out to Daddy. He stopped picking us up on weekends, and then, when I was about fourteen, I would call him and he wouldn't even return my calls. Royce didn't care, but I never got over it, I guess."

Nancy started to get angry as she realized she had been wrong about Chrystal. The anger was directed towards all the people who hadn't noticed this child suffering. She realized, sadly, that she was just as guilty.

Yes, scratches and cuts on hands and knees were easy to see. You could heal those with some ointment and a bandage. But what about the deep gouges to her heart? The twisted knife of mental abuse and hurtful words was more deadly than the sharpest blade. Those kinds of hurts were never taken out, examined, and healed. They were left to fester and run with rancid pus.

What did it take to make people really start protecting the ones they love? She had to include herself amongst the numbers, for she too had not noticed nor done anything to help. It was so much easier to lay blame at someone else's feet. Even the person wronged usually blamed themselves. This child—this woman—felt she wasn't even deserving of love because nobody had shown her she was worth the effort.

Now, hearing her say the words, it was crystal clear all her acting out had been cries for help. With each and every child she birthed, Chrystal had cried louder and longer. With every run-in with the police, thugs, and felons, she screamed in agony at the unfairness of it all. Nancy felt as if the worst injustice in history had been perpetrated upon this woman. She had misjudged her niece so badly. She had only seen what she wanted to see.

Not one of them had listened. Every nonsense action, every no-good friend, every day she moved backwards, she was clearly begging for someone to remove the twisted blade left hanging from her heart. Everyone labeled her a spoiled brat, a mean and hateful girl-child. No one saw the emotional scars, the self-loathing blisters, and the pulsing aneurisms of anger. Here stood the proof of their bitterly intolerant judgment, their apathy.

Nancy made a move to hug Chrystal, but she pulled away.

"Don't you go soft on me! I'm fine. I don't need hugs and kisses over my boo-boos now. I'm a grown-ass woman with my own small children. I understand the game. Besides, things once done can never be undone. My mother made that very clear to me."

"It doesn't have to be this way. I'm here and I want to help. I'm not going to give you a lecture. It's too late for that now, as you said, but I—"

"Come on. Grandma is probably about to die from thirst. Watching The Rock is probably making her drool and drying her mouth out."

"Sure, I guess so. But I'm not giving up. I'm here for you. I love you and I know your mother does too. And I'm sorry, so very sorry we didn't show you that."

BEG

I am not going to beg you
I don't need your smile to make my day
But I want the heat from your sunshine
To make my world less cold and gray

I am not going to beg you
I don't need your arms to hold me close

CRYSTAL CLEAR

But I want to feel your gentle touch
To comfort me when I need it most

I am not going to beg you
I don't need you to keep me safe
But I want to feel less frightened
To keep the fear from my face

I am not going to beg you
I don't need you to want me too
But I want you to just say the words
To let me know you feel as I do

I am not going to beg you
I don't need your love that bad
But I want your gentle caresses
To make me believe that's what we had

No, I am not going to beg you
No, I don't need you to see me cry
But sometimes, very late at night
I think . . . I really do want to try

Chapter Four

Late Saturday Night - Jackie's house

Jackie and Eric talked about everything that happened at the wedding and later on at Ms. Sylvi's house. There was no holding back. It was a catharsis that was long overdue. They were seated at the kitchen table and had just finished eating two delicious omelets that Eric made.

Jackie stood up and took the dirty dishes to the sink. "Do you think Chrystal will be all right? She looked devastated."

"I really don't know. I feel so inadequate when it comes to understanding either Chrystal or Royce. All these years, I thought of them as my children, but only in the sense of paternity. I never really got a chance to see them as individual people. You know, with their own personalities, desires, and wants."

"Well, I raised them both and I'm just as perplexed. I've never really communicated well with Chrystal. There was always something missing there. I always felt as if we were in a competition for Jimmy's love. There wasn't much of that to go around, I guess. I know it was hard for her after the divorce.

She really is a daddy's girl and to be separated from Jimmy hurt her deeply. I guess I felt guilty for breaking that up, but I had no choice. I couldn't stay in that marriage. I had to get out before it was too late."

Eric looked at Jackie and felt the remorse and hurt she was experiencing as if it was his own.

Jackie slowly confessed. "I guess I didn't do all the things I could have done for her. There was a period of time when I didn't even know what I was doing. Let alone what Chrystal was feeling. By the time I saw what was going on, it was too late. I couldn't break through the tough exterior she put up. I guess I really didn't try hard enough. I thought, if I helped with the babies, then that was enough, but I'd forgotten Chrystal was my baby also."

Eric stood up and went to Jackie at the sink. He put his arms around her and said, "I know in my heart all this will come out positively in the end, but the getting there is going to be difficult. One thing I want you to remember though is I am here for you, Chrystal, and Royce. I will never leave again like I did. I love you, Jackie, and I love our children."

"I love you too, and I feel the same way, that in the end it will be a positive thing. But for now and after all the revelations today, I don't know how she feels about either me or Jimmy. She looked like her entire world had collapsed."

"Yeah, I guess it's pretty hard to take all this in at once, and she probably feels really betrayed because Jimmy never told her the real truth."

"Yes, she probably does feel that way, but I never wanted them to know the real Jimmy. He's such a terrible person, evil personified. I didn't want them to know their father was gay and Uncle Bryan was really the dude on the side either." Jackie laughed a sad little laugh. "I thought I was protecting them, and now I find out I really didn't have a clue. Imagine, Chrystal and Royce had been in contact with Jimmy all these years. I thought I knew Royce and we had a great relationship, but I don't know him as well as I thought either. To finally know Chrystal is Jimmy's child and only Royce is yours, I think I need to really understand what this has cost all of us."

Eric kissed Jackie again. "We'll make it work out because now we know. There's no more secrets and hidden agendas. We can all start over."

"Yes, you're right. Everyone has been hurt by all the revelations. I'm going to give it a day or two and talk to Chrystal. And I mean really talk to her as a mother should. I want us to really work on trusting each other. And Eric, I pray to God all the secrets have finally been exposed."

Ms. Sylvi was watching The Rock's movie and urging him on to destroy the bad guys. Every now and then, she took a sip from her wineglass.

Nancy had been back to the kitchen already to refill her drink. They both were talking loudly and laughing over parts of the movie. Both were clearly loving their time together and an almost-naked Rock.

Chrystal sat in the midst of all the fun, but her mind reached backwards in time. A time when she knew she was in love again, for the second time.

Five years ago

His name was Omar Terek. He was twenty-three and his father owned a convenience store. She remembered the first time she saw him. She was eighteen and thoroughly bored with her life. She was working on her GED and planned on going to nursing school in the fall when she ran into Omar. Again, her life took a detour to parts unknown and unplanned.

She walked to the store on a sunny May afternoon. It was mainly for exercise. Although she hadn't gained an ounce with Jewell, Chrystal always felt she was too fat. She knew the good-looking guys didn't like fatties, and she was determined she was going to get her a good-looking guy. She already had one strike against her, but she was going to be smarter this time.

Jewell was only about six months old when Chrystal pushed her in her baby stroller to the store to get a diet soda. No matter where she was going, Chrystal always had her hair styled and cut in the latest trend. Her clothes (a cute little blue short set) were from pre-pregnancy, but they were still stylish. A pair of gladiator-style sandals completed the outfit. She looked more like she was the babysitter than the mother.

She was looking around when she heard a deep voice ask her if she needed some help. Chrystal turned around so quickly she almost fell into Omar's arms. He was standing too close behind her. He had the deepest, darkest eyes she'd ever seen. And when he smiled, a set of perfectly dazzling white teeth lit up his face. She had to tell herself to breathe. This had to be the most gorgeous man she had ever seen. He was about six-two and very fit. He had the prettiest caramel-colored skin. His hair was jet black and tied into a short ponytail.

Chrystal flipped her hair back out of her face in a casual manner. "No, I was just getting a diet soda. I'm good." She backed up a little and turned Jewell around in the stroller.

Jewell's face lit up like a beacon and she gurgled and cooed at the man standing tall above her. She didn't get a chance to see many tall men in her home, so this was a special treat for the baby.

Omar stooped down and exclaimed over the baby. "Wow! What a beautiful little girl. She's the cutest little one I've ever seen. Her mother obviously trusts you a lot to let you out with her beautiful baby. It's a wonder some big bad wolf hasn't gobbled both of you up."

Chrystal laughed, "Well, really this is my baby girl, Jewell. We were out walking, catching some sunshine. My name is Chrystal and I live down the street. Well, actually a couple of streets over."

Chrystal didn't want to blow her chances, so she decided to be upfront and honest to begin with. If having a baby was a turnoff to him, then she wouldn't have wasted any time.

The young man looked shocked at Chrystal's words, but he continued to smile at them. "I can see where she gets her beautiful looks from. You both are as pretty as a spring flower."

The man's kind words worked their magic on Chrystal, and she blushed as an excited Jewell blew spit bubbles. "Do you work here? I've never seen you around before. I would have remembered if I had."

"Technically, no, my name is Omar, and my family owns this store. I finished my master's at the university, and my dad thought it would be good if I came and helped out in the store from time to time. You know, to get some practical business experience."

"Wow, that's really great. You're probably like his right hand man, then. But you look too young to have already have your master's degree."

They both turned when an older man called Omar's name. "That's my dad. Let me see what he wants. Don't go anywhere. I'll be right back."

For once, Chrystal felt she'd made a great first impression on a good-looking guy. This one seemed to be smart and funny and had money. It had never been easy for her to talk to boys, and now that she was older, it hadn't gotten any better. Deep down, she was shy and easily flustered. Her self-esteem was at an all-time low, and she felt she would never find true love.

From that day forward, things seemed to finally have changed. Chrystal made frequent trips down to the store with little Jewell. Omar asked if there were a husband or boyfriend in the picture. Chrystal felt embarrassed to tell him there wasn't. It never occurred to her to ask him the same questions.

At first, she was a little hesitant about being at the store so much, but Omar assured her it was all right. He flirted shamelessly with her and the baby. Every time she came in, he had a special treat for Jewell. Eventually, he saw them in the back office and entertained them during his free time. He helped Chrystal with her GED tests and actually made studying fun. She had Jewell with her, but the baby usually fell asleep almost immediately and stayed that way during most of the time at the store.

Finally, Chrystal got up enough nerve to tell her mother a little bit about Omar. She kept it in general terms and made it seem like no big deal. "Mama, you know the son of the guy who owns the convenience store is kind of good-looking, and he's so nice to me and Jewell whenever we go there." Chrystal was in such a big rush to get the words out that she garbled most of it.

Jackie said, "Well, that's good. I'm glad you're out and about again. But don't make yourself a nuisance down there. You know how they think about us. I wouldn't want them to think you might steal something."

Chrystal tried to not let her mother's words hurt her, but she was so sensitive about everything that any negative words from her mother stung her. Still, she didn't let it stop her from seeing Omar. In fact, it made her want to get to know him even more, just to show her mother how wrong she was.

She loved to talk to Omar and found out he and his family were all from a little region in Pakistan that she couldn't pronounce. They had come to the US about sixteen years earlier. She thought they had done very well for themselves since.

Every time she came to the store, Omar's father found an excuse to talk to Omar in their native language.

Mr. Terek was a small man, but he talked with a loud voice. She had no idea what they were saying, but she guessed it was about her being there so much. He would say something rapid fire to Omar and throw up his hands while looking at her at the same time. Omar would say something back in their native language. This went on so much she finally asked Omar about it.

"Your dad doesn't seem to want me here. If there's a problem, I can wait outside, or you can come and visit me at my house."

"Oh, no, Chrystal," he said with his beautiful accent. "There's no problem. My father likes to explain over and over his ideas about arranging the store. It's nothing. Don't worry."

He took her hand and rubbed up and down her arm with his strong fingers. With every warm touch, her fears melted away.

Omar started out slowly, but soon he moved up to convincing Chrystal they should go out on a date. She begged her mom to look after Jewell. She said she wanted to go out with her cousin Nikki to the movies without the baby. She wasn't ready yet to tell anyone she was actually dating Omar. She wasn't that sure how she felt about him.

When she and Omar finally went out, it was everything she imagined and more. Omar was a complete gentleman and treated her with so much respect she felt positively special. He drove a new red Camaro and took her to the movies. He held her hand during the chase scenes, and he even put his arm around her shoulder several times during the love scenes.

If he thought it strange she wanted to meet him at the theatre, he didn't say. But he was adamant about taking her to her house and dropping her off after the date was over.

The next time, she asked her grandmother to keep Jewell for her. Chrystal said she wanted to spend some time alone with her girlfriends. She told her grandmother none of her friends had babies and she wanted to feel like a teenager again. She needed time to gossip and catch up with her friends.

Her grandmother didn't know Chrystal had very few girlfriends. Her family never noticed the only person besides Jewell that Chrystal was ever around was her cousin Nikki and occasionally her old school pal, Chantrelle.

It wouldn't have taken much to figure out what was going on if they really wanted to, but her mother was drowning in her own fears and Chrystal's feelings weren't her major concern. It was all her mother could do to keep up with Royce, who she felt hadn't let her down yet.

The first time Chrystal and Omar were really alone, he took her to his friend's apartment because he couldn't take her to his house. He lived with his parents, grandparents, and four younger siblings. That was their culture, and he said he didn't feel it was proper to take her there. She was so nervous she kept rubbing her arms and jumping at every little movement he made. She almost made herself sick with her nervous thoughts.

"Chrystal, relax and go with the feeling," he said. "You are so beautiful and kind. I can't believe you'd be interested in someone like me."

77

"I like you a lot, Omar, but I don't know if I'm really ready for another relationship. I'm still trying to come to terms with Jewell's father's disappearing act. I still can't even say his name out loud."

"You don't have to worry about me. I would never treat you like that. You're much too special to me already. I want us to have a real relationship. I'm not holding anything back and I want you to do the same. Trust me. I would never betray you."

Omar was still the perfect gentleman, and they only sat and talked in the small living room. It felt so good to finally have someone she felt comfortable with. The only problem was his best friend Jacob.

Chrystal got chills every time his friend came around. He was a good-looking man, but he was way too blondish for her taste. Although he hadn't technically said anything wrong, there was something about him that made her uneasy. He always gave her a creepy smile when she came over. Asking her too many times how she was. Commenting on how gorgeous she was. Asking her if Omar treated her right and on and on. She'd learned never to trust anyone who gave you a full-tooth smile. There was nothing she could say because it was Omar's friend and he thought the guy was really generous to let them use his apartment.

By the fifth date, Omar introduced her to weed. She knew what it was but had never done it. Her mother would never believe she hadn't, but Chrystal had never tried any drugs or alcohol of any kind. After a few puffs, she started feeling mellow, or so she thought.

Chrystal had asked her aunt Nancy to keep Jewell for her overnight. She told her aunt she was going to a party at a friend's house and then staying over to spend the night. No one though too much of Chrystal's requests. Her aunt was just glad she seemed to be having some fun for a change. For too long, it had seemed she'd given up on life.

Omar had taken her to his friend's apartment again. His friend was out of town, so this time, they had the whole night to indulge. Omar fixed dinner for them both. Chrystal was so impressed that he cared enough to share his native dishes with her. The food was unrecognizable, but tasty. He kept pushing alcoholic drinks on her, and before she knew it, she was stretched out on the sofa, very intoxicated. She knew what was going on and what this was leading up to, but somewhere in the back of her mind, she wanted it to occur. She equated love with sex and felt that was the only thing she had to offer someone.

Chrystal wasn't on any kind of birth control. Her mother made sure she received some after Jewell was born, but Chrystal felt she didn't need any. She'd had the prescription filled but threw the pills in the toilet. She was convinced she would never love again and therefore didn't need any birth control. She'd had no intention of having sex ever again, but here she was, ready to indulge. And the thought of STD's never entered her mind. Jewell was nine months old when Chrystal ventured into those deep waters again.

After every last bite of dinner had been eaten, Omar took Chrystal to the bedroom he was using. He had another joint ready and quietly lit it and took a puff.

"Here, take another pull. This is some really good stuff. Jacob only gets the best. I'm sorry there's no chair in here, but you can sit on the bed. Do you like his place? It's a nice place, but my parent's house is a mansion. I wish I could take you there and show you my room. I've decorated with some special pieces from my homeland."

Omar was nervous as well and continued to ramble on about his family's house and his bedroom.

Chrystal sat down on the bed and tried to relax, but she was so jumpy she couldn't sit still. "I'm sure it's beautiful, but I don't know about this weed. I thought Muslims didn't drink alcohol or smoke weed. Like I told you, I've never done this before tonight. Can't we just watch some TV, or you can tell me about the little town you're from again?"

Chrystal wasn't as dumb as everyone thought. She had done some research on Omar's native homeland and its people. Omar side-stepped the question of alcohol and drugs. He chose instead to talk about his family and how they came to the US. He didn't want Chrystal to know he was actively going against everything his Islamic teachings had instilled in him.

"Well, my family and I had to leave our homeland because of the last military coup in 1999. It was so dangerous we never knew if we would be blown to pieces or imprisoned. My father was a very wealthy merchant, and he had a large store in the marketplace that sold carpets. Politically, he sided with the wrong government party that wanted all the power. He and others who thought like him were often singled out and had to give bribes to the local militia to stay in business. Even with that, it was a good living for us. I was about eight when I noticed what was happening. I used to play with a group of boys about my age and—"

Omar paused and looked at Chrystal. She had passed out. "Hey, wake up sleepyhead. I was telling you all about my childhood, and here you go to sleep on me. I know it must be boring to a girl like you."

"Oh, I'm sorry. I guess I had too much good food, drink, and whatever. It's making me so tired I want to jump into bed. I guess that sounds kind of 'bad girl' of me, but I just want to go to sleep." Chrystal laid her head back on the pillow and looked up at him with large sparkling eyes.

"You have the most beautiful eyes. You could never be a bad girl. You're too sweet. I want to taste just how sweet you are. Let me make love to you, Chrystal."

Chrystal loved all the compliments Omar gave her. No one had ever treated her this special in her life. Not even her father, whom she loved dearly, had given her such praise. None of her family members realized how little Chrystal thought of herself. She believed she had disappointed everyone by getting pregnant and dropping out of high school. She was very careful to remain in the background. She didn't want them to think even worse of her.

Now, it was the moment of truth. Did she trust Omar enough to let him into her heart? Would he hurt her? Chrystal didn't know the answers to these questions, but she had to admit she was very attracted to Omar. From the way he was looking at her, he was very attracted to her too.

"I don't know about this. I want us to be good friends, but not necessarily friends with benefits. You know what I mean?"

"I know what you mean, but this is so much more to me than casual sex. I don't give my heart lightly, but I feel you are the right woman for me. I even love to watch out for little Jewell.

Believe me. I'm not a kid kind of guy, but you and Jewell make me feel something special. I want to protect both of you."

"Can we take it slow? I'm really not used to all this, and I don't want you to think badly of me. I mean I'm not that experienced."

"Chrystal, just relax and let me take care of you. You are so beautiful. Your skin is so soft and radiant. I love how you smell. Everything about you turns me on."

"I don't know. I do like you a lot, but I—"

"Here, take my hand and let me hold you. I won't do anything you don't want to. Okay?"

Chrystal put her hand in Omar's and decided to tell him the truth. "I've been hurt in the past and I don't think I can take another letdown. Jewell's father doesn't even deserve that title. He was the only person I ever had sex with. I was young and stupid and thought he loved me. All he wanted was the panties, and now I'm an unwed mom who didn't even finish high school. I want to let you into my world, but I know deep down your world is so different from mine."

"What do you mean? I've been here in the US for the past fifteen years and finished my graduate courses right here at the University State College."

"Well, for one thing, you're Muslim and I'm not. I don't see how your family could accept someone who isn't Islamic and has a baby already. And I don't have any intentions on becoming Muslim. There's too much there I don't understand. When I do go to church, it's with my mother and grandparents, and they're just plain old-fashioned Baptist. And for another thing, I thought it was common in your culture to have arranged marriages and even multiple wives. At least that's what I learned in school."

"Chrystal, you're thinking too much. Yes, arranged marriages are common in Pakistan, but we have adapted well to the US. I don't want to think about my family right now or your family either. I want to kiss you and make love to you. I know you want to, but like I said, I'm not going to push you. I can wait."

"But if we're to have something more, then our families are important. I don't want to feel like an outsider. I feel enough of that now with my own family. I couldn't stand it if I knew your family didn't like me. I see the way your dad looks at me. I don't want that."

"I understand, and I want more also. I'll let you decide when you're ready and I won't push. But I don't know how I'm going to keep my hands off you. You're so beautiful. I can't stop touching you. The things I want to do to you. It will be wonderful, I know."

Omar kept his word that night, and all they did was cuddle and sleep.

As time moved on, Chrystal eventually gave in to her desires.

The differences between Omar and Jason were like the differences between a small stream and the ocean. Omar was a man, and with Jason, Chrystal had been dealing with a boy. Omar showed her what real passion was. He took over her senses and left her breathless.

"Chrystal, when I make love to you, I want you to know who's giving you passion. Open your eyes and let me see those beautiful amber eyes." Omar kissed her senseless and Chrystal gave back all she had in her. As he removed each piece of her clothing, he licked her naked flesh and left scorching-hot kisses all over her body.

"I don't know how to love you," said Chrystal as Omar kissed her neck. "I've never done anything close to this. I thought I knew what sex was about, but now I see I don't know a thing. I can't even call what I'd been doing lovemaking. I feel so . . . I don't know. I just feel bad about my past."

"From now on, our past is just that. Gone and forgotten. All that matters are you and me now. Just let me love you and we won't think about what is to come, but only what is now."

Chrystal did just that and let go of the past. While Omar held her, the troubles of her life seemed to disappear. One by one, she let him take over the empty spaces in her heart. One passionate night led to another and another. Before she knew what happened, she was in way over her head. Omar was like her drug. She needed him to calm her and center her world. She continued to meet him as often as possible at Jacob's apartment, but eventually things would have to change.

Jacob smirked at her every time Omar brought her over. He even hinted that sometimes he and Omar shared everything. He made it sound as if Omar was doing things she didn't know about and he wanted to help her see the true Omar.

Chrystal was ashamed to let Omar know how his friend disrespected her. She kept quiet about the things Jacob said behind Omar's back. She tried her best to never be left alone with Jacob, but sometimes Omar would leave the room to go to the bathroom or elsewhere. She couldn't very well ask to go with him. He would definitely know something was up. She had no choice but to endure Jacob's comments. She didn't want to be the cause of trouble between the two. Besides, Jacob's apartment was the only place they could be together.

Chrystal hoped she hadn't misread all the signs again. She tried to believe what Omar said, but she was confused and didn't know who to trust. She couldn't talk to her mother, who would only tell her she was being stupid to even think someone like him was doing anything other than using her. Chrystal knew Nikki's advice wasn't reliable, and she knew not to trust Nikki too far.

Then there was her father. He had finally reached out to her after Jewell was born, and Chrystal didn't hesitate to jump in the lifeboat. She'd received a phone call from Jimmy totally out of the blue, and she almost hadn't recognized his voice. It had been so long since she talked to him.

It started out slowly, but soon she felt she could open up to him again. She wanted so badly to trust him; she was willing to believe anything he told her about her mother, even though she knew some of the things he said about her mother couldn't possibly be true. They talked about everything, and she finally felt someone was on her side again. She could never talk to her mother this way and her father convinced her she didn't need to.

Jimmy persuaded Chrystal to come and visit him. She was overjoyed, and she and the baby happily got in the car her father arranged to pick them up and deliver them to his house in Alpharetta.

It was a lavish estate, much bigger than the old house in Midtown. It had more rooms than she could count, and to top it all off, there was a huge pool she and Jewell loved to lounge around. Chrystal felt like everything was going great until her father asked her about Royce. She didn't want to share her father with Royce. Besides, she was Daddy's little princess. Royce was a mama's boy in her eyes. He always spoiled everything for her. When he was involved, no one paid any attention to her. He had their mother eating out of his hand and now their father would be too.

Jimmy finally got his way. Chrystal was left with no choice but to tell her brother about their father wanting to reconcile. Royce wasn't as overjoyed as Chrystal to visit his father, but he tolerated it out of respect for the man.

Chrystal and the baby visited as often as Jimmy let her. He even introduced her to Bryan and confessed that Bryan was his partner in life now. Eventually, they built a working relationship that all three enjoyed. Royce didn't visit as often as Chrystal, but Jimmy cautioned both of them not to tell their mother. He told them she would never understand his lifestyle and she didn't have a forgiving bone in her body. Just to keep the peace, they both agreed.

Now, Chrystal saw no reason not to confide to her father how she felt about Omar Terek. Unfortunately, Jimmy wasn't overjoyed to hear she was seeing someone outside her race.

It all came to a head one day when she was visiting. They were in Jimmy's office when the interrogation started.

"Chrystal, how does this Omar person treat you? And please tell me you haven't had sex with him."

"What do you mean by that? He told me he loved me, and he treats me with the utmost respect. In fact, I've never had anyone treat me as nice as Omar does. He buys me and Jewell very nice gifts and takes us to great places. Daddy, every relationship isn't based on sex. Even I know that." Chrystal said this out loud, but secretly she had her suspicions that everything was not as it should be with Omar.

"Baby don't you see? There's red caution flags waving all over the place. You have to be careful of who you trust these days. Everybody is not your friend. People will use you to get what they want."

"What? Why would you say something like that. I know I can trust Omar."

"Well, what about 9-11? Have you forgotten it was his people that toppled two skyscrapers and brought down several airplanes, killing thousands of people? I know you read about that horror in school." Jimmy said this while holding Chrystal's hands and looking deeply into her eyes. He wanted her to understand the seriousness of what she was doing.

Hot red highlighted Chrystal's cheeks, and she snatched her hands out of her father's. She practically shouted at him, "That was not Omar's people who did that. We had a very in-depth conversation about that. Those were some crazy Arab terrorists that have no respect for the US. In fact, they are some of the same people that forced Omar and his family to flee Pakistan in the first place. They're worse than animals, and Omar and his family despise them. I believe what he told me, and there's no way any of his people were involved in that horror."

"Look I didn't mean to upset you, and I think we woke up the baby, but don't be so naive. They're all the same. Don't let them fool you. They can be very convincing when they want to be. You young people now-a-days rush into things so quickly.

I love you and Jewell, but, baby, you don't need another fatherless child. And that's exactly what I see coming."

Chrystal grew angrier and angrier with every word her father uttered. She was trying hard to be respectful, but she was tired of her father treating her like a child. She made an angry sound of distress.

"Calm down, okay. I'm just speaking what's on my mind. I don't want anything bad to happen to you. So, have you at least met his mother or any other family members? I know for a fact that how a man treats his mother is very indicative of how he will treat you."

"I met his father, but we're waiting for the right time to visit with the rest of his family. He said they're very old fashioned in a lot of their ways and he has to sort of pave the way first."

Chrystal heard the disbelieve in her father's next statement as he quietly spoke.

"Baby, I don't want to see you hurt, but these people are traitorous. Besides, what do you know about their culture? He could already have several wives waiting for him back in Pakistan."

Jimmy sat back down behind his desk. "You can't believe anything they say. If everything was all right, why would he have to pave the way, as you say? Believe me, he's not to be trusted. All men want is to use you. You should know that by now. Don't make another mistake. I have never liked those people, and I will not start now. Not even for you."

"No, Daddy, I can't believe that. I know you're wrong. I just know." Chrystal went to Jewell and picked her up and held her tight. She prayed to God that her father was wrong, but deep inside she thought he just might be right. *Dear Lord, please don't let Daddy be right. Please let Omar be the one, please.*

Chrystal caught her aunt looking at her strangely. "Is everything all right, baby? You look lost in thought. The Rock is pretty good in this movie. Why don't you come back to Earth and join us?"

"I'm okay. I was just thinking about something Grandma said."

"You mean you really heard me? I thought I was wasting my breath," said Ms. Sylvi as she stood up and stretched.

"No, I heard you, and I understand what you're saying. The kids do need a positive male figure in the house. In fact, anyone positive would be good right now. I want to . . . I don't know. I don't know what I want."

"Yes, you do know what you want," said Nancy as she stood up to go in the kitchen for another drink. "Maybe you're afraid we won't understand, or maybe you don't feel like you deserve it."

Chrystal's next words stopped Nancy in her tracks. "Yeah, you're right. I don't deserve it. I've made so many mistakes and trusted the wrong people. I thought my cousin Nikki had my back, and now I find out she's just stabbing me in the back, in my face, and all over my body. She set me up, and I almost got the shit beat out of me. Sorry, Grandma, but they're some really bad people."

"Is that what the handprint on your face is about?" Nancy came over to Chrystal and lifted her face by the chin.

"What are you involved in? Please don't tell me its drugs again."

Ms. Sylvi looked ready to faint as she clutched her hands to her chest. "What? Oh, my Lord! Baby, you haven't been involved with drugs, have you? Why didn't anybody tell me? What in the name of the Lord has been going on? When did all this happen?"

Nancy didn't give Chrystal time to answer before she took over the conversation. "It was a long time ago. Jackie and I decided not to upset you with it. It was after Oro was born and so much was going on, what with Daddy and . . ."

Nancy trailed off, not wanting to bring up the subject of her father's tragic accident again.

Chrystal took over and answered her grandmother. "Well, I guess I was depressed after Oro was born, and Nikki said she had some stuff that would help me sleep and feel better. I swear I didn't know what it was at first, but I really didn't ask." Chrystal hung her head and rubbed her hands up and down her arms as if she was cold.

"Oh, baby. Why didn't you go to your mom for help or even come to me? I would've helped you any way I could," said Ms. Sylvi as she teared up at the thought of her granddaughter's suffering.

"I don't know why I did what I did. I just know I was so unhappy and I . . ." Chrystal looked up at the ceiling of the family room as if hoping the answer would fall from the sky right through the rooftop.

"Go on," said Nancy with a sorrowful look on her face.

"I felt lost, you know. Here I was again with another baby and no baby's father in sight. I knew everybody was thinking how ridiculous and pitiful I was. I loved my baby. Don't get me wrong, but something was so . . . I guess it was too much. I felt like I was out here on my own and nobody really cared. I couldn't sleep, I couldn't think, so I went with what Nikki gave me. Then she stopped giving me the pills. She said she had to pay for them and I needed to pay her back."

Ms. Sylvi took Chrystal's hands in her own and said, "Baby, what exactly did you do to get these pills?"

"I started stealing from department stores. Stuff like perfume and small jewelry. Stuff that was easy to get into my baby bag or the stroller I had Jewell and Oro in. Then I would give it to Nikki to resell. But the store security people caught me on camera, and I ended up detained and a bunch of stuff like that."

Chrystal wouldn't look at her grandmother as she told the story, but Ms. Sylvi quietly held on to her hands and rubbed over her cold knuckles back and forth.

"Lord have mercy on my granddaughter. I never knew. I would've never thought all this was going on. My poor baby, and with two little ones and feeling like this, so depressed. My Lord!" Ms. Sylvi continued to rub Chrystal's hands.

Chrystal stood silently with tears shimmering in her eyes, remembering the past, the hurt, the pain, and the humiliation of being jailed and going to court.

Nancy looked to her mother still holding on to Chrystal.

"Okay, I understand about then, and I'm sorry. I had no idea you were feeling that way, but what in the world do you need so much money for now? Are they still selling drugs and things like that?"

"Well, I wasn't really involved in that part of what they were doing. I was just supposed to do a video shoot. This guy, Smoke, I mean Calvin, is a producer, and he has a lot of connections. But they tricked me. Nikki said all I had to do was entertain some of Calvin's friends from time to time. You know, be a fun date and the money would really flow. They said they were filming it to be part of the background scenes for a new video."

"Oh, baby. I know you didn't fall for that. You have got to know Nikki has been hustling all her short life," said Nancy as she sat back down and clasped her hands together.

Ms. Sylvi looked on, shaking her head all the while with tears in her eyes.

"Yeah, I know it sounds stupid now, but I was desperate for money, and my job at the nursing center wasn't bringing in enough." Chrystal let go of her grandmother's hands and turned to go into the kitchen but turned back when her grandmother called her name.

"Chrystal, why do you need so much more money? Just what were you going to do with it?"

Nancy and her mother both waited for Chrystal to answer.

She thought a while. "If I tell you, you'll probably laugh at me. I don't want that. I want to be taken seriously."

"Give us a chance first. Just because others may laugh doesn't mean we will," said Nancy as she brought Chrystal back to the sofa to sit with her. "I promise we'll take whatever you say seriously, and no one is going to laugh at you."

Chrystal thought for a while and finally came to some internal decision. Not sure what to do with her hands, she twisted her nightgown almost into a knot. "Well, you know I never got a chance to finish nursing school since Jade came along. So I thought I would try to do that full time. That way, I would only have a year to go. The only thing is I can't work, take care of the kids, and go to school full time."

That's a wonderful idea," said Ms. Sylvi as she clapped her hands together and gave Chrystal a big smile. "I know you can do it. And like I said, I want to help you any way I can."

"So I wanted enough money to support me and the kids for at least a year. I figured I could put the kids in day care and really put my all into it. But like I said, I need enough money to keep up my share of the rent, pay for day care, and put food on the table."

Chrystal stood up from the sofa. She looked at her grandmother and really wanted to believe what she was saying, but to trust anyone now was very difficult. "Okay, you can go ahead and laugh now. I know it sounds really stupid, but I honestly think I can do it." She waited for them to tell her she was crazy to even think she was capable of doing it. She was one tear away from a real downpour.

Nancy stood too, and she turned Chrystal around to face her. "I don't think it's a stupid idea. I think it's a fantastic idea. But why didn't you go to your mom or dad? Why risk your safety messing around with these criminals?"

"I don't know. I did try to ask Daddy, but he wanted to know what I needed the money for and I wasn't ready to tell him everything. I never go to Mama with much, and I didn't think she would believe me anyway. I guess I thought Nikki would be honest for once since she had done so much wrong before."

Chrystal sat down again and slowly let out a big breath. She looked around the large room and, suddenly, tears clouded her eyes.

Ms. Sylvi went over to her and laid a gentle hand on her shoulder. "Look at me, child. I know I haven't always been there for you, and right now, I want to say how sorry I am that I neglected you."

Chrystal looked up at her grandmother and tried to smile, but her heart just wasn't in it. "I believe you're sorry, but I know I haven't helped to improve any ideas you have about me. I keep a lot of things to myself, but I didn't—I mean I don't know how to let go and open up now." Chrystal glanced at her aunt as she said, "Really, I don't know how to trust anyone anymore." She stood up and Ms. Sylvi hugged her tight.

Nancy watched her niece, who she had so neglected for most of her young life and thought about her own life. Chrystal wasn't the only one who held back in sharing how she really thought and felt. Nancy too had pretended to be someone she wasn't for more years than she could count. As she saw the silent tears fall from Chrystal's eyes onto her grandmother's shoulder, Nancy thought about all the times she'd hidden behind a false persona.

She thought about the first young man who had broken her heart. She was probably no older than Chrystal had been when she gave away her virginity to someone who wasn't worth it. What followed was man after man who she thought would make her feel better about herself, but in reality, they only made her feel worse. She lost her identity, her very self, trying to fit into a mold that was inadequate no matter which way she turned herself around trying to fit in. For a long while, she doubted her own femininity.

Some of the men hinted that she was too masculine, too butch. They said she had too-wide shoulders, not enough breasts, and a flat ass. She towered over most of the boys in school, and later, she stood shoulder to shoulder with the rest. Just because she didn't want to put up with their bullshit, demanding they respect her, they labeled her manly, even a lesbian.

She wasn't, never had been, but so deep did their claws dig that even she began to wonder. She would look in the mirror and see the wide shoulders they didn't like and the much-too-long legs that weren't feminine in the least. She always felt her sister, Jackie, inherited all the good looks while she only got the bossiness.

To say her love life sucked was to be too generous. It became a joke to even her. But no one saw just how depressed it really made her feel. She hid it too well, and to her family, Nancy was the solid rock on which everyone else stood. She supposed, if drugs had been available for her, she probably would have taken them too.

Once she reached adulthood their father depended on Nancy for her wise council. He always said she had a good head on her. She frowned to herself, thinking no one ever said "pretty head" when it came to her. She was always labelled the strong and cautious one. Dependable, no matter what the situation was. She guessed with her wide shoulders she was supposed to support the world. Unfortunately, she always tried to do just that.

She went into teaching the young with the hope that she could influence their growing minds. Hopeful that she could guide them to have more respect for themselves and each other, she wanted them to have more empathy for those around them who were different and to grow up to believe in themselves, even when no one else did. She had done this while constantly fighting a school system that pushed conformity down her and her students' throats every day. She didn't fit the school system's model of a teacher any more than she had filled the role of a desirable woman in the minds of the men she dated.

The memories now were as amorphous as a shadow on a cold wintry day. Oftentimes, you step in a different direction from the way you were going, and the shadow disappears altogether. Or finally, the sun comes out and a whole new shadow appears. But the hurt, the pain still cut deep. Either way, it was enough to chill her very soul. She was happy she was now fifty-four and old enough that her memory sometimes failed her.

Nancy now realized she didn't fit any model. Much like Chrystal, she didn't know exactly where or with whom she belonged or which direction and shadow appealed to her. She felt misplaced, out of sync with this new world of texting and emojis. Unlike Chrystal, who wanted to blame her mother for all her mistakes, Nancy couldn't place the blame on any one person. She didn't know about Chrystal, but she was deathly afraid to look herself in the mirror and start there.

Chrystal finally laid her head down on her pillow. She had checked on her babies, and they were sleeping peacefully. She knew she needed her rest, but her mind was racing. So many hurtful secrets had been revealed. Her heart ached from facing the many truths she never dreamed could be so.

Just imagine! Her mother had been grinding with Uncle Eric. Chrystal would have never thought that in a million years. She'd told Nancy a lie when she said she'd suspected something was going on. In truth, she'd never even thought about it being a possibility. She just didn't want her aunt to know she hadn't notice what was going on around her.

She honestly loved her brother, but evidently, Jackie knew the truth in her heart and loved Royce more because he was Eric's son. She wondered if that was the reason she always felt something was missing between her and Royce.

On the other hand, Chrystal must have looked too much like her father, Jimmy, and their mother just couldn't stand that. *Yeah,* she thought, *that must be why. Deep in her heart, Mama knew I was Daddy's biological daughter, and that just wasn't what she wanted.*

She looked at her phone and saw the time was a quarter past one in the morning. She had let her phone charge after she talked to Tyler earlier. There were several messages from him that she read.

"Baby pls. I'm so sorry I missed the wedding and the opportunity to be with you and your family. Pls text me back."

Again she shook her head at the unfairness of it all. *Why can't I find Mr. Right? Why do all the childish so-called men keep getting in my life? And he's older than me too, but still acts like a baby. Him and his damn music career.*

She continued on to the next message.

"Chrystal pls answer me. What do you want from me? I'm trying my best to be the man for you, but you keep pushing me out. What can I do to make this up to you? Call me, I'm staying at the Hilton downtown, call me pls."

Finally, the last message was the heartbreaker.

"I know ur mad and I know I disappointed you again. But I love you and want to be with you and the kids. Don't shut me out, pls answer. I love you."

Two and a half years ago

Chrystal thought she's met the love of her life when she met Tyler Jamison. She and Chantrelle had gone on a rare night out at a club in Midtown. Chantrelle's mother was babysitting all the kids at her house to give the girls a much-needed break. Chantrelle had seen an ad for complimentary tickets to a new jazz club and persuaded Chrystal to join her.

They put on their best club outfits and were nervous about being out on a Friday night to anything other than the kiddie pizza parlor, but it was super cool and both young women were impressed.

Their seats were right down front, and they had a perfect view of the stage. They were enjoying a sultry songstress who introduced a talented guitarist to join her onstage. A young black man came out and started to accompany the singer on an acoustic guitar. He played a beautiful love song, and Chrystal swore the guitarist was playing just for her.

He was so handsome. He looked to be in his late twenties, with a shadow-like beard that matched a thick head of sandy, kinky hair. He was tanned a rich golden brown as if he lived in the sunshine. Slim, but not too slim. Tall, but not too tall, just right.

He smiled at Chrystal as he played his heart out to the sad love song the singer performed, and Chrystal couldn't help being mesmerized. She felt a connection unlike anything she had ever felt before. To her amazement, he joined them at the table when his set was finished. Everyone introduced themselves, but the conversation was only between Chrystal and Tyler. Chantrelle, seeing where the chat was going, excused herself to the club's bar area to give them some privacy.

"I believe we were meant to meet tonight," said Tyler as he purred in Chrystal's ear. "Do you believe in soulmates?"

Chrystal stammered. Her heart raced a thousand miles a minute. The proverbial butterflies fluttered in her stomach, and for once, she was struck dumb by this handsome man sitting beside her. She couldn't answer out loud, but her heart sang loudly. *Yes, yes, I truly do!*

Later that night, they said goodnight to Chantrelle and the two of them went to an after-hours night spot. It was a dark and hazy club, but it gave them an opportunity to talk.

Chrystal found herself telling Tyler more about herself than she had ever divulged to anyone before. Even Chantrelle didn't know all the details of Chrystal's dismal love life. She was barely twenty-one and had two babies already, but she showed off with pride pictures of a three-year-old Jewell and fifteen-month-old Oro. Even though it was obvious they had different paternity, Tyler praised her for her care and devotion to her children.

Tyler, in turn, shared with her his hopes and dreams. He was a struggling musician. A product of an alcoholic father and a downtrodden mother. He was an only child from upstate New York, but his miserable childhood gave a soulfulness to his music that otherwise would never have developed. It seemed they had a lot in common.

They laughed and talked until the early hours of the morning. Chrystal had never felt so alive. This didn't compare to the early childish fumbling she had with Jewell's father or even the love she thought she had with Oro's. This was something so much more, so much deeper and soul sharing.

Tyler called them a car service and Chrystal entered her phone number into his cell while they waited. He called it right away. "Just to be sure," he laughingly said. They held hands as they rode to Chrystal's house, and she practically floated into her home after Tyler kissed her goodnight. It had been perfect. So romantic, and again, for the third and final time, Chrystal knew she was in love.

Early Sunday morning, Midtown Atlanta - Nikki

"Nik, you and your damn cousin play too much. Y'all gonna make me fuck y'all up real bad, and it's gonna be y'all own damn fault."

Nikki knew Smoke was really pissed this time. Not only had Chrystal messed up the deal he'd set up with his fellow felons, but Nikki felt he blamed her for sending Chrystal to the Bluff in the first place. Now he had to come up off ten grand, and Smoke didn't like to part with his money. Especially since Chrystal had been the one to mess up.

Nikki sucked her teeth and tried to throw her braids over her left shoulder. Somehow they got caught in the ripped tee-shirt she was wearing and stuck to her chest. "Look here, I ain't the one that went over there and acted the fool. Chrystal did that shit on her own. I told you that chick wasn't shit. But you wanted some of that ass and now look."

She really had tried to make Chrystal look as bad as possible to Smoke. She couldn't help it, but she was so jealous of Chrystal and what she thought Chrystal had; she wanted to cry about her own sorry state.

Nikki thought back to when they were younger. Chrystal always showed up in the newest outfits, while Nikki had too-tight hand-me-downs from her mother's cousins. Chrystal's hair was long, thick and wavy, while her hair was short, thin, and kinky. Chrystal has perfect light pecan brown skin. She had acne and scars, trying hard to cover her brown skin with tons of makeup.

Then there was Chrystal's exotic eyes that seemed to sparkle, while her eyes wouldn't look that way with colored contacts. To top it all off Chrystal had a body to die for, model thin in all the right places, while Nikki was chunky and thick in all the wrong places. Chrystal had all the handsome young men lusting after her, while she was stuck with losers like Smoke.

Still thinking of why she hated Chrystal, Nikki spoke without thinking. "Besides, Duck and them squashed all that. I don't know why the count was low. Do you?"

"I know you didn't just question me about my own damn business. Who you think you is? I know how much I had, and I know what happened to it too. I'm gonna go over to that ho's house and get what's owed me. One way or another, I'm gonna take what's mine." Smoke looked at Nikki and blew out a loud breath. "Besides, why didn't you tell me that Chrystal's old man was gonna be at that wedding. You know I ain't got time to mess around with that. That man ain't right in the head. I'm through messing with him and the people he play with."

Nikki trembled nervously as she watched Smoke strut back and forth in her cramped apartment. She also noticed how old and tired everything looked, including herself.

Hell, she wasn't but twenty-five, but she felt like fifty. She knew she was at least thirty pounds overweight, and nothing she had in her tiny wardrobe fit. This wasn't the kind of life she'd pictured herself in at this stage. The apartment was little more than a studio with a pull-out sofa bed. Everything was dark, drab, and dingy.

She knew better, but her temper was starting to get the best of her, and as her blood boiled so did her mouth spew like a volcano.

"What you mean? You knew he was Chrystal's daddy when you started messing around with them. What? You thought he wouldn't come to his own son's wedding? You stupid too if you didn't see that one coming."

Smoke gave Nikki an evil look as he slapped her across her face. "Now who look stupid, ho? I gave you too much credit too. You as dumb as yo cousin. You know better than to talk to me like that. Go wipe all that snot off your face and stop that damn crying. I ain't hurt you yet. Just keep acting the fool though and you really gonna get a whipping. You need to learn to shut up too. I swear y'all heads as hard as bricks, and don't be telling them folks I'm your fiancé either. I heard you tell Chrystal's old man that we were getting married. You'd be the last bitch I would marry."

For the first time since being with Smoke, Nikki felt like she was in over her head. She wished she was as brave as Chrystal and could stand up to him. In her mind, she heard herself tell Smoke to get the hell out of her apartment and take his funky ass straight to hell, but in reality, all she managed to get out were some hiccups and a string of snot.

"Calvin, Smoke, I didn't mean nothing by that." Nikki stuttered and whimpered as she tried to rub his arm. She had overestimated how far she could go with Smoke. As much as she hated it, she still needed the stuff Smoke was giving her. Now she knew what she had to do to make peace. "You know I don't know how to shut up. I'm sorry. Just let me make it right. That's all I want to do is make it right."

Nikki's mind was in turmoil as she tried to wipe away the snot as Smoke had commanded. *Lord,* she thought, *if you let me get away from Smoke, I promise I'll do right. I promise, Lord. Please just help me get away!*

Smoke looked at Nikki with a slight smile on his dusty brown face as he pulled her hand to his crotch. He scratched in his tangled mess of dreads and looked at his nails for dirt. "Yeah, you need to make it up to me and tonight you gonna do just that. You need to stop stressing me with all this bullshit and get on your knees. I know what I'm doing, and from now on you better remember that too."

Chapter Five

Sunday Morning, 9:00am - Jimmy and Bryan's house

"Jim! Jim! Jimmy! Are you coming to get breakfast before it gets cold? I've been cooking for the past half hour, and I will not let you have it go to waste." Bryan was fed up with Jimmy's attitude. He wanted to call Jim on his behavior, but he knew it wouldn't do any good.

Jim had been complaining late into the night and again all morning, and Bryan was so over the whole thing. If he had to hear any more about what Jackie and Eric might be doing, he was going to hurl. Yesterday had been a long and trying day. Too many secrets, too many lies and too many voices were still ringing loudly in his ears.

"Jim, do you hear me?" Bryan was a step away from throwing the meal away. He couldn't understand why Jim wouldn't leave it alone. What was there about Jackie that made him go crazy? Did he still want her after all these years? Was that the answer? Bryan didn't know what to think anymore, but he did know he was about at the end of his patience with Jim and the whole situation.

"I'm coming. You don't have to shout," Jimmy hollered down the hallway as he was coming out of the master suite's adjoining bathroom. Jimmy was mumbling to himself as he strode down the hallway dressed casually in tailored khaki pants and a polo shirt. "That damn Jackie needs to be taught a lesson. I need a way to do it without it coming back to me."

"What did you say? Are you talking to me or yourself?" Bryan turned from the gas stovetop to watch Jimmy striding happily into the kitchen. He heard what Jimmy said, but he still couldn't believe Jim wouldn't let it go.

Bryan looked around their kitchen. Theirs was a gourmet kitchen that held every appliance known to man. It was a chef's dream with off-white cabinets and white, lightly streaked with gold, marble countertops. The blinding Georgia sunlight coming through the kitchen window was more of a distraction than an enhancement. Expensive coffee and espresso makers sat upon a gleaming section of the counter. A shiny Viking range and refrigerator complemented the décor.

"I was just thinking about the wedding yesterday. Did you hear what Ms. Sylvi said to me?

"No Jim. What did Ms. Sylvi say to you that's so important you make me wait breakfast for you all morning?

"You don't have to be so snippy. Anyway, she said, Jimmy you just as handsome as ever. You haven't aged a day. And she told me my skin was as tight and smooth as any fifty-five-year-old black man could want." Jimmy crowed with laughter as he looked at Bryan, waiting for him to say something smart back to him.

"Soooooo, all this time you've been looking in the mirror? Admiring your smooth mocha colored skin. You, who never has a hair on your head out of place. You, who spends his time getting twice weekly salon appointments just for your moustache. Of course she would say that.

Bryan mused to himself. And of course the color is as natural as the day he was born. Whereas my hair has turned an unnatural shade of orange with gray streaks, and I have to continually beat a path to the salon for dye jobs. Jim's hair is still a lustrous black with a natural curl pattern that any woman would die to have.

Jimmy perched himself on an upholstered, cream-colored stool at the huge island as he watched Bryan critically. "You know this better be worth all the hollering you've been doing. You're acting like you're in here creating a soufflé or something. All I smell is bacon and eggs." Jimmy crossed his legs and picked up his juice and took a sip.

Bryan tried hard to keep the sarcasm out of his voice, but he was way past caring what Jim thought about him this morning. Along with his now depressed, self-loathing thoughts about his appearance, he let his angry words fly. "Well, if you can do better, then by all means, take the spatula. I do my best to take care of you and cook nutritious and delicious meals, and you lay around and complain. You don't appreciate me or what I do for you. One day you'll miss all the things I've done for you."

Bryan brought over a plate and plopped it down on the counter in front of Jimmy. "Here you go, Mr. Mattock. I hope you enjoy your damn meal." He didn't wait for Jimmy's answer but turned swiftly and retreated down the hallway.

Sunday Morning - Ms. Sylvi's house

Nancy came into the kitchen as her mother turned from the stovetop. "Good morning Mama. You know you didn't have to get up this early to make us breakfast." Nancy tried to make light of what Ms. Sylvi was doing, but she really didn't feel right with her mother waiting on her as she did.

"Morning. It's all right. You know I love to cook, and usually, I get up earlier than this. Today I just felt like cooking a big meal for all y'all instead of going to church. I figured we had enough church yesterday. Lord knows we got an ear full of truths."

Nancy took a seat at the table. She knew it was no use trying to get her mother to sit down. Besides, she didn't want to insult her by taking over her kitchen. She decided to move on to other topics. "Mama, what do you think about Chrystal wanting to go back to school full time?"

Ms. Sylvi came over to the table and set a cup of coffee down in front of Nancy. "You take sugar and creamer with your coffee, don't you? Here's both if you want them."

"I just take mine with sugar. I don't like all that creamer you and Jackie like. I like my coffee just like my imaginary men, black and sweet." Nancy laughed along with her mother at her joke, but it was a sad laugh, full of longing. "Anyway, what about Chrystal? I was thinking about asking her and the kids to move in with me until she finishes her nursing degree. I figured Jackie would be busy making up with Eric and wouldn't want all the kids there."

Finally, Ms. Sylvi sat down at the table with her own cup of creamy coffee. She took her time answering as she sipped her coffee.

"You know, I thought about that very thing all last night in bed. I think that's a good idea, and you're right about Jackie and Eric. They need some alone time. But I think a much better idea would be for her and the babies to stay here with me."

Ms. Sylvi looked around her spotless kitchen, avoiding Nancy's eyes and quietly said, "You know, I can imagine little toddlers playing on the floor, laughing at some silly game they play. I haven't really had the chance to be a full-time great grandmother, only babysitting now and then, but I want it so badly. Until now, I hadn't realized just how desperately I need it.

"Oh . . . well, I guess I didn't think you would want all that responsibility at your age. Chrystal and three little ones all up in here. That's way too much for you to handle." Nancy knew she had said the wrong thing the minute the shining light left her mother's eyes.

Ms. Sylvi got up from the table and slowly walked over to the sink. She took a dishrag and started washing dishes.

"Mama, I didn't mean it the way it sounded. I just meant that this is your retirement life now, and Chrystal and the kids would bring so much disruption to your everyday . . . you know, lifestyle." Nancy trailed off, not knowing what to say, but knowing she still had said the wrong thing.

Ms. Sylvi looked away, deep in thought. "I need a disruption Nancy. All I do now is sit here in this big old house, waiting for somebody to need me. You know I cook a big meal every day, just hoping Royce or somebody will drop by to eat it."

"Oh, I didn't know it was that bad. I had no idea. I'm so sorry, I . . ." Nancy trailed off again and looked at her coffee.

"It's so quiet here most days that all I hear is my own breathing. I'd even let that annoying old man next door come over just to have some company."

Ms. Sylvi continued to wash dishes, but her back curved until she was almost lying across the sink.

"Hey, what y'all doing? I smell something good to eat." Chrystal, carrying Jade, came into the kitchen from the back bedrooms. Jewell and Oro trotted along behind her. She and the kids had been happily picking out clothes to wear. Her grandmother had enough clothes in the closet to outfit the babies for weeks. Chrystal had on a loaned caftan. It was a beautiful, red, patterned gown and Chrystal, Jewell, Oro, and Jade, as usual, looked pretty.

She took in the scene in front of her and felt a sadness in the room. Ms. Sylvi was draped over the sink and Nancy was seated, bent over a cup on the table. They both looked like all the life had been sucked from their bodies.

"Is everything okay? You guys look like somebody died." *Uh, I wonder what in the world has happened now*, Chrystal thought.

"Mommy, I want sumthin to eat," said Oro as he scratched his nose. "My nose telling my tummy it's time to eat."

The kids all giggled at Oro's comments, but Ms. Sylvi and Nancy still hadn't said a word.

"Mommy, did you hear me? I think Jewee is hungry too. Ain't you Jewee?

"Here, you kids sit down at the table and Mommy will get you something to eat. Just wait a second."

Chrystal placed Oro and Jade together in a chair at the table and Jewell climbed up into her own chair. The kids happily sang the ABC song and clapped their hands.

"Grandma, you okay? Is everything all right?" Chrystal went about getting the toddler plates filled with the grits and eggs her grandmother had already cooked. She took the plates over to the table and got out some milk for the children.

"Yes, child, everything's all right," said Ms. Sylvi, "I got a little crook in my back is all. Let me help you get the kids fed." She moved over to the table and picked up Jade and sat at the chair she'd vacated earlier. She sat Jade on her lap, and Jade immediately started pulling on her great-grandmother's lovely silver hair.

"All right, Miss Jade. Let's eat something good this morning. I know you hungry because you all slept good all night long." Ms. Sylvi hummed a little song as she hugged Jade to her and picked up the spoon to feed her.

"Mama, I didn't mean how that sounded. I know how much you love your great-grands. I also know that you're not frail and can stand up to anything and everybody. It's just that I want to help too."

Chrystal looked from her grandmother to her aunt. She didn't know what had happened before she came into the kitchen, but she could feel the tension still oozing in the air.

"Come on, Oro," she said. "Let's get the eggs and grits in your mouth, not all over your face. Jewell, baby, you're doing so good. Now eat the eggs too, okay?" Chrystal turned her attention to her aunt after Oro started trying to feed himself. "Aunt Nancy, what's going on? What are you guys talking about?"

Nancy looked at her mother, who was feeding Jade. Finally, she answered. "We were actually talking about your and the kids' living arrangements. I, well, I thought maybe you and the kids could come and stay with me while you went back to school. You know your mom and Eric are trying to reconcile, and that might be a little awkward for everyone."

"You don't have to offer that. Really, I'm okay."

"Let me finish. Your grandmother thought it would be a better idea if you all came to stay with her. You know, she has a bigger house and you guys wouldn't have to double up. I think that's a better idea too." Nancy gave her Mother a smile as Ms. Sylvi looked at her with astonishment in her eyes.

Chrystal looked at both women sitting at the table. After her soul searching last night, she felt differently about her family. She had never considered that, like she was, they were misunderstood. Maybe they weren't as terrible as she always thought. Maybe they did care about her.

She looked around the kitchen. It was a beautiful room, light and airy, painted a beautiful shade of pale peach. There was a big picture window at one end of the room, overlooking the back yard. A back door led out to the patio that had all types of potted flowers arranged around the patio furniture. The women sat around a huge, carved wooden table that she remembered her grandfather, Buddy, bringing home. It had happened so long ago, when she was a little girl. So many memories were in this kitchen. Could she see herself in it, not as a guest, but as family?

"I don't know. I don't want to intrude. Me and the kids are a lot to take in." She turned her attention to her grandmother. "Grandma, do you really want us to come and stay here? I mean, it would help me so much. But I don't know."

Chrystal saw the smile all over her grandmother's face and knew she was sincere. But could she handle her grandmother in her life like that? Clocking her comings and goings. Telling her how to raise her own children. Was she willing to give up her freedom for security and the help she needed so desperately to make her dreams come true?

"I would love to have you and the little ones stay here. I would finally have somebody to eat all the food I cook."

She thought to herself, *Grandma is nosy, so I know she'll be full of questions about my private life. Not that I have that much going on, but Tyler is still kinda in my life.*

Nancy looked back and forth between Chrystal and her mother. "Well if nothing else, I think staying here with Ms. Sylvi is the best idea."

Ms. Sylvi's smile was as bright as a sunflower, and she clasped her hands together around Jade, holding her tight.

"I only hope Chrystal, that you can see this as a positive answer to your dilemma and not as an intrusion into your privacy. I know you young people live differently than when me and your mother were young. I know I wouldn't have dared do the things I see on tv and the internet. Heck, we barely had a party-line telephone to talk on. Now kids are playing with computers and tablets liked we played with a etch-a-sketch. And the dating world or whatever you call it. Hooking up, I guess. That's just too much for me to even guess at."

"What are you trying to say? You act like I'm out wilding in the streets. I can't help it if people flock to me and my three kids. We're just popular I guess." Chrystal laughed at her aunt's statement and said, "I'm just kidding. You know I be home most of the time. Believe me there won't be much going on to worry about."

Nancy smiled at her mother and nodded at Chrystal. "Just think about it. You don't have to agree right now," said Nancy as she took a sip of her coffee. "I'm sure Mama didn't mean pack up and come over right now. You would have to get a lot of things squared away before you could possibly move. You do have your roommate to consider."

Ms. Sylvi let Jade try to feed herself, and she was stuffing eggs into her mouth as Ms. Sylvi answered. "No, I didn't mean right now. I know a lot of planning will need to be done before a move like that, but please consider it. I would love to have you, Jewell, Oro, and Jade come and stay with me. Look at it like this. I need you and the children probably much more than you will ever need me."

She paused and Chrystal could tell her grandmother had a revelation. "Did I ever tell you the story my grandmother told me about life?"

Nancy finally smiled and nodded her head. "I remember that story about the spider's web. I always thought it was so beautiful and meaningful. Yes, please tell it to Chrystal."

"Well," said Ms. Sylvi, "there's this old African tale, according to my Granny Tina. She said her granny told them as children from what her gran said was told to them as children. The story says there's a web, you know, kinda like a thread of mankind's life, that comes out from an ocean. It's the source. She said the strands are thinner than the finest spider's silk. There are tens of millions of these strands, intersecting and twisting about, just like a spider's web caught in the wind."

Chrystal and the children all sat enraptured as their grandmother continued the tale in her mesmerizing voice. Too young to understand, Jade appeared to know the words were powerful, nevertheless.

"Granny said that every man's and woman's life comes from that ocean, and it goes out like a silken spider's web. But somewhere in there, we choose the path it takes. While we are on this path, it can cross others over and over again. Some folks are so stubborn that, even if they hate the path they're on, they keep going on it anyway, saying they can't help it, they can't change. Blaming everybody else for their ways." Ms. Sylvi stopped for a moment to take a sip from her cup of coffee.

"Don't stop. This story, I never heard it before, but I love it. I really do," said Chrystal as she pulled Jewell, who had finished eating, to her side.

"Well, like I said, my granny said people were getting angry about how their life thread was going. They didn't like who they picked to marry or what trade they ended up getting or where they lived. You know how folks are. The chief of the village said, 'We gonna pray to our God to clear this up,' because that's how the chief got the information in the first place. So the people and the chief prayed for enlightenment from their mighty God."

Everyone around the big wooden kitchen table sat in anticipation of the next words from Ms. Sylvi's mouth. Even though Nancy had heard the tale several times as a child, she still enjoyed hearing it again.

Ms. Sylvi continued speaking as she glanced around the table. "So after a few hours of everybody praying, the chief comes out of his house and says to the people that he got enlightenment. He said, 'Your path can change directions and you got free will to jump off one path and on to another.' Along this journey are other folks, and you cross their path or join them and travel along together for a ways. Because the strands are so thin, they are close together and one may look just like another at first."

Jade squirmed a little in Ms. Sylvi's lap and reached for another handful of eggs. She giggled as she stuffed the eggs in her tiny mouth.

Ms. Sylvi continued in her sing-song voice while juggling Jade. "But every one of these tens of millions of threads are different. You never know where it leads or who you gonna meet. But all the people you come across are there for a reason. Some help you, you help others, and some are just there to get on our nerves to make us change paths. The chief said, 'It's up to you people to pick the thread and travel it to your liking. Nobody but you can change the strand you step upon.'"

Ms. Sylvi hesitated and took a sip of her coffee. After she cleared her throat, she continued. "Granny Tina said a lot of folks still thought you didn't have control of the way your life strands go, but like I said, you can choose to change anywhere along a given thread until the day your thread ends. You can do this anywhere along the way, as often as you choose. It's up to you what path your life thread takes." Ms. Sylvi finally stilled and took a big breath, "Well, what'd you think about that?"

Chrystal lowered her head and took a moment to collect her thoughts. She didn't want to answer without thinking over her options. Finally, she raised her head and looked directly at her grandmother with tears in her eyes. "Yes, we want to come and stay. Thank you, Grandmama. Thank you."

Ms. Sylvi was overjoyed. She hugged Jade closer still, until Jade squirmed to get down. "Down, Gran-gran, down."

"I'm so full of joy right now." Tears of joy were indeed streaming down Ms. Sylvi's cheeks. "I prayed for a way to help, and I believe the Lord heard me and answered your prayers and mine, Chrystal. Let's finish this breakfast, and then we can talk about details. Oh Lord, I'm so happy," said Ms. Sylvi as she gently placed Jade on the floor.

As soon as she was released, Jade toddled over to Chrystal and gave her a huge hug. "Yes," said Ms. Sylvi, "I'm full of joy right now."

LIFE'S THREAD

Finer than the thinnest spider's silk
Is the web of mankind's time
Each line, each thread, uncountable
Holding ten million times ten million strands

And each thread could hold much more
Streaming from the ocean of sources
Each piece intertwined like silken yarn
Finer than the thinnest spider's silk

The path, the strands, they twist
They turn, they circle, but ever straight
As if the line was drawn with a compass
Directly from the beginning to the end

Each strand gives us free will
To follow to the end of the beginning
To spiral from one to another
Intersecting, dissecting, blending, blurring

Once chosen and it is a choice
Traveling it's given length until
Becoming one, starting another
Finding love, leaving life, ending

Sunday afternoon, Bermuda - Royce and Jessica

Royce and Jessica, newly married, finally had a moment to themselves. The day before had not only been their wedding day, but it had been the most stressful day of their lives.

It started with his mother, Jackie, confronting Royce about the vows she'd written for him to bind himself to Jessica. He couldn't understand why she was so upset. She denied giving him the poetry and instead accused him of stealing it. It had upset him and Jessica so much.

Then Chrystal's raggedly friend, Smoke, had shown up to the wedding on the arm of their cousin Nikki. Royce had never trusted Nikki either. She always dragged Chrystal into trouble whenever she showed up. Smoke looked like a bad cartoon character in an old clownish suit from the fifties, and Nikki, as usual, was dressed like a stripper.

But the motherlode was hit when Eric, who Royce had invited, showed up and Jackie fainted. The mess that created was almost beyond his comprehension. His father, Jimmy, instigated most of the ridiculousness with his accusations, which unbeknownst to Royce at the time, turned out to be true.

Chrystal was devastated, but what could he do? He hadn't planned that mess. All it had done was add a new level of distrust and tension to his and Chrystal's relationship. He loved Chrystal, but she acted as if she hated him most of the time. Royce didn't know what to do about that.

Chrystal had looked at him like he planned it all. It was his and Jessica's wedding day. No one in their right mind would want all that dysfunction to mar that special day, but there was no way he was going to call off the honeymoon. He'd told Jimmy whatever they had to say could wait until they got back. And now he was glad he had.

He awakened his wife with a deep kiss.

"I love you so much. I can't think of a better way to wake up from a nap." Jessica stretched in Royce's embrace. "I can't believe we're finally on our honeymoon. I had my doubts there for a while. So much was going on at the reception. I wish—I don't know—I just wish it hadn't happened."

Royce turned Jessica in his arms. "Well, for one thing the honeymoon's just starting, and you can certainly believe that."

He gave her one of his loving smiles. "And for another, if it hadn't happened, then we wouldn't be luxuriating in this beautiful king-sized bed right now."

Royce tried to make light of yesterday's mess because he didn't want Jessica to worry. "When we get back home, there will be a lot of questions that have answers. That, my lovely bride, is a good thing. But I promise you we'll still be honeymooning for a very long time, way after we get back home."

Jessica sighed and whispered, "I wonder how your mom is doing?" Louder, she said, "That's the one thing I can't get out of my mind. The look on her face, it was like she'd lost her entire world. And poor Chrystal, she looked like she was totally confused. Wow! You and Chrystal have different fathers. That really is a lot to wrap my head around."

"Yeah, I know. But I talked to Mom this morning, and she's been with Eric. He's helping her work through everything. And Chrystal will have to realize that everything isn't about her. It's way past time she grew up and accepted things as they are."

"What about you, babe? Was it as much of a shock to you? I know you put a lot of time and work into locating Eric, but you didn't know all this, did you?"

Royce hugged Jessica closer to him. "Well, it's like I told you. I was suspicious of some things, but no, I had no idea about all of it. And no, I didn't know that Eric is actually my biological father. But if nothing else, Mom sounded happy, so whatever may come, we did one thing right in getting Eric back in our lives."

Royce and Jessica finally climbed out of bed. "Okay, let's make this afternoon one of the best before we have to go back to reality. We can go hiking or parasailing. It's all up to us what we make of it. But no matter what, we have each other, and no one can change that. I love you, Jessica Mattock, and always will."

"I love you too, Royce Mattock. And like you said, no one can ever change that."

Sunday evening - Jimmy and Bryan

Jimmy and Bryan had dinner at a restaurant they both loved, but the conversation was stifled as if Jimmy didn't want to confront the issues at hand. Bryan, being the compassionate person he was, tried several times to broach the subject of family unity, love, and forgiveness. Jimmy either pretended not to hear or gave one-syllable answers.

Eventually Bryan gave up. Not even the generous glasses of wine and tender, juicy steaks softened the gloomy mood. It was painfully obvious Jimmy's true emotions and thoughts were being withheld. Bryan remembered the difficult conversation they had earlier at breakfast. Jimmy didn't want to forgive and forget. It was apparent he still had something up his sleeve.

Later, after they returned home from dinner, Jimmy seemed to be sleeping in his favorite chair in the family room. The chair was an Italian, handmade, cocoa-colored leather recliner. It had a soft buttery texture that conformed to Jimmy's body shape and size. His hands were clasped behind his head and his feet were crossed at the ankles, resting on the footrest. By all appearances, he was comfortably taking a nap. But Jimmy was seething and very close to exploding.

Jackie, Jackie, Jackie. The mantra running through Jimmy's mind was deafening. Jimmy was fuming, but he had almost put together a plan to derail Jackie and Eric's plans for a happy ever after. *Just need to get in touch with—*

Bryan made the mistake of coming into the family room at that moment. "Jim. Hey, Jim." Bryan touched Jimmy softly on the shoulder, and Jimmy shot up out of the chair and turned on Bryan.

"What the fuck is wrong with you? Can't you see I was sleeping. Are you that dense?" Jimmy knew he'd let his temper get the best of him, again.

Bryan cringed. Tears of hurt appeared in his eyes. He blanched and started to back out of the room as if Jimmy was a wild animal and Bryan needed to keep a wary eye on him. "I'm sorry. I didn't think you were that deeply asleep."

He turned to slip from the room and Jimmy grabbed him by the arm. "I said I was sorry. Stop Jim, you're treating me like an intruder in my own home. I can't even remember what I came in here for."

"Wait. I'm sorry. I didn't mean that like it sounded." Jimmy shook his head.

Bryan turned back and looked him in the eyes. "How else could you have possibly meant that? I'm not dense enough to misinterpret your words. You've changed Jim. I can't figure you out anymore. The kind young man I grew to love has changed into this awful, angry person I see now."

Bryan watched Jimmy. "I'll get out of your way. You can get back to thinking up horrific tortures for whomever. Maybe I'll take a walk and get some clean air in my lungs. The murderous haze in this house is too much for me."

"No, don't go away hurt. I really didn't mean that. I was thinking—"

"Yes, that's the problem. You're always thinking about Jackie and now Eric. You've got to let it go. If not for you, then at least think about our relationship. It can't take too much more of this craziness you keep sending us through. I love you, but it has got to stop. It's been twenty-five years for God's sake." Bryan smiled a sad little smile, full of bitter tears of resignation.

"I've stood beside you and sheltered you through a lot of storms. I didn't say much when you wanted to marry Jackie for all the wrong reasons. I kept silent when you decided that same marriage needed to end. I let you hide me in the corner like a poor relation you were ashamed of. I stood right there when you shredded your children's affection by pushing them away, and then you bring them back in, but only if they behave by your rules. They must love who you say, and if not, you end it."

Jimmy was so flustered by Bryan's accusations that, for once, he was left relatively speechless. "Wait, wait. You're making me sound like an evil villain. I'm not that bad of a man. I want things to be right for everyone and—"

"That's the trouble with your thinking. You do not know what is right, correct, or even best for everyone. People have their own ideas about what they want out of life. You just command, snap your fingers, and expect it to be so. Have you ever asked what it is that someone wants? For instance, me?"

Jimmy stammered but couldn't come up with a clear answer.

"Well, I'll answer my own question. No, you haven't. Why? Because you want to dominate and control everyone and everything around you. I'm so tired of that. I'm so tired of it all." Bryan walked slowly towards the door, heading out of the room.

"I don't know what to do or say anymore. I'm probably just wasting my breath talking to you now. It probably won't make any difference. I'm tired Jim. I'm tired of trying to break through the emotional roadblocks you've erected."

"Wait. You're right. I wasn't thinking clearly. I was caught off guard. Sit down here with me. Let's talk. I honestly want you to understand how I feel. I have been too domineering, too aggressive, I guess, as you say. Too angry over this entire situation. But I don't want you to feel like our relationship isn't worth saving. Besides, it's not at all like you say."

Bryan rolled his eyes at Jimmy's statements. He made a move to leave the lavishly decorated room again. One of the male figures in the framed artwork on the wall looked on in silent disapproval of the scene unfolding in front of him.

"You just don't want to understand!" Jimmy threw his hands out, helplessly. He rubbed his hair and slowly exhaled and held his hands out to Bryan. It was clear he didn't know what to say and certainly not what to make of this new Bryan, who dared to confront him. Every word Bryan uttered was like a punch to his guts. Jimmy felt Bryan shooting him couldn't hurt worst.

Bryan turned back to face Jimmy again. "What're you going to say next? You're really the victim in all this? You're the one that's hurting? You're the one who's been mistreated? By whom, Jim? Your father? You're not the only person who had a shitty childhood. In fact, your children can probably say the same of you. No one else made you take this direction in life and certainly not the way you've gone about it. You've ostracized and hurt a lot of people getting to where you are."

Jimmy squirmed and had the nerve to look uncomfortable for a heartbeat. Again, he wondered where this Bryan had come from.

Bryan took one huge breath and slowly let it out. He looked Jimmy directly in his chocolate-brown eyes and said, "My wish for you, my prayer for you, is that it was all worth it. As you've told me repeatedly, the end always justifies the means. I hope this end was worth it."

Jimmy finally dropped his hands. He watched Bryan turn away. There was nothing he could say, and for the first time in his life, he wondered if he'd finally gone too far.

Chapter Six

Sunday Night, 11:00pm - Ms. Sylvi's house

*M*s. *Sylvi* was still puttering around her immaculate kitchen. Nancy, Chrystal, and the children had left several hours ago in the van Nancy rented to take everyone to the wedding. Ms. Sylvi had talked with Jackie and Jackie sounded so happy. It was wonderful to hear the joy in her daughter's voice after all the tears yesterday. She had to make it up to Jackie. She'd always thought Jackie was the problem behind the breakup between her and Jimmy. She now realized no woman could have put up with what Jimmy had done. She didn't need to know any more details than she'd already heard, and frankly, she didn't want to hear any more.

She wanted to help Chrystal and Jackie become closer, so she told Jackie about the plans for Chrystal returning to nursing school. And Ms. Sylvi was so happy that Chrystal had agreed to come and stay with her. Jackie had her doubts, which was understandable considering her relationship with

126

Chrystal, but Jackie, like Nancy, gave her blessing to the idea. It had indeed been a blessed day.

At first, Ms. Sylvi had thought it wasn't going to happen. Nancy seemed intent on stopping her, telling her she was too feeble, too old to have them in the house with her. Her memory wasn't as good as it used to be, but she could still handle the children. That was a talent you never lost.

Ms. Sylvi thought of Chrystal and remembered how frustrating it could be for people to change, realizing with a start she would have to change also. She thought back to the spider-web origin story her grandma told her and which she, in turn, had told Chrystal and the children. She was just as guilty of wanting to hold on to what was known and comfortable as everyone else. Even if it wasn't good for her. This arrangement would change her life greatly, but she needed that change. In fact, she felt she would perish if change didn't come as soon as possible.

At seventy-six, soon to be seventy-seven years old, she needed some light in her life, some joy. It had all disappeared along with her Buddy. She was just existing. Struggling to find some meaning to her life.

She continued her cleanup, putting dishes and glasses in the cabinets. Straightening an already straight silverware drawer. Pots and pans were put away. Even a fairly large casserole dish had been cleaned of the pot roast, potatoes, and other vegetables it had held earlier for dinner. The leftovers were wrapped up and refrigerated. The final thing to do was clean the floor. She took out her duster mop and cleaned up the crumbs from the great-grands. It actually was fun looking for all the little crumbs left in their wake.

127

All too soon, there was nothing left to do in her huge kitchen that contained too many memories. Memories of happier times. Awful memories of sad times. Memories of her Buddy Stinson. Memories of the only man she ever loved.

Unlike her granddaughter's, Ms. Sylvi's love life had been simple. She was raised in a strict, God-fearing home on a small farm in South Georgia. Her parents, George and Evelyn Johnson, produced seven children to help on the farm. They had all been given their chores at an early age. Her father needed all his children to help grow vegetables to make a decent living. But Sylvia Johnson, the third youngest, wanted more out of life.

After finishing high school at eighteen, she was on the first Greyhound out of Sumner County. One of her mother's younger sisters, Minnie, agreed to let Sylvia come and stay with her family in the big city of Atlanta. Armed with her Bible and a list of rules from her mother and father, Sylvia left home with her one suitcase.

Unbeknownst to her at the time, her new job was to look after her three younger cousins so their parents could work in the textile mills on the outskirts of the city.

Sylvia didn't mind it. Anything was preferable to country life on a farm, even if it meant changing her baby cousin's diapers and having dinner ready when her aunt and uncle came home. Her job around their house wasn't that bad, and her extended family was good to her.

Sylvia had learned how to sew at her grandmother's knee, giving her an education she wouldn't have otherwise gotten. Since her aunt worked at the textile mill, where there were plenty of discarded seconds of fabric, she was able to bring home the unwanted materials, a boon for working there.

128

Sylvia made beautiful dresses for her aunt and herself on the old sewing machine. She learned how to make men's clothes also. Her little cousins were some of the best-dressed babies and children around their neighborhood. Best of all, Sylvia had an opportunity to wear her creations to church.

She washed her thick dark hair once a month on Saturday night. Adding Bergamot hair pomade to the mass made it shine, and she twisted it up with rags for the perfect curls. By the next morning, she had a head full of natural shiny curls.

The church was the mainstay in most black families' lives during those years. On this particular Sunday morning, after a breakfast of fat biscuits, homemade jam, and ham, Sylvia put on her favorite homemade church dress. The one with the beautiful blue satin sash around the waist. She sashayed into the Big Bethel Baptist church with her head held high, wearing her shiny, black patent-leather shoes. She felt today would be special and she wanted to look her very best.

Sylvia joined the choir the first chance she got. Singing lifted her spirits and gave her hope for a better tomorrow. She was a tiny little thing and was barely able to see over the shoulders of the more prominent choir members. But her eyes always sought out the tall, good-looking boy in the back of the church.

This special Sunday, while her lips were singing "Steal away to my Jesus," her eyes were saying, "Look at me, pretty boy." She couldn't wait to get out of her choir robes to show off her newest dress. She ran from the choir room to join her family as they were exiting the church.

Her Aunt Minnie took her aside and whispered in her ear, "Ain't that the boy you sweet on? He keeps looking over here. Go on and talk to him. We can wait." Her aunt smiled tenderly, remembering her first love.

Now was the moment of truth. Sylvia gathered her small strength and strolled over to him. "Hi. You a member of Big Bethel?" Sylvia knew that was a stupid thing to say and her cheeks blushed at the knowing.

"Hi to you too, young lady. I am a member, baptized and all. You sure looking pretty today and you sing real nice too." The young man left the door open for more conversation as he looked down at what he considered to be the prettiest girl in the church.

"Ooh, you talk real nice. What's your name? Mine is Sylvia Johnson." She stumbled over the last part, thinking she had been too forward to give him her name. She knew she should have waited for someone to introduce them, but she really didn't know anyone but her family. Besides, her aunt had given her the okay to talk to him. She could see the smile on her aunt's face from way across the church.

"I'm Robert Stinson, but everybody calls me Buddy. I see you all the time when you come to church with the Tally family. Is she your auntie or something? You do look a lot like her. Pretty that is." Buddy stopped talking at that point and hung his head while he shuffled his large feet. He acted as if he had said too much also.

"Yes, that's my auntie. I'm staying with them for the summer. I just graduated from high school and wanted a chance to see the big city. If I can get a paying job, I might be able to stay. You know, stay on with them permanently. And everybody calls me Sylvi." She rambled on and on. But the best part was Buddy did also.

Oh, what a whirlwind that summer had been! To Ms. Sylvi it was something right out of a movie. Robert "Buddy" Stinson became the man of her dreams. He was twenty-one when they first met and had a job driving a delivery truck. He had big dreams of owning his own business one day. Ms. Sylvi loved everything about him. He took her out to the fried chicken and fish places and ordered all kinds of food. He always said she was too small and delicate and needed more food.

The summer turned into the fall and Sylvi was able to stay on with her aunt's family. She found a job working in the same textile mill as her aunt. She dreamed of her own home with Buddy and a house full of babies. Buddy courted her as if she was so special and precious. They had a love that was full, and it grew into a marriage that lasted over fifty years. Not once did she ever regret meeting Robert "Buddy" Stinson.

But now, she was so lonely, so lost. Her mate, her life, was lost in that hospital bed two years ago. She was still a healthy and vibrant woman and she prayed for something, for someone to help ease the loneliness in her heart. Her heart that shattered right along with Buddy's.

Buddy, Buddy, why did you leave me? I miss you so much, she thought. As always that ghastly Friday night came back to haunt her. A fatal crash and her whole world changed. All the plans they'd made. All the love they still wanted to lavish on each other. All gone. The only things she had left were her crystal clear memories and her silent tears.

Two years ago, Midtown Atlanta - Grady Hospital

"Buddy, what you gone and done now? You weren't supposed to be gone this long. You know it's way past your bedtime. Come on and get up." Ms. Sylvi could barely get the words out and ended on a strangled sob. She was inconsolable and hardly made sense as she spoke to Buddy. Her husband was wrapped up in bandages and was only just recognizable.

It had been a horrific accident, involving three vehicles. Buddy's truck had been struck repeatedly and flipped several times. A fire complicated matters further. He was now in the emergency room at the hospital.

"Sylvi, what you cry-crying 'bout?" croaked Buddy from the bed. He tried to cup Ms. Sylvi's chin, but his fingers wouldn't work. "You know it's all right. You gonna be all right. I guess I won't get to bed on time tonight. Don't you forget I have always loved you and always will. Don't you worry, everything gonna be fine . . ."

"Buddy, don't you dare leave me. Buddy, do you hear me? Buddy, please! Please, doctor, do something for my, for Buddy. Lord, it wasn't supposed to be this way. Please, Lord, don't let it be this way." Ms. Sylvi's voice was choked with tears. The front of her blouse was soaked with her anguish.

The doctor came around to the other side of the bed to check one of the machines hooked up to Buddy's chest. Then, he went to the curtain and asked one of the nurses to come inside. "Ma'am," he said to Ms. Sylvi, "I'm afraid there isn't anything else we can do for Mr. Stinson."

Ms. Sylvi moved slowly down the hall to her bedroom. Now, all she had left were her memories. She kneeled down beside her bed. She prayed so earnestly and for so long for all her family. *Lord, please let me do the right thing for my granddaughter and her babies. I know I haven't always treated her right, but please forgive me. Help me to be a better granny. Don't let the past take over the future. Give us another chance to be loving and giving towards each other.*

But most of all she prayed for an end to the loneliness caused by the loss of her Buddy. *And please, Lord, take away this emptiness and fill my heart and my home with love. I know it's only been two years, but oh Lord, I can't take it. I'm so lonely in this big old house. You took my Buddy on to his reward, and Lord, I praise your name for your mercy. But please, Lord, help me. Help me to find love again. In Jesus name, Amen.*

She stayed for a long time on her knees. Quietly crying and rocking back and forth. The pain, the lonesomeness was a live and deadly beast preying on her very being. Her heart felt as if it would shred into a thousand pieces. She cried long into the night, pleading for her prayers to be heard.

Chapter Seven

Friday afternoon, June 9th - Ms. Sylvi's house

"Chrystal, how did your roommate take the news?" Ms. Sylvi barely let Chrystal and the children in before she was questioning her granddaughter.

Chrystal took a moment to settle the children as she came into her grandmother's kitchen. It had been a hell of a Friday, but she'd enrolled in the nursing program for the upcoming semester at Atlanta Central College. With the help of her mother, aunt, and grandmother, she even had enough money to put down for the deposit and cover the first semester.

Now it was do-or-die time. The next semester started August first, and that was only a month and a half away. There were so many things she had to do before then. She had given her resignation to the head nurse at the facility. In one week she would be without a job. They weren't pleased with her leaving, but understood she wanted to get her degree. They even told her she was welcome to come back once she finished.

No one would believe it, but Chrystal was a really good nurse's assistant. She talked as if she didn't care about the residents of the nursing home, but in truth, she cared a great deal. Often, she went out of her way to help the elderly and infirm patients. The residents would greatly miss her when she returned to nursing school.

"Well, she didn't love the idea, but she understood," Chrystal said in answer to Ms. Sylvi's question about her roommate. "I told Chantrelle that me and the kids were moving in with you so I could finally finish nursing school, and she was happy for us. But when I said I would be moving at the end of June, she kind of got a little sad."

Chrystal shook her head at the memory of Chantrelle's sad face. "You know we've been housemates for a while, and I guess she'll miss us. It only gives us a couple of weeks to get everything taken care of. I really don't want to leave my girl hanging with the rent and all by herself, but I don't have any other choice."

Ms. Sylvi didn't want to upset the roommate, but she was overjoyed Chrystal was moving in. "Believe me, baby. I know change gonna be hard for all of us, but I know God is directing our footsteps and this will be the best for us all."

Chrystal looked thoughtful for a moment. "Well, yes, I hope so. Anyway, I told her I was leaving all the furniture I bought for the kitchen and bedrooms. Since you have everything here for us, I figured there was no reason to bring all that here. That seemed to help some. So all I really have to bring is our clothes and a few little things, like the crib Mama bought. I want to keep that."

"That's really sweet of you, baby. I bet that will make a difference, and she can probably use that as a selling point to get another roommate. You know. Just tell them it's already furnished and all."

"Mommy!" Jewell jumped around the large kitchen, tugging little Oro behind her. "We hungry. Ain't you hungry, Jade? I bet Oro hungry too. We didn't get enough to eat with Miss Chanty today. Did we, Oro?"

Oro was sleepy and rubbed at his eyes. Chrystal gently set Jade down on the floor. Chrystal could tell Jade was sleepy also.

"Well, Great-gran got you something to eat," said Ms. Sylvi. "Don't worry none. Y'all go wash your hands and come right back and sit down here at this table. I got chicken strips, rice and peas, and a nice green salad, just for all my babies." Ms. Sylvi moved around the kitchen setting out plates, glasses, and utensils for everyone. "Chrystal just get the kids washed up and we all can eat. We can talk better with a full belly anyway. Your mama and auntie will be here in a little bit, and we can all talk about the rest of the plans."

"Okay, we'll be right back. I want to say you shouldn't have, but I know what you're gonna say to that, so I'll just say thank you." Chrystal started down the hall with the children just as Nancy and Jackie came through the kitchen door.

Ms. Sylvi gave Chrystal a dazzling smile and said, "I wouldn't have it any other way, and you are so welcome." To her daughters she said, "Oh, y'all just in time. I was just setting the table."

She busied herself with setting plates for Nancy and Jackie as they came in and gave their mother a kiss on the cheek. Jackie sat down at the table, but Nancy hovered near the sink.

"I'm good, Mama," said Nancy. "I ate before I came over. I'll just have a glass of water, please. I had a wonderful idea. I was telling Jackie and I wanted to shoot it past you and Chrystal. I think I hear them coming down the hall now."

"Well, I haven't had anything to eat since lunch and I'm famished." Jackie rubbed her stomach as she moved to the sink to wash her hands and dry them with a paper towel. "I will definitely have a plate. But Mama, I can fix my own. You just go and sit down."

Jackie took her time looking at the delicious meal her mother had prepared. She couldn't help but think back to the last time she was in the kitchen with Eric. In her mind, she could still hear the arguing going on out in the living room.

"Chrystal, how could you do your mother like that? You know she has done everything she could for you." That was Nancy. *No matter what, she's always on my side, whatever the situation. Whether I deserve it or not.*

"You don't understand. You weren't there. You don't know or care how I felt." Chrystal was right of course. Nancy couldn't know.

Jackie was so nervous when she called Chrystal and asked her if she could come over to Chrystal's place and talk. Chrystal said sure, but Jackie almost chickened out. But she gathered her injured dignity about her and climbed into her older model Porsche and drove over to Chrystal's house.

It was late, about nine-thirty on Tuesday night, but Jackie felt she needed to come clean about her role in this old mess that had resurrected itself. Chrystal answered the front door dressed in a tee-shirt and red sweats.

"Come on in, Mama. I put the kids down a little while ago, so we can talk or whatever in the kitchen."

Jackie followed Chrystal into the kitchen and sat down at the small round dinette table.

"I really don't know how to start this conversation. But let me begin by saying how sorry I am that you had to go through that. Last Saturday was a day like no other. It was almost like a dream, a very bad dream. But I pray I never see another one as crazy as that one. It was pure hell, but again, I need to tell you that I'm so sorry. I never meant to hurt you by my foolish actions. Eric and I . . . well, that's a long story, and I don't even know how it all happened myself."

Jackie twisted her hands together and dropped her head. Her thick, curly hair flopped over her forehead. She was wearing a loose workout top and pants. Chrystal went over to the refrigerator and came back with a bottled water and handed it to her mother. She took a seat opposite her.

Jackie looked up and said, "Thank you. Well, like I was saying I really don't know where to begin. I . . . I thought your father, Jimmy." Jackie hesitated so long that Chrystal cleared her throat, and Jackie continued as if she never stopped. "Had hung the moon when we first began dating. He was nothing like he is now. I guess I wasn't either. I wanted so badly to catch a good man, a man with an education and a good job. I chose to overlook what my sixth sense was telling me wasn't quite right."

Jackie took a drink from the bottle of water and looked off into the kitchen.

Chrystal stood back up and went over to the sink. There was a curtained window there, and she looked out into the darkness of the night. "You don't have to tell me all this. I understand you did what you did because you were in love or something. I understand. I've made a mess of my own life, thinking I was in love. I really understand." You know we really aren't that different when it comes right down to it. Except you got Eric fighting like a ninja to be with you. I can't keep a man by my side for the world. I feel like a fool. A loser and a fool for believing I could get a man to show me real love."

"Ha, I guess you're right. We do have a lot in common when it comes to men. But it hasn't always been easy and love just didn't fall in my lap. I struggled just like you for more years than I can count. I put my trust and faith in the wrong people. I made foolish choices, but I never regretted once having you or Royce. I want you to understand this was never meant to hurt you. I love you both so much."

Jackie buried her face in her hands and trailed off in her speech. She finally looked up, "I never realized how much until it looked like I would lose everyone I cared about." *The things we do to be loved.* "I was wrong for blaming you for the foolish things your father and I did. Even more so, I'm so sorry for the way I treated you when you needed me most. I, of all people, should have seen your suffering as a teenager and then as a young mother. I know what it feels like to be cast aside. For that, I pray you can forgive me."

Chrystal turned back and looked into her mother's eyes as tears fell onto Jackie's shirt. "Don't worry about it. I told you

I've done my share of dodging the real issues. I promise you this. If you can forgive me, then I can certainly forgive you."

Jackie filled her plate and sat down at the table. Slowly, she folded her hands in her lap, waiting on the others. *I have treated Chrystal like a pariah. I blamed her for Jimmy's treatment of me. I should've done better as a mother. I should've tried more. She said she understood when I talked to her earlier this week, but how can she when I don't understand myself. I can only hope she can really forgive me.*

Jackie smiled as Chrystal came into the kitchen. She soon had the children situated. They were all so beautiful. Little Jewell with her head of dark curly hair in a little short set with mustard all over the front, scooted up into her seat. She was so tiny, more like a three-year-old in size than her true age of five.

Caramel-colored Oro smiled at Jackie and said, "Hi, Grandma," as he tried to climb up into one of the table's chairs. His black wavy hair was way too long. *He needs a haircut,* Jackie thought.

Chrystal was carrying Jade, who was slow with her toddler steps. Jade, of all the children, looked just like Chrystal, but she had gray eyes and almost blondish hair. Chrystal had dressed her in a yellow, sunflower-patterned dress. She was so beautiful in her own exotic way.

And Chrystal. Chrystal had been a beautiful baby, and now she was a gorgeous woman. She had the thickest, waviest, dark-brown hair. Jackie was glad Chrystal had taken the weave out, finally. Her body shape was so much like Jimmy's side of the family. Not as tall, but slim with a generous behind that gave her a model's physique.

Her face was beautiful also. Big, light-brown eyes, almost amber colored, with a heart-shaped face and clear, shining skin. It was no wonder she drew men to her in droves.

Jackie realized she loved them all so much and wondered if a new beginning was possible for them or if it really was too late.

Once everyone was settled, Nancy took a deep breath and spoke. "I was thinking we all need a big and exciting way to celebrate this new beginning. What would be better than a cruise to the Caribbean? Just us girls. Mama, Jackie, Chrystal, and me. A kind of womanhood celebration, all on me."

Ms. Sylvi stood up from the table to grab another paper towel for Oro's spill. "You know that's not a bad idea. We could get on one of those huge hotel-like ships, like the Crown Caribbean."

Oro raised his hands from the spill on the table so his great-grand could wipe up the messy milk, giving her a big missing-tooth smile in the process.

"But what about the kids? We can't take three little kids on a cruise ship." Chrystal looked back and forth between all three children as she raised the question.

As if on cue, all three children started in on another loud singalong. They were cute if not correct in the actual lyrics.

"Hey, you guys, quiet please," said Chrystal as she held her fingers up to her lips. "Anyway, I do like the idea. I've never been on a cruise ship before, but I heard they were slamming.

All you can eat and everything else too. Nightclubs, Broadway shows, and casinos."

"They sure are lavish. I remember the one time we went on a cruise vacation on the Royal Princess."

Jackie's face took on a look of distress as she said that. She stopped the fork full of food halfway to her mouth. "I guess that wasn't such a great cruise. Not because of the ship, but the company. Anyway, cruise ships have everything you could possibly want or need. It was a great way to travel and see exotic places." She continued the fork to her lips and chewed slowly with a thoughtful look.

Chrystal reached over to wipe Jewell's mouth as she juggled Jade on her lap. Jade fidgeted more than she ate but was happy as she clapped her hands to a song Jewell sang softly in her little-girl voice.

Nancy continued on with her ideas about the vacation. "I thought about the babies too. What do you think if we asked your dad to keep the kids for a week? I think he would actually do it, and we could go knowing they were in good hands. At least I hope so," Nancy said softly.

"I think his partner, Bryan, would jump at the chance to keep the kids," said Ms. Sylvi. "I saw how he kept playing with them when they were here last weekend. Maybe he's not as bad as we thought. Jackie, Chrystal, what do you guys think?"

Chrystal pushed her plate aside. As usual her food was only half eaten. "Yeah, I guess so. He always liked to take the kids out with him when I came to visit Daddy and him. But I have never left all the kids with only one person, besides Mama, for that long. I don't know if he can handle all that. Daddy has a bit of a temper sometimes, and I wouldn't want the kids to get on his nerves. But it doesn't hurt to ask. I mean if we really want to go, somebody has to keep my babies."

Chrystal lowered her head and looked at her mother shyly. She didn't know what to think of this new announcement. A vacation with her mother, aunt, and grandmother might be too much love too quickly. She and her mother had managed to have a long conversation earlier in the week. Tears were shed and promises were made, but was it for real?

It had been genuine on her part at least. She really wanted to forgive and forget, but could her mother really do that? She'd told Jackie so many lies and halfway truths over the years. Among other things, could her mother really forgive her sneaking behind her back and reconciling with her father? She felt that, if she was her mother, she would have a hard time forgiving someone like her. Chrystal held her breath, waiting for her mother to speak.

Jackie toyed with her plate as Nancy looked at her skeptically. "Well, what do you think, Jackie? Do you think the great and masterful Jimmy can handle three little children?"

"I want to say yes because I believe Bryan is actually a calming influence on Jimmy, as much as I hate to say that, but Chrystal is right. Jimmy has a terrible personality and temper. He's so vindictive. But I don't think he would do anything to the kids. At least, not on purpose."

Ms. Sylvi slowly stood up and started clearing the table. "Well, we can at least ask him if he would be able to watch the little ones. When are we talking about doing this?"

Chrystal set Jade down and stood up. "If we do this, then it has to be before August first. My new semester starts then. I want to be ready for whatever that may take." Chrystal cleaned Oro and Jade's faces with damp paper towels and cleared their plates from the table.

Nancy said, "I was thinking about the second or third week in July. I was looking at the Crown Caribbean, like Mama suggested. It's one of the biggest cruise lines. Here, let me bring up the information on my phone. I already started looking at itineraries." She pulled out her cell phone, pulled up the details, and passed the phone to Jackie.

"Oh, Nancy! This is fantastic. I love this six-day cruise to Cozumel out of Tampa. This one looks like a lot of fun. It stops at Jamaica too." Jackie passed the phone over to Ms. Sylvi. "Look Mama, this one would work perfectly."

Chrystal came over and stood behind her grandmother to look at the phone. "Oh wow, that one does look fantastic. But look at the cost! I don't have that kind of money."

"I said it was on me," said Nancy. "Please let me do something for everyone. I was going to take a vacation anyway to celebrate my retirement. My coworkers took up a collection when I left, remember? What better way to spend the money than to treat us all to a wonderful, fun-filled vacation. Besides, I know I deserve it, and I believe the rest of you do too."

Chrystal looked at the photos on her aunt's cell phone. *I don't really deserve a vacation, but if that's what they want, I'll try and go along with it. But honestly, I don't feel right about this.*

144

Chapter Eight

Saturday night, June 10th - Jimmy

" " I need you to complete another little task for me." Jimmy
was sequestered in his office at the back of his house in
Alpharetta. This time, he'd made sure the door was
securely locked. He didn't want Bryan barging in on this
conversation.

As with every other part of the house, Jimmy's office was
decorated extravagantly. Behind an ornate Edwardian-style
desk, he hunched over some notes on his laptop. His chair was
a complement to the desk. It was big, dark, and bulky, and it
made Jimmy feel like a king. Across from his desk, framed
artwork depicted a serene country setting.

The person on the other end of the cell phone almost
growled at Jimmy. "Man, you know it's gonna cost you fifty
stacks this time. Me and my crew almost caught a case messing
with that fucking foreign guy."

"I told you to be more careful. You were messy, and that's
not my fault. This time, you stick to the plan, like I told you, and

145

the police won't get involved. I don't want any mistakes or it's gonna be your ass. Do you understand me?" Jimmy reclined in his chair and waited for confirmation from Duck. He smiled as he looked out the window on the wall opposite his desk. He could see the illuminated pool area and manicured grounds.

"Yeah, man. What the fuck? I ain't your bitch. I know my business. You want somebody fucked up; you better be ready for the backlash. I ain't doing time for nobody. Your name gonna be flying out of my mouth the minute 12 pop up. Do you understand?"

Jimmy leapt from his chair and shouted into the phone. "Look here, you shithead. Do what I tell you and you get paid. Don't try to fuck me over. I got enough on you to bury you for fifty years. Who you think the police gonna believe, a three-time felon or an upstanding businessman?"

Jimmy sat back down and continued the conversation as if nothing had happened. "Now, I'm going to send you a picture of them, my ex, Jackie Mattock, and her lover, Eric Henderson. I'll send her address, and I want them to have a little accident. Do you think you can follow directions this time, or do I need to get somebody else?"

"Man, I should of never took that first crazy ass job for you in the first place. Why you always trying to fuck people up? I thought you said you was a businessman. If they owe you money, I'm cool with that, but all this feelings shit is nonsense."

Jimmy heard the hesitation in Duck's voice. "Look can you do this, minus all your bullshit on my motives, or not?"

"I got you man, but since it's two this time, the price has doubled. It's fucking hard to make some accident happen to two of them at the same time. That other guy was always walking around by himself. I'm gonna have to get these two together. I'm gonna need more people to pull it off."

Jimmy heard another voice laughing as Duck spoke. He figured it was Smoke hanging around in the background.

"That's not a problem if you do what I need," said Jimmy. "But remember if you fuck this one up, you and Smoke better be ready because I'll be coming for you two. And nobody, and I mean nobody, will be able to stop me."

Saturday night, 11:00pm - Chrystal

Chrystal settled down in bed. Jewell, Oro, and Jade had completely worn her out. She'd finally put them down after a long day, and they were sleeping peacefully. She was so thankful they all slept through the night. There was nothing worse than having to get up and do bottle feedings. She didn't breastfeed with any of her children. It never felt right to her. She never really felt like a true mother even though she birthed them all. She didn't have a good example or anyone to guide her, so after several attempts, she gave up and took the old formula route.

Chrystal had been packing up their things, getting ready for the big move. They were so excited to be staying with Gran-gran, as Jade called her. *I pray this is the right thing to do*, she mused. *I love my family. I really do, but sometimes I just don't know. Everybody wants something from me, and I don't know if I have anything left to give.*

147

Here she was again, a single mom, trying to do the best she could with what she had. After next week, she wouldn't have a job for a while. No money coming in concerned her greatly. All she would have was what Tyler put into her account every month. He tried to do right and she wanted to believe he cared, but she had been hurt too many times to start believing in true love now.

Her grandmother's offer was really a life-saver. Grandmama insisted she not pay a penny for room and board. Chrystal did feel bad about the free ride, but she was going to make it up to her. She wouldn't be a burden. She was going to help out as much as she could before and after school.

Jewell would be in kindergarten this year, and Chrystal needed help getting her to and from school. They had already talked about the schedule, and her grandmother was delighted to keep Oro and Jade and then get Jewell after the school day was over. All Chrystal had to do was get to her classes and do the work. She wanted to get all As. That was her goal and she was determined to make it work this time.

Yeah, Grandmama's idea is right on time. I think I can really make this all work. I got to put on my big-girl panties. Swallow my pride. Start being a woman and make amends to my family for being such a bitch. She turned over in the bed just as her cellphone rang.

It was Royce. She was actually glad to hear from him.

"Hey Chrystal. How you doing?"

At first, she didn't know exactly what to say. But after a week and more crying than she ever thought she would do; she was finally able to face the facts. They weren't as terrible as they'd first appeared. She could hear the hesitation in Royce's voice.

He probably thought she would cuss him out, and the old Chrystal probably would have. But she knew it wasn't Royce's fault any more than it was her fault. It was just the way things were.

"Hi, Royce. I'm good. In fact, I was going to call you. How you and Miss Th— uh, Jessica? The honeymoon's over, huh?"

She had almost said her old derogatory name for Royce's wife, the one Chrystal used to say to get on their nerves. But it was time for a new day and she was determined to start now. This was going to be the start of a new Chrystal.

"We're good. But the honeymoon isn't over. We're going to keep it going. Just here instead of Bermuda. Well, I was just checking on you. I can only imagine how rough last weekend must have been. I'm sorry it went like that. I never meant to hurt you, sis."

Chrystal let Royce's words sink in before she answered. She knew it wasn't his fault. It wasn't even their mother's fault. In truth, she was glad it had all come out.

"I know, lil' bro. I know. I don't blame you. You know Daddy was behind so much stuff that nobody had any idea about, and Mama . . . well, Mama was just in love, I guess."

She couldn't help but think of Tyler and their situation. She was still dodging his phone calls and text messages. She needed to do something about that too.

"Right. I know, but this is still blowing my mind. I guess I kinda always knew something wasn't right about Mom and Dad's relationship, but I never would've guessed all this."

"Neither did I. This is like something from *The Jerry Springer Show*. And I really don't like how it's going," mumbled Chrystal.

"Well, anyway, I was just checking in with you. Jessica and I want to take you guys out for a meal or maybe meet at Grandma's house or maybe even Dad's. I need to go over there and pick up their gift. I'll let you know what we come up with."

"Okay, that sounds good. Just let me know. Talk to you later."

Chrystal looked up at the dark ceiling. She had the ceiling fan on, blowing cool air down on her. A streetlight threw some dim light through the sheer blue curtains at the window. She turned over again, lonely as usual in her bed. She threw off the light sheet, suddenly too warm. *Why, why, why? Why can't I hold on to a good man? Why do they always betray me? Leave me?*

She knew Jason, Jewell's daddy, was nothing but a silly boy. She had been young and naive and hadn't known a thing about real love or sex. There was no way that could have worked out. But Omar—Omar was a man and she thought he loved her just as much as she thought she loved him. Why did it have to end like it did?

Three and a half years ago

Omar had been overjoyed when he found out Chrystal was pregnant. He had treated her like his queen, lavishing special treats on her and Jewell. They made plans, so she thought, to be together. Then something happened, something changed, and Omar started making demands. Suddenly, he no longer talked about them being together. Instead, he talked about him and the baby and his family. She didn't understand. What was he trying to tell her?

"You already have one fatherless child," he told her. "I don't intend to have my child be a bastard. I will make sure he or she is with me and my family. I will take care of it. Don't worry."

But she did worry. What the hell did he mean by that. How could he not have the child be a bastard? When she asked him what he meant, he skipped over her questions. He started totally ignoring her. His only concern seemed to be the health of the baby. Chrystal's health didn't concern him. He didn't refer to them as a couple and he certainly didn't talk about marriage. In fact, he completely backed away from saying they would be together. His conversation was about going back to his homeland and the property his family had there. She was scared and didn't know what to do. Omar wasn't as loving and attentive as he had been. She was eight months pregnant when it all boiled over.

Omar had been paying for her doctor's visits. He even had the finances arranged at the hospital for the delivery. But he insisted on having a test done to determine the baby's sex. She was nervous and didn't think it was a good idea, but Omar made her. When they found out it was going to be a boy, Omar was ecstatic. He never spoke about the four of them. He only talked about his son and the life he was going to make for him.

Chrystal was very frightened. She'd been careful to keep her pregnancy secret from her family. She didn't want them talking about her and questioning who the father was. Here she was again, without the child's father in her life and maybe even unable to keep her baby. She was so terrified.

She didn't want her mother, and especially not her father, looking at her with derision. Besides, her father had told her what he thought about Omar and his family, and it wasn't good. She tried her best to avoid them, but her father demanded she and Jewell come over to see him and Bryan.

Chrystal had no choice but to go to her father when he sent a car for them. She wore a loose top that completely covered the small bulge in her middle. But as she was coming back from the bathroom rubbing her back, Jimmy looked at her and suddenly said, "You're pregnant, aren't you? Chrystal, what did I tell you?"

Chrystal broke down and cried. "Daddy, I'm so scared. You were right about Omar. He's talking about taking my baby from me. He doesn't want me. He only wants his son."

The more Chrystal cried the more Jewell cried. Chrystal took the baby from her father and tried to calm Jewell down. She was only eighteen months old and her mother's crying set her to crying also.

Bryan heard the commotion and ran into the family room from the kitchen, where he'd been preparing some lunch for them all. "What's going on? Chrystal, baby, why are you crying? What's happened?" Bryan looked from Chrystal to Jimmy as he took a crying Jewell from Chrystal's arms.

Jimmy was furious. "What the hell are you talking about? Chrystal, calm down and tell me everything. I mean everything." To Bryan he added, "Chrystal's pregnant with that terrorist's baby."

Jimmy was so angry he strode back and forth from Bryan to Chrystal. Blazing red spots danced in his eyes. "I bet this is that damn mother of yours fault. She is so neglectful of you and Jewell. Well, tell us what that lying bastard has done to you."

"Oh, my God Jim. I knew Chrystal has been seeing Omar, but I had no idea it had progressed to this point. I just thought you were complaining and overreacting about him as usual. But now, oh my Lord, look at what's happened." Bryan continued to hug a crying Jewell to his chest.

"Daddy, I'm so sorry. I should have listened to you. I never thought he would demand my baby. And now, now I don't know what to do." Chrystal sobbed even more and poor Jewell just wouldn't be consoled. Chrystal tried to finish the story while Bryan tried to hush Jewell.

"He started acting funny a few months ago. At first, he said we all would be together, and then, he kept talking about his family and what they expected from him. I didn't understand. I didn't know what he meant."

Jimmy took Chrystal by the hands to keep her from shaking. "Okay, then what? What happened to make you think he wants to take the baby from you?"

Chrystal took one of her hands from her father and wiped at her eyes. Bryan found some tissues and shoved them into her hands as he continued to soothe Jewell. "Oh, my God. Go on, baby," he said.

"He made me take that test to determine the baby's sex. I thought he just wanted to make more plans for us. You know, like picking out clothes and stuff like that. But when they told us it was a boy and Omar saw the pictures himself, he changed." Chrystal finally sat down on the sofa and Jimmy sat beside her, still holding on to one hand.

"Okay, and then what happened?" Jimmy looked at Bryan and shook his head while Chrystal tried to collect herself. "I knew it. I just knew it. I told you not to trust him, and now see how they do."

"I know, Daddy. But I thought he really loved me. He treated me and Jewell so good. I would have never believed he would do this. But he flipped on me so suddenly. He kept talking about his son and what he was gonna do for him. He said he was gonna take him back to Pakistan, to his homeland. He said there was no way he could take me. He said it just wasn't done."

Chrystal cried even more after she said the last words. Her beautiful eyes were puffy and red. She shook her head from side to side in denial and suddenly stood up, clinching her fists.

"Daddy, please don't let him take my baby. Please! You've got to stop him. Please!"

"Baby, when are you due?" asked Brian

Chrystal looked at Bryan as if she didn't understand the question.

Bryan repeated, "When is the baby due? How far along are you?"

"Oh, they said at the doctor's office that I had three more weeks. Around the end of September was what they said. But I think he's coming before then. The pictures of him looked like he's such a big beautiful baby, and I can't—I won't let him take my baby boy."

"Okay, today is September second, so we have a little time." Jimmy calmly said. "Does your mother know? How she couldn't is beyond me, but anyway."

154

"Well, I haven't told her. Unless she guessed like you. No, I don't think so." Chrystal went over to Bryan and took Jewell, who had finally calmed down, from his arms.

Bryan looked on with sadness in his eyes. He had such a concerned look on his face. It was as if Chrystal was his own flesh and blood. "Jim, what are we going to do? We can't let him take the baby."

With steel in his voice and determination in his eyes, Jimmy said, "I'll take care of it. Don't worry. He will not take my grandson. If it's the last thing I do, I won't let that happen."

Jimmy told Chrystal to go home and tell her mother. "There's no use in denying it any longer," he told her. "But remember not to tell her anything about me or Bryan."

He took both Chrystal and Jewell in his arms and hugged them tightly.

"But let me handle it, and do not go back to that man, that Omar. I will take care of him. Trust me. I'll get him out of your life. Do you trust me, Chrystal?"

"Yes, Daddy, I do, and thank you. Thank you so much."

Monday evening, June 12th - Ms. Sylvi's house

Nancy and Jackie were making plans for the upcoming trip and waiting for Chrystal to come over. Nancy wanted so badly for this vacation to be the best ever, but it all depended on Chrystal getting her father to look after the kids while they cruised.

"Did you tell Royce about the trip?" Nancy took a sip of her cold sweet tea and watched their mother moving around her spacious kitchen. She seemed to be cleaning up, but there really wasn't anything to clean.

"Yes, I did," said Jackie. "I thought maybe Jessica might want to come, but then it hit me like a brick that they're still honeymooning. They wouldn't want to hang around us." Jackie laughed as her mother turned from the sink and laughed along with her.

"I would have thought the same thing about you and Eric. Not honeymooning necessarily but getting to know each other again. It has been a number of years since you two were together. You sure you have time to come with us?" asked Ms. Sylvi as she wiped at an already immaculate countertop.

Nancy cleared her throat and snickered. "They've definitely been getting to know each other—if you know what I mean. Besides, didn't Eric go back to Chicago for a while?"

Remembering the last night she and Eric spent together, Jackie blushed at Nancy's comments. "Well, Ms. Nosy, we have gotten to know each other again, and it's been wonderful. But you're right. Eric is back in Chicago tending to his job. He won't be able to come back until the first of August, so I have plenty of time to take a vacation with you guys."

"I'm really happy for you two. You deserve Eric and all the love you've both missed out on for the past how many years." Nancy wistfully stated. She turned away for a second, not wanting Jackie or their mother to see the unshed tears in her eyes. She couldn't help but compare her life to Jackie's, and it only made her sadder.

Even though Nancy turned her head, she knew both Jackie and her mother heard the longing in her comments. She turned around just as they passed an uncomfortable look between them, seeming to say they both realized just how lonely Nancy really was.

Fortunately, the kitchen door burst open and Chrystal came through with an armload of clothes and other items. "Hey, everybody. I thought I'd get a start on moving. Chantrelle has all the kids with her over her mother's house. She let me use her car and there's plenty more outside."

Nancy took the opportunity to clear her head by jumping up to help Chrystal. "Here, give me that and you can go get another armful. I'll take all this stuff on back to the bedroom."

Ms. Sylvi dried her hands on a towel and moved to join Nancy. "Wait a minute, Nancy. I'll show you where to put everything. I got the babies' room ready, but I still need to set up Chrystal's."

"Here, let me come with you and give you a hand getting the stuff out of the car." Jackie got up from the kitchen table to join Chrystal at the back door.

After four trips back and forth to the car, all the clothes, toys, and incidentals Chrystal brought over were finally put away. Everyone gathered around the kitchen table, drinking iced tea.

"Well, I think we've made a big dent in the moving already," said Ms. Sylvi. "I can hardly wait for the final, big move. This is right for all of us. I just know it." She arranged roses picked from her garden in a vase.

Nancy wiped her face with a paper towel. She was perspiring from the trips in and out to the car. She sipped at her tea and lazily fanned at her face with the towel. "Whew! I'm glad it's done for now. It's too hot and humid out there. I think I lost five pounds going back and forth. Chrystal you know you have a lot of stuff. How much more is at your house?"

"Not too much more. My clothes, the crib, and just some odds and ends. I left some of the kids clothes and stuff until we actually move in. I figured I'd work out of both houses until we got everything situated."

Jackie spoke up after she took a big sip of her iced tea. "That sounds like a smart thing to do. That way, you all can get dressed at your place and bring the kids here where Mama can look after them. This is your last week working, right?"

Chrystal rubbed at her eyes as if she was tired. "Right, I'm kinda sad about leaving. I worked there for so long it became like home in a way. I really will miss some of the patients. But this is definitely the right move for me. I really want to finish nursing school and get my license."

"Well, we're proud of you for taking this big step," said Jackie. "I know it hasn't been easy for you, but I promise I'm behind you, one hundred percent. You will get that license and a whole lot more. I just know it."

Jackie raised her glass and said, "Here's to a new beginning for us all, and may the good Lord guide our steps."

Everyone around the table raised their glasses in turn. A chorus of "Amen" was happily spoken around the table.

"Now, on to the vacation planning," said Nancy as she set her glass down. "Did you get a chance to talk to your father about keeping the kids?"

Chrystal hesitated. She mumbled, "He can be such an asshole sometimes." Louder she said, "Yes, I asked him about it. He said he had to think about it, he needed to check his calendar, and he would get back to me. Something about he and Bryan were thinking about a vacation then too."

"Okay," said Jackie. "I knew he would be an ass about it. That's Jimmy through and through."

"Did you tell him about moving in with me?" Ms. Sylvi asked as she set the flowers in the center of the table.

"I did, and believe it or not, he said he thought that was a wonderful idea. I almost didn't believe it myself."

Chrystal's cell started buzzing. "That's Daddy calling now. Let me take it in the other room."

Jackie and Nancy looked at each other as Chrystal left the room. They both wondered why she didn't want to take the call in front of them.

"That damn Jimmy!" Jackie spoke with venom in her voice. "I didn't want to say this in front of Chrystal, but I will never forgive Jimmy for what he's done to our family. He is so despicable."

Ms. Sylvi rubbed her hand across her forehead and exclaimed, "I think you're right. I didn't want to believe it. He always acted so caring, saying such pretty words to me. I'm so sorry I blamed you . . . I just didn't know. He had me completely fooled."

"That's all right. I understand. For so long, I was just as confused. I blamed myself for how he acted towards me. Then, I think I took it out on Chrystal. Lord help me. I have been such a fool." Jackie slumped down further in her chair. The same old doubts and insecurities were rearing their ugly heads. The thoughts swirling through her mind brought tears to her eyes.

159

"That's enough," said Nancy. "There's enough blame to keep us all occupied for the next twenty-five years. It still wouldn't help the situation."

Jackie sighed, "I know, but I want our lives to have some sort of normalcy. It's been so crazy for so long that I just want us to be an ordinary family. A loving, kind family without pretense."

Silence reigned in the kitchen as each woman was lost in her own thoughts.

"Okay," Chrystal announced as she came back from the other room. She had a smile on her face that brightened the mood considerably.

"Daddy said he and Bryan can keep the kids if it's the second week of July. I told him that would work. So let's get these plans together. We need to book everything right now if we're going to make this happen."

Chapter Nine

Late Monday night, June 12th - Chrystal's house

C hrystal had put the kids to bed. They were too excited after spending the afternoon with Chantrelle and her son, Christian. He was just a few months older than Oro. Fortunately, all the children got along amazingly well.

She would miss Chantrelle babysitting all the kids, but she felt her grandmother could handle it. Besides, Chantrelle said to not leave her out of their lives. She really wanted to continue to let the kids play together. They had a lot of fun, and Chrystal didn't want to give that up either. Chantrelle was one of the rare true friends she had. She finally realized that real friends were hard to come by.

The only problem was the distance between Chantrelle's place and her grandmother's. *I really need my own car. I can't keep borrowing Chantrelle's, and Grandma needs hers to get the kids from place to place.* Chrystal was turning these thoughts over in her mind when her cell phone rang.

Oh shit it's Tyler. I really don't want to talk to him, but I know I need to. Chrystal reluctantly answered, "Hello."

"Hey, babe. I'm glad you finally answered. I know you're mad at me, but please don't hang up. Give me a chance to explain."

"I'm listening but make it quick. I've got to go to work in the morning."

Chrystal wasn't so much angry as disappointed with Tyler. She wanted badly to believe what he was telling her about loving her and Jade, but too much had happened between them. She didn't know if she could forgive him for not being there when she needed him most.

"First, let me say again that I love you, babe. I love Jade and Jewell and Oro too. I know you probably don't believe me, but it's true." Tyler exhaled a big breath and tried to continue, but Chrystal cut him off.

"Sure you do. That's why you did a disappearing act when I needed you most. All hell broke loose at the wedding and things and people I thought I could trust . . ." Chrystal's voice broke and she faltered in her speech.

"I tried to be there. You're not being fair. First of all, I told you I was probably gonna be late. You know that, and second, how was I to know things were gonna go to shit? Besides, I still don't know what you're talking about. Just tell me what happened."

Tyler stopped talking and waited for Chrystal to answer him. "Tell me what happened. I want to help you, but I can't if you won't be honest with me."

Chrystal was trying not to cry, but the tears pooled in her eyes anyway. She looked around her small bedroom and decided to trust Tyler. She figured she had nothing left to lose. She had been emotionally wrung out over the past two weeks. Tyler couldn't do much more damage to her.

Chrystal went over the scene at the wedding when Eric had shown up and her mother fainted. She talked about the turmoil that erupted later when her father confronted her mother in the small room in the chapel. But she didn't mention her run in with Smoke or Duck and how she had been hurt the night before.

"Oh no, babe, I had no idea." Tyler sounded so sincere that Chrystal continued with the story.

She told him about the final showdown at her grandmother's house and how all the secrets from twenty something years came tumbling out of her mother's mouth. Lastly, she told him how she was blamed for keeping the fact that she and Royce had been communicating with their estranged father from their mother.

"Chrystal, I can't believe all that drama was going down. I'm so sorry, baby. I had no idea all that was going on, and I know it wasn't your idea to keep this information from your mother. I tried my best to get in touch with you, but I couldn't get through."

"I know. I know. But so much was going on that I just left my phone back in the bedroom. Anyway, to add to the crap, Royce is my half-brother. It turns out my mother was a lot more than just friends with Eric. He's Royce's biological father."

"Wow! That's a lot to take in. That's really deep. I'm so sorry. How do you feel about all this? Did you have any idea what was going on?"

Chrystal dried her teary eyes on the sheet. She felt a little better since Tyler was being so sympathetic. She continued with her story, but she wanted Tyler to know she wasn't a pushover. "I had no idea my mom had been doing this stuff, but after my father came out with being gay since forever, I can understand why she had to do what she did. Lowdown, down-low, doggish men seem to have no age limits or sexual preferences. All this stuff was going on way back then too."

Tyler decided to let the "lowdown" comment go. Instead of responding to that, he said, "I want to see you, babe. I'm gonna be back on Friday. I have a gig at The Central—you know that jazz club where we first met. Please come, please. I want us to get back together."

Chrystal took her time answering. She could hear Tyler breathing heavily over the phone. A piece of her wanted to say, "Yes, I'll be there." Another part was still wary. She knew Tyler wasn't another Omar, but still she wasn't sure just what he was to her. "Look, I can tell you're sorry, but honestly, I don't know what to think about us. Is there even an us anymore? You're always gone to all these fancy places, playing at these clubs in big cities that I'll never see. I'm here with my kids, and only one is your daughter. So you tell me how should I feel about us."

"Again, I don't have all the answers to your questions, but what I do know is that I want to be with you. When you wouldn't answer me, I felt so helpless."

She could hear the pain in Tyler's voice, but he continued on with his confession, and Chrystal sighed heavily into the phone.

"I'm trying so hard to be with you," said Tyler, "but sometimes, I don't know. I get the feeling you want this magical, make-believe guy. A superman. That's just not me. Honestly, I guess it's not anybody."

Chrystal thought hard about what Tyler said. *He's probably right. I do want a superman. And it's about time I got one. After all the shit I've gone through, I know I deserve a good man.* But to Tyler she said, "Maybe you're right, and maybe you're the one for me, but right now, I just don't know. I don't know if there's an us anymore."

"If nothing else, please meet me. I want to work this out between us. I want there to be an us. I love and want you. Really, I need you in my life. I need our baby. I love you all so much. I'm willing to do anything and everything to prove that to you. Do you understand?"

Chrystal listened to Tyler and heard the honesty in his voice, but she was afraid. Afraid of another Jason, another Omar. Too many times she'd been hurt by those who claimed to love her. Too many times she'd seen the truth much too late.

"Okay, I'll come to the club, but I'm not promising anything. I'll come and listen to what you have to say. That's all. Then I'll make up my mind where we go from there.

She thought of all she'd given Tyler for the past two and half years. Not only her body, but her heart as well. Did she really want to throw all that away? If she had to be honest with herself, the answer was no.

Over two years ago

In the beginning, it was awesome. He surprised her with his visits to town. Even though most of the time they were in her small bedroom at her house. Or better still were the times they spent at the hotel rooms he rented while he was in town. it was still so romantic and, she thought, special. He filled her room with beautiful, perfumed roses and tulips in an array of colors. She wasn't much of a drinker, but Tyler brought rare wines to toast their times together. But most special of all were the songs he claimed he wrote just for her. He serenaded her on his guitar and her heart melted for him.

He took her mind away from the mundane, miserable life she led. She loved her two babies, but that was about all she had to look forward to in her life. Until Tyler, her world was dark and dismal. Little more than drudgery. Not only did they connect physically, but mentally as well. He often said out loud what she was thinking. It was so uncanny, but she loved it and she loved him too. It was no wonder, when they made love for the first time, that she believed what he'd said when she first met him. She did believe she'd found her soulmate.

It seemed so long ago, that Saturday that changed her and brought her baby Jade into existence. She'd left Jewell and Oro with her mother, who for the first time didn't give her a lecture or a hard time about it. He sent a car for her as usual. She was meeting Tyler at his hotel in downtown Atlanta, and she was so nervous she forgot to bring the small bag she had packed. She had met him there before, but this time she knew it was going to be different. This time she was ready to give all of herself to Tyler.

"Chrystal, babe, come on in." Tyler hugged her tightly to his chest as he led her into his king room at the Hilton. This was "their" hotel, as she thought of it. He always stayed there when he was in town, which wasn't often enough for her. He kissed her lightly on her lips and led her inside to the small sofa. "Your mom kept the kids with no problems?"

Chrystal was flustered, but she answered, "Oh, yeah. For once she didn't give me grief about it. Of course, I didn't tell her about us. I just said I needed a little 'me' time."

"Well, that's true. We need a little 'us' time." Tyler moved around the room to the nightstand and came back with a little box in his hand. "This is for you. I hope you like it."

She took the small box he gave her and wondered what could possibly be in it. "You didn't have to get me a gift," she said out loud, but inside she was overjoyed with the love and attention he showed her. She opened the box and pulled out a beautiful gold necklace. It had a heart that appeared to have a jagged line through the middle. On the back it read: "Two halves makes one whole."

She was so nervous that her hands shook as she held it up. "It's the most beautiful necklace I've ever seen. I love it."

She jumped up from the sofa and hugged him and kissed his sweetly smiling lips.

He was much taller than her, so he bent to hug her back. "I love how you feel. I could hold onto you forever." Finally, he took the necklace from her hands and fastened it around her slender neck. "The gold looks just right with your beautiful skin tone. I knew it would. Come on. Let's sit down and get comfortable. Do you want anything to eat? I can order something from room service."

"Maybe later. Right now I just want to get comfortable and talk." She leaned back against Tyler.

They talked all afternoon about their dreams, their hopes. They talked about being together like many young couples, and finally, the big empty king bed in the middle of the room brought them together.

It was a good thing they hadn't eaten first. She was full of nervous tension, and the food would have come flying out of her mouth and ruined the special moment. Tyler's hands shook, and it calmed her somewhat to know he was as nervous as she was. But he was so gentle with her. He touched her as if she were rarer than the fine wines he brought to her little house.

"You probably won't believe this, but I'm not that experienced when it comes to . . . sex," she admitted to Tyler. "I haven't even been intimate with anyone for over a year and —"

"You don't have to say anything. It's just you and me. But if it helps, I haven't been with anyone in over a year either." Then, Tyler laughed and said, "So really, we're both kinda virgins."

She had laughed at his silliness, and it put her at ease. They sat nervously on the side of the bed, both knowing what was coming, and their heartbeats increased with the tension. Tyler continued to kiss her and rubbed her back. Slowly, she leaned into him, calming down more with every pass of his warm hands.

"I have a condom. Do you need me to use it?"

"No, no," she breathlessly answered. "I take that shot for birth control. We should be okay." Chrystal was so caught up in the heat moving through her veins that she only heard every other word Tyler said. But she understood what he was asking her and felt even more loved and protected because he asked.

He removed her knit top and placed gentle kisses on her flushed skin. "You're so beautiful. Your skin is so soft and perfect. You're so kind and sweet. Everything about you is perfect. I didn't know you had this tattoo on your back. But, it's just as beautiful as the rest of you."

Chrystal had never felt comfortable with compliments. Truthfully, she didn't think she was beautiful or talented or kind or anything worthwhile. But she wanted to believe what Tyler was saying. She had gotten the tattoo after Oro was born. It was a full moon that appeared to be rising towards her neck. She thought of it as her new beginning, her new cycle of life. She wanted to believe making love with Tyler, her soulmate, brought it all to fruition.

He continued to compliment her as he removed her jeans and bra. "I want to make love to you. You're so lovely. Will you let me love you?"

"Yes, yes, I want you to make love to me. I want to make love to you too."

Tyler continued to take off Chrystal's clothes. He removed her panties and she was completely nude. Chrystal tried to cover herself with her hands and arms, crossing them in front of her. She was self-conscious about what she considered her flawed figure. She always thought she was too big in her ass and too small in her breasts.

But he held her hands in his and said, "Don't. You're the most beautiful woman I've ever seen. You're perfect and you're mine."

Chrystal smiled, "Well, in that case, you're mine too and I want to see all of you." Chrystal took charge and took his shirt in her hands and helped him pull it over his head. He shook out his kinky hair and kissed her lips again. He jumped up to kick off his shoes and take off his jeans and underwear.

"Wow, you're so big. I . . . I don't know what to say." Chrystal was still looking at Tyler's penis as he moved her back onto the bed.

"You don't have to say anything else. The look on your face speaks for itself." He smiled and puffed out his chest in response to the praise she gave his manhood.

Tyler caressed Chrystal's breasts with his large hands. He gently palmed her entire breast in one hand. "I love how my hands look against your skin. Your breasts are like golden peaches, so soft and smooth. They're just the right size and I love even more how sweet and juicy they look and will taste."

He sucked her nipple into his mouth and then tongued each one as if they were made from the foods of the gods. "Hmm, I knew it. Sweet and delicious. I love them. I love you."

Chrystal held on to Tyler's shoulders and then moved her hands around and down his back. She came back to the tattoo covering the top part of his shoulder and arm. It had been partially visible to her earlier, when they had been kissing and holding on to each other. But now she saw the entire tattoo of a golden dragon perched on his shoulder with its tail wrapped around his upper arm. In her daze, she meant to ask him about it, but she lost the thought as Tyler continued to kiss her.

All her rational thoughts fled her mind as she heated up fast with the tender suction Tyler had on her breasts. He moved lower to her belly button and licked and then nipped around her hip bones. The lower he went the more breathless she became. No man had ever shown her this much love and adoration. Everywhere his fingers and lips trailed left ribbons of fire. He worked her body like the fine-tuned instrument he played. Every note he stroked upon her body stirred her blood to a boiling symphony. He licked and kissed her swollen sex until she positively drooled.

She didn't want to think about what she was doing or even about tomorrow; she only wanted to feel what was happening now. All she could do was call his name over and over as she spiraled out of control.

He easily held her in his strong arms and joined with her in a sensual dance that was as old as humankind. He filled her with his rigid member and two became one.

Chrystal was wordless. Never in her life had she experienced this kind of hunger. Every stroke filled her to overflowing and she heard him murmuring sweet words of love that fed her until she thought she would burst. She was slick and wet with passion, brimming over with this scorching need only he could fuel. She offered him all the love she had within her. She kissed him over and over, demanding more with every caress of her slender hands.

Tyler, in return, gave her everything he had. He filled her as if there would be no tomorrow. As if today was all that was given them. And he thanked the gods he was here in this moment with Chrystal.

All the doubts and the fears she had were burned away in their blazing desire that flowed like molten lava. In all her failed attempts at sex and love, she had never known it could be like this. This was magic and Tyler was her magician. She would never be the same again and she thanked God she wouldn't.

Chapter Ten

Wednesday Evening, June 14th - Jimmy

Jimmy had just gotten home from his office. He still ran some of the operations of his multimillion-dollar tech business, but now at fifty-five, he had slowed down some, and he only went into the office when some high-level decision needed to be made. He'd barely made it out of his Jaguar and into the house from the garage when his cell phone rang and, at the same time, Bryan confronted him.

"I'm glad you're finally here," said Bryan. "It's been a long, hellish day and—"

Jimmy raised his hand to cut Bryan off as he took the call on his cell. He'd looked at the number, but it wasn't familiar. But with the type of people he dealt with, he didn't want to miss an important call. He answered his phone, hoping it wasn't Duck calling him back.

"Son, how are you?"

Jimmy almost fell on Bryan when he heard his father's voice. Of all the people who could be on the other end of the phone, he never would have believed it to be James Sr. He hadn't heard from the senior Mattock in over a year. Even more importantly, Jimmy didn't want to hear from him now. He was in such shock that he couldn't answer.

"James, are you there? Do you hear me?"

Jimmy finally stammered, "Yeah, I'm here. What do you want?"

"Well, you don't have to be so insolent. Your mother and I are in town. In fact, we came by your house earlier, and your, your uh, friend answered the door."

Bryan urgently mouthed at Jimmy to hang up. He looked ready to explode as he dragged Jimmy deeper into the house and sat him down at the kitchen countertop.

Jimmy was so flustered that he clicked the end button on his phone. "What the hell is going on? That was my father, and he said they came by here earlier."

"That's what I've been trying to reach you to tell you. You should have answered my calls, or at least you should have listened to my message." Bryan was clearly distressed as a flush broke out all over his face and he was sweating profusely. His faced turned red as he fanned himself and sat down heavily on a barstool next to Jimmy.

"Of all the people in this world, he's the last person I would have ever expected to drop by my home as if he was a wanted, invited guest. When did they show up, and what did they want?" Jimmy grabbed a napkin from the countertop and wiped sweat from his brow. He was so angry he thought he would be physically ill.

"They stopped by a couple of hours ago. I was cooking and heard the doorbell," said Bryan. "I was expecting the UPS guy, so I answered the door without thinking. At first I was speechless, and then your mother, bless her heart, was looking so frail . . ."

"What? What? Get on with it. What did that old man want?" Jimmy stood up and paced back and forth. Nothing gave him heartburn more than his father. The very idea of having to talk to him made Jimmy angrier and angrier.

Bryan shuddered and clasped his hands together. "He was looking for you. He said he'd gotten our address from your sister, Teresa, and wanted to know if this was your home. So like I said, your mother was looking so pale, and I didn't want them standing on the doorstep, so I invited them in."

"So why? I mean what in the hell did they want?" Jimmy couldn't continue; he was so rattled. His cell phone rang again, and he looked down at it as if it was a deadly cobra ready to strike.

Bryan visibly shuddered as he watched Jimmy to see what he would do about the phone. When Jimmy didn't answer Bryan, continued with his story.

"They wanted to see you. They said Teresa told them about Royce's wedding, but they were informed after the fact. Then your mother asked me who I was, and I didn't know what to say. So I said I was a friend of yours. Oh, Jim, I'm so sorry. It was so difficult. I didn't know what to do."

"How did they get this cell phone number? I never gave it to Teresa. At least I don't remember doing that." Jimmy sat back down and looked at his phone. He had the sudden impulse to throw it across the room.

"I gave them your number. After I let them in, they stood around awkwardly, so I said you were at work and that I kind of cook for you and . . ." Bryan trailed off and looked apologetically at Jimmy.

"It's all right. You did the best you could. So you gave them my number and then they left?" Jimmy continued to look at his phone.

"Sort of. Your father kept asking me questions about where you were and who I was, so I told them to call you and I gave him your number. Your father is so intimidating and strong-willed. He made me feel dirty, like I shouldn't have been here. It was terrible. I just wanted them to leave. When they finally left, I tried to reach you, but you didn't answer and I left you a message and . . ." Bryan couldn't go on. He collapsed in a crying heap on the countertop.

"Okay, stop crying. It's all right. I'll talk to them. Don't worry. I'll take care of it, like I always do. Just let me handle it."

7:00pm - Royce and Jessica

"Was that your father on the phone?" Jessica came out of the kitchen of the townhouse wiping her hands on a towel. "I finished your favorite dinner. It's baked chicken with yellow rice. It's all ready when you are."

Royce sat at the small dining table and stared at his cell phone. "Yeah, thanks babe and yes that was Dad. He said he needs to see us right away. He asked if we could come over. He said his mother and father were in town." Royce reached out his hand to Jessica. "He didn't sound happy. In fact, he sounded very upset."

Jessica moved to stand in front of Royce, holding his hand. "But that should be a good thing, right? I mean he hasn't seen them in forever. And these are your grandparents. When was the last time you saw them?"

"That would be a good thing in a normal family, but you know my family is anything but normal. And I haven't seen them since I was a little kid. They're not your typical loving grandparents. Believe me. They're nothing like Ms. Sylvi. Let's put the dinner away and get this visit over with." Royce looked at Jessica with love in his eyes. He hugged her tightly to his chest, rubbing her back as they stood together. They had barely been married a week and already so much family drama had occurred that he was wondering about the sanity of his family.

"Babe, do you think we should call Chrystal and include her in this? Because I hate to say this, but there have been so many lies and betrayals, and it doesn't look like it's over yet." Jessica stepped into the small kitchen to put away dinner and save it for later.

Royce followed her and leaned against the countertop. "Sure, we might as well. Let me call her now and see if she can come too. We can swing by there and pick her up if she'll come. They're her grandparents too. I have a funny feeling, though, that this is going to be a hell of an evening."

7:30pm - Jimmy and Bryan

"Calm down. Please calm down," said Jimmy. "You're going to give yourself a heart attack with all your worrying. Royce and Jessica are on their way over. It won't take them long to get here."

He wiped more sweat from his brow with his napkin and set the thermostat to sixty-five, hoping to cool down himself and the house.

"But Jim, your father and mother will be here any minute. I don't want them to beat Royce and Jessica to the door. Oh, my Lord! I can't take it. I just can't. I still remember the look your father gave me. I should leave. I don't want to see them again."

"I don't want you to leave. I care more about you and your stability than that of my father. Besides my father is nothing if not punctual, and I told him to come back at nine. I won't open the door to them before then. So relax and breathe deep. You have nothing to be afraid of. This is our home. No one can change that."

"Okay, all right. Just let me go freshen up. I must look a mess. I'll be down the hall. Call me when Royce and Jessica get here. Oh, and we want to give them their gift also. Don't forget."

"Right, let me get that too. It's going to be all right. They'll love the gift." Jimmy's words were just as much to comfort himself as they were to calm Bryan. He had no delusions his father would be courteous and certainly not kind towards Bryan or about their living arrangements. His mother, he hoped, would at least be more understanding and accepting. Although she couldn't exert any influence whatsoever over his father, he hoped she would at least not make the situation worst. Most of all, Jimmy really wished his horrid father had died years ago.

177

8:30pm - Jimmy and Bryan's house

"Come in, come in." Bryan hugged Royce and Jessica tightly to his chest as they came through the front door.

"And Chrystal too! My beautiful baby. I'm so happy to see you all. Come on in, and let's go to the family room." He led them down the hallway to a beautiful, comfortable family room, where Jimmy was waiting for them.

This room, like every other room in the house, had been decorated beautifully. The decor reflected Bryan's cheerful, sunny attitude. It was full of warm yellows, cool blues, and emerald floral patterns. It looked like a garden in bloom. Comfy upholstered chairs and long, deep sofas were scattered around a beautiful marble fireplace. The lighting reflected off the people in the room beautifully.

"It's so good to see all my children here together." Jimmy smiled from ear to ear. Carrying an envelope, he came over from the mantel where he stood and gave them all big hugs. He gave a big kiss to Chrystal and held her longest.

"How's my baby and all her babies? And where are they anyway?" Jimmy held her back from him while looking her over from head to toe.

Chrystal, as usual, was dressed casually in dark jeans, a tee-shirt, and flip-flops. She flipped her wavy natural hair back off her face and struggled to answer her father. *Okay, here we go already with the questions. Isn't it enough that I'm here? What's with the scrutiny?* "The kids are with Mama. She took them all over to Grandmama's house for a sleepover. So what's all this about? Royce said your mother and father were in town." Chrystal hoped to deflect the conversation from her back to her father's dilemma. *Stop asking me so many damn questions and take care of your own business.*

"Oh, Chrystal, that's so wonderful," replied Bryan loudly, "but I was looking forward to seeing my handsome and lovely little ones." Bryan held on to Jessica as if she were his life raft while he gave Chrystal a curious look.

Chrystal looked from Bryan to Jimmy. *Bryan seems so upset. He's trying too hard to not let it show. I hope everything will be all right.*

"Bryan, come on and let's sit down. I'd forgotten how lovely this room is," said Jessica as she patted the floral sofa's seat.

"Yes, let's all sit down." Jimmy sat in his comfortable chair opposite the sofa. "Chrystal, Royce, take a seat. First, Bryan and I want to apologize to you both in person about the unfortunate events at your wedding."

"Dad, it's okay. Jessica and I understand things happen. We're all adults, and well, stuff happens in everyone's lives." Royce looked to Jessica for help. "We really don't want to rehash the disastrous reception again. It's done, it's over."

"Mr. Mattock, there's really no need to apologize. We, um, understand. It wasn't your fault." Jessica looked to Royce and shrugged. It all was so awkward.

You wouldn't be saying this shit if you'd been at Grandmama's house. It's his damn fault most of this stuff happened. Chrystal sat at the edge of her seat and crossed her legs, one of which swung back and forth in agitation.

"Well, thank you for being so understanding. Anyway, Bryan and I didn't get a chance to give you our gift." Jimmy handed a lovely embossed envelope to Bryan, who leaned over to get it. "We hope you enjoy it."

Bryan took the envelope and grandly handed it to Jessica. Royce came over and sat on the arm of the sofa next to her. She hesitantly opened the envelope and read the card silently.

"Oh, my goodness!" Jessica jumped up and squealed. "It's the most creative and thoughtful gift I've ever received. You shouldn't have."

"What is it? What did they give you two?" Chrystal came over and read the card over Royce's shoulder.

Royce read out loud. "Dear son and daughter-in-law. To make your new home as welcoming as you are, we are gifting you with a total renovation of your condo with the Atlanta company *Full Bloom*. Whether it's bedroom, kitchen, living room or all three, a professional will be at your disposal to make your new home your dream home. Love, your dads."

"Wow, that sure is generous," said Chrystal as she looked at the card in Royce's hand. "It seems you guys get a butt-load of stuff no matter what else goes on."

Royce and Jessica looked at Chrystal as she went back to her chair. It was clear that the gift had upset her. Bryan looked to Jimmy for direction.

Jimmy finally answered Chrystal after an uncomfortable silence. "Don't be that way, sweetheart. We would do no less for you if you were getting married." He looked directly at Chrystal with a slight frown on his face.

Chrystal crossed her shapely legs again and swung a leg in an aggressive way. She glared at her father and gave Royce and Jessica a look of contempt. *Sure, you would do that for me. Like hell. You wouldn't even give me enough to get a used car,* she thought as she stared back at her father. *I'm your daughter, not Miss Thang. And Royce's not even your biological child.*

Chrystal acted belligerent, but really, she was sadden by what she considered as Royce once again getting all the attention and love. *I get the shitty end of the stick every damn time.*

Jessica tried to defuse the situation by going over to Jimmy and giving him a big hug. "Thank you both," she said, looking back to include Bryan. "This means so much to me and Royce. I can't tell you how much." Jessica looked at Royce with tears in her eyes.

"Well, this is just one of the reasons we wanted you all to come over." Jimmy hesitated a moment and looked at Bryan. He continued in a quieter voice.

"My father and mother made a surprise visit to Atlanta and to our home. It seems your Aunt Teresa shared with them the wedding details."

Royce stood up from the arm of the sofa and said, "I'm the one responsible for that, Dad. I wanted to include your side of the family too, and I was able to get some info on your sister. So I called her, and Jessica and I told her about the wedding."

Royce had a calm look on his face as he went over to Jessica and put his arm around her. "I didn't mean to open up old wounds, knowing how you feel about your father, but I didn't see any harm in contacting Aunt Teresa."

Chrystal couldn't help herself. She said, "So Royce not only contacted Eric, but he called up Aunt Teresa too. So now Grandfather James and Grandmother MaryBeth are on their way over?" Chrystal barely held back the snicker in her voice. "So you guys rewarded all that backstabbing with a big-ass expensive gift. That's so special." Chrystal laughed an evil and ugly sound.

"Chrystal, that's not necessary. Stop acting so childish." Jimmy gave Chrystal a disapproving look and shook his head at her. "Although, there is some truth to what you're saying. It seems we all underestimated Royce's detective skills again. Well, now we know the rest of the story. I think the important issue here is this visit from them is not something any of us are looking forward to."

"I don't understand, Mr. Mattock," said Jessica. "These are your parents. They can't be that bad. Besides, Royce was doing what he thought was right in talking to your sister. I don't see anything wrong with that either. She said she was out of the country doing photography shoots. Otherwise, she would have loved to come. I talked to her and—"

Chrystal leapt from her seat and shouted, "What do you know about our family? You've just married into it. You couldn't possibly know what these people are capable of. You need to stay out of our business! I don't blame Daddy for not wanting to have anything to do with them."

Chrystal knew she was acting like a spoiled brat. But she saw again how Royce always came out on top. No matter how good she tried to be, she was overlooked in favor of Royce. She took a big breath and tried to calm herself. She counted backwards from one hundred and sat back down. *Get yourself together girl. This isn't about me. So I just got to let it go. They're looking at me like I'm crazy. Calm down, calm down and just let it go.*

Jessica paled at Chrystal's remarks. She looked regrettably at Chrystal's face.

"Chrystal, that's enough! Thank you for standing up for me, but I don't need your help. I didn't mean for this to become a competition between you, Royce, and Jessica. The real issue

182

here is that my father does not know about my— Bryan's and my—relationship. And frankly, I don't want to have to discuss it with him. He is one evil old man, and there's definitely no love lost to be found between us."

Jimmy suddenly looked deflated. He went over to Bryan and gently rubbed his knee. "Bryan doesn't deserve the hatred that I know my father is capable of. I don't want to expose any of you to that, but I felt, at least I thought, we could all rally together to protect Bryan."

Bryan gazed at Jimmy with a soft smile. "That's so wonderful of you Jim, but I know how much you don't want to talk to him. This is turning out to be a—"

The doorbell cut Bryan short.

Jimmy looked at Bryan. "Well, I guess it's show time. Everyone wait here while I get the door."

Chapter Eleven

Jimmy cautiously walked to the front door, as if his greatest adversary was standing behind it. The door's details were as ornate as everything else in the house. Wrought iron intertwined with cut glass stood out beautifully in the nine-foot tall double doors.

He wiped his sweaty palms on his pants and took a deep breath. *It's about time I stop hiding my true self. I don't care what my father thinks. I am my own man, and I will not be afraid to confront a seventy-five-year-old tyrant.*

He could see the distorted image of his parents standing under the lavish overhead lights. Even with the glass separating them, he spied his mother's pale face and the stern visage of his father standing over her. Jimmy slowly opened the door and stood back. *Well, here goes nothing.*

"James, oh my God! It's been too long, way too long. It's so wonderful to actually see you." MaryBeth Mattock rushed into Jimmy's arms and hugged her son tightly. Tears shone in her bright eyes. In her haste to hug her only son, she dropped the Louis Vuitton purse casually thrown over her arm.

"Come in, come in. It's good to see you too." Jimmy was surprised because, for once, he meant what he said. He hugged his mother back just as tightly as she hugged him. She reached up to pull him to her and kissed him several times. His father picked up his wife's forgotten purse as Jimmy ushered them both into the house and closed the door.

"Hello, son." James Sr. towered over his tiny wife. He looked over her head to Jimmy as she hugged her son again. Even though he had a harsh look on his face, his eyes appeared teary. He held out a hand to Jimmy and waited.

"Hello, Father," said Jimmy. He looked at the hand his father held out to him in greeting, and he released the tight hold he had on his mother and shook his father's hand. "Come on back to the family room. There's some people I want to finally introduce you to."

MaryBeth took her purse from her husband, but she held on to Jimmy's arm as he walked her down the expansive hallway lined with contemporary artwork. "Your house is so beautiful. I love the paintings. Who did the decorating? It's exquisite."

Bryan came down the hallway and stood hesitantly waiting for Jimmy to acknowledge him. "That's one of the people I want to introduce you to. Come in and meet Bryan Denveue, my decorator, and more importantly, my partner in life." Jimmy watched his father for a reaction.

For a moment, his mother hesitated and a little color blushed across her cheeks, but she held out her hand to Bryan and he drew her to him for a small hug. "It's so nice to see you again, Bryan," said MaryBeth. "Your taste is superb. It seems you not only cook but decorate as well. You are very talented. Your family must be Creole? That is a Creole name, isn't it?"

MaryBeth turned to James Sr. with a hesitant look on her weary face.

Her husband finally held his hand out to Bryan also.

"Thank you, Mrs. Mattock, and yes, my family is from Louisiana." Bryan shook James Sr.'s hand as he answered Marybeth's question.

"It's good to see you again, Bryan," said James Sr. "Thank you for getting our message to James and for letting us in earlier. It was a long and exhausting flight from Denver."

Jimmy was astonished. Who was this old man standing in front of him sounding sane and human? This couldn't possibly be his father, the monster of his nightmares. Jimmy glanced at Bryan and shrugged. The look Bryan gave him back seemed to say he was just as perplexed as Jimmy was.

Chrystal heard her father talking to his parents as he led them down the hallway. Her grandmother led the way into the family room on Jimmy's arm.

"Oh my goodness, look at my grandchildren," gushed MaryBeth. "Chrystal, Royce, come give your grandfather and me a hug. The last time I saw you both, you were nothing but little children. Look at you now, all grown up with your own children. Chrystal, you look like a beautiful fashion model, just like your Aunt Teresa. And Royce, this must be your lovely bride."

Chrystal looked at her grandparents as they stood beside Bryan. Her grandmother looked so old and frail. Her coloring had always been light, but now it was downright white. Her once black, lustrous hair was silver and pulled back from her face in a tight knot at the back of her head. But she was genuinely smiling.

Grandmother looks like she could faint at any moment, Chrystal thought as she hugged her grandmother and received a kiss on her cheek. *All I feel is bones, and she's so tiny. But she is slaying that designer outfit, and that Bvlgari perfume is definitely on point.*

Seeing her grandfather standing beside her father was unsettling. Jimmy looked so much like his father it was eerie. They were the same height, except James Sr. had started to stoop some, and they both had the same dark, tightly curled hair and chocolate-brown eyes. The same high, sharp cheekbones and tight, cruel-looking mouth adorned both their faces. Jimmy was slimmer than his father, but you could tell they had similar builds. One could easily see her grandfather still retained a powerful build. Chrystal reached up to give her grandfather a hug, but he held her to him and gave her a small kiss on her cheek.

Chrystal looked to Royce as he led Jessica over to his grandparents. They had heard a small portion of the conversation as her father along with Bryan led the grandparents down the hallway. She wondered where these calm-looking people suddenly came from. They were nothing like she remembered, but she was happy they weren't.

Royce gave his grandmother a hug, and she held him tight and gave him a kiss on the cheek. He shook his grandfather's hand as he said, "Grandmother, Grandfather, this is my love, my beautiful bride, Jessica. Jessica, these are my father's parents, Mr. and Mrs. James and MaryBeth Mattock Sr."

Jessica blushed at the compliment Royce paid her as she reached out her hand to his grandparents. "It's a pleasure to meet you, Mrs. Mattock," she said. "Royce told me you all live in Denver. I'm sure you must be exhausted if you just got in today."

Royce's grandmother hugged Jessica. "Please call me Grandmother. You're one of the family now. Oh, Royce, she is beautiful. I see a little Creole in you too. Where're your people from, dear?"

Jessica stammered as James Sr. gave her a small hug. "Yes, yes, my mother was a Bijoux before she married my father. She was born and raised in St. Charles Parish."

"Wonderful, just wonderful. I was a Jadeaux before I married James. My mother's people were famous for the Jadeaux float every year during Mardi Gras."

Chrystal couldn't believe these were the same grandparents she had last seen years ago. *Who in hell are these people? Zombies or something must have stolen their bodies.. They both must be about to die. That must be it. They're about to die and need somebody to take care of them. Well, that ain't gonna be me.*

Chrystal looked to her father. From the expression on his face he was thinking the exact same thing. She never knew her grandmother could string together more than two words, and here she was talking up a storm. *And grandfather is holding his shit together too. That must be a record for him not losing his temper and cussing everybody out,* she snickered to herself.

188

"Well, come in and sit down. You must be so tired with all the traveling." Bryan quickly moved them towards the sofa to sit them down. Of all the people in the room, Chrystal thought Bryan looked like he was the only one who wasn't totally confused. In fact, he looked like he wanted to do a cheer that things seemed to be going so well. But Chrystal above anything else, knew that looks could definitely be deceiving.

"Yes, Mrs. Mattock and I have been traveling since early this morning. She's especially worn out. You know we are getting older." James Sr. hugged his wife to him on the sofa.

"Well, it's true. I am a little drained, but no more so than usual." MaryBeth leaned back into the comfortable sofa and crossed her slim legs.

Jimmy sat down in a brightly upholstered chair. "Mother, Father, where are you staying? If I had known you were coming, I could have made the arrangements for you." Jimmy was smiling. His look said he still couldn't believe these people were his parents. They were acting way too normal.

James Sr. leaned forward and looked around the room with a scowl on his face. "If you had bothered to let us know that Royce and Jessica were getting married, then you certainly could have made arrangements for us."

His comment took a moment to sink in. Everyone in the room looked uncomfortable as they passed glances back and forth.

"If it hadn't been for Teresa, who graciously informed us of the nuptials, I daresay we would still be sitting in Denver unaware of what our only grandson was doing." James Sr. leaned back in the sofa as if he had stated the absolute truth. "May I please have a glass of water? My throat is very dry."

189

Bryan shook himself out of his stupor and said, "Oh, my goodness. Of course you can. I'm so sorry. Mrs. Mattock, would you like something also?" He quickly moved towards the hallway that led to the kitchen, but he stumbled as he moved to leave the room.

"Yes, dear. That would be wonderful." To Jimmy, MaryBeth said, "so to answer your question, we're staying in a hotel not too far from here. We'll be here through the weekend. Your father is very good at locating the best places to stay. I think it's called the Grand Royale. Is that right, James?"

"No, it's called the Grand Resort, but names don't matter. Actions do."

Now this is the grandfather I've seen, thought Chrystal. He's already trying to be an asshole. But I got to give it to him for snapping back like that.

"Really! Father, I tried several times to reach you. I left messages that went unanswered over and over again. Frankly, I got the impression from your actions that you weren't interested in me or anyone else in my family."

Chrystal wanted to laugh at the people carrying on, but one look at her father's face let her know how serious things had suddenly gotten. Her father looked ready to go ballistic and Royce was squeezing Jessica's hand so hard it had probably cramped.

"So you're telling me you tried to contact me and I didn't answer the phone or reply to your messages? I don't recall any messages from you or anyone else in this room." James Sr. turned to his wife for confirmation, and she silently looked to her hands in her lap. An uncomfortable hush moved in like a dark cloud and took over the room.

Bryan hurried into the room with a tray of refreshments. He set it down on the coffee table in front of MaryBeth. "I have some water here and started some coffee. There's also a light snack of cheese and crackers if you're hungry." He looked at Jimmy's silent, hostile looking face. It was obvious things had gotten much worse since he left the room. He shrewdly glanced at Royce looking for confirmation.

"Thank you, Bryan. That's very nice of you," said MaryBeth. She picked up her glass of water and slowly brought it to her lips. "That's just what I needed."

James Sr. looked his son in the eyes. It was clear to Chrystal that a lot of hurt and angry emotions were materializing full grown in front of her.

"That's exactly what I'm telling you. I could even get the phone records to verify the calls I made to you if I wanted to. But you probably still wouldn't believe me. None of my calls were answered by you or Mother. How many times do you think someone should keep being ignored before they give up?"

James Sr. picked up his glass and took a sip. "That's the problem with you, son. If you really want to reach someone, you never give up. That is, if you really want to do what's right." He set his glass down on the coffee table and looked at the silent faces staring back at him. "If it hadn't been for your sister, Teresa, who stays in contact with your mother and me, we'd be ignorant of all this. Even though she lives in Europe, she hasn't forgotten her parents. She also told me she hasn't heard from you in years. And if not for my grandson contacting her, we would still be in the dark."

"That's not what Aunt Teresa said to me." Royce looked from his father to his grandfather. "She said she talks to Dad every now and then, but not as much as she wishes. She also said she talked to Dad about six months ago."

"Thank you, Royce, but I don't feel I need to prove anything to this man anymore." Jimmy looked at his father and shook his head sadly. "I thought you had changed for the better. After all these years, I see you're still the same old arrogant bastard I grew up with."

MaryBeth gasped. "Oh, James, please don't talk about your father like that." With tears in her eyes, she continued, "We love you all and wanted this visit to be a sort of reconciliation. I've missed so much of you all's lives. I don't want to miss any more. I refuse to sit back and be left out."

"That's all right, dear. What can you expect from him? He's never given me the respect a son should give his father. He's an ungrateful, deceitful liar. He's never done as he should, so I don't expect any difference now. Of course, he's always had some other agenda. His purpose in life seems to be to cause tension between everyone."

Chrystal sat silently in her chair and looked back and forth between father, son and, grandson. *Humph! Now you know Royce don't look nothing like Daddy or Grandfather. He got all that red hair just like Eric. Come to think of it, he got the same eyes too. I wonder how long before they realize that.* "Grandmother's right," she said. "They've come a long way. That has to count for something. I know I wouldn't have come that far just to argue with everybody."

"Yes, I agree with Chrystal," said Jessica as she wrung her hands together.

Chrystal looked at Jessica. *I bet she never thought she would be caught up in the middle of this shitty family drama. I know everybody's family has issues, but our family takes the cake. I wish I could change the atmosphere in here though. It's so tight and angry.*

"They're here now," Jessica said, "so that means a lot. At least give them a chance to explain before you throw away a chance at understanding what everyone is feeling." Jessica sat back in her chair.

Royce, sitting on the arm of her chair, rubbed her back and started to say more, but Jimmy interrupted him.

"Thank you Chrystal and Jessica, but I've had enough of trying to get through to my father. I realize I'm a failure in his eyes. I never followed his orders. and he has held that against me for years. Apparently, he's the one who doesn't want to understand the feelings of others. It's crystal clear he doesn't want to reconcile. He only wants to blame and cause dissension. If you feel this way, then why in the hell did you come here?"

"Please, everyone. Let's take a big breath and calm down." Bryan stood up and clasped his hands together. "This is truly upsetting Mrs. Mattock. Look at her. She's even paler than before." Bryan moved to her side and touched her on the back. "Mrs. Mattock, are you all right? Do you need anything?"

MaryBeth clutched the cool glass of water in her hand and sat rigidly in her seat. Her face was whiter than white. She took shallow breaths and started to shake. "Please, please don't argue. This isn't the reason we're here. I want peace. I want time with my grandchildren. I want to see my great-grandchildren. Please stop this arguing." Suddenly, she dropped the glass and water splashed over James Sr.'s shoes.

"Becky, are you all right? What is it?" He took MaryBeth in his arms and cradled her like a baby. "Do you hear me? Answer me, please!"

Her voice shaking, she answered, "I'm all right, but I won't be if my husband and my son don't stop this feud this minute. I swore I wouldn't sit quietly anymore and allow this to happen. You promised me you wouldn't do this. You promised. Do you hear me, James?" MaryBeth pushed against her husband. She sat back in her seat and glared at him with misty tears in her eyes.

Bryan came around with napkins and dabbed at James Sr.'s shoes. "There now, all better."

"I'm not the one picking a fight, Mother. Your husband is being his intolerable self as usual. I've done everything in my power to be respectful, but it seems Father doesn't want me to be that way." Jimmy came over to the sofa and rubbed his mother's shoulder. "I'm willing to get along with him for the sake of everyone in this room. But I will not be disrespected in my own home. Not by Father, not by anyone."

Another uncomfortable silence gripped the room at large. Chrystal looked back and forth from her grandmother to Royce. *Becky, huh? Grandmother sure doesn't look like a Becky. But whatever.* As she thought about the scene in front of her, she wanted to say something to ease the tension, but no words came to mind. She pleaded with her eyes for Royce to say something.

Finally, Royce stood up and went to his grandfather. "Grandfather, please let's not spoil what could be the best reunion ever. Dad is trying to get along. I know your feelings are hurt. That's obvious to everyone here. But Grandmother is right. Let's not waste this opportunity to reconnect." Royce

194

looked to his father. "Dad, you have to know that just them being here is a sign they want to at least try. Put away some of the past mistakes, that clearly have been made by both of you, and try to move past it."

Royce waited for them to acknowledge what he said, but both Jimmy and James Sr. were still being mulish, so Royce continued. "Everybody's right in their own minds, and you can't get in there with them to dispute the facts. Who in their right mind would want to? I understand how you both feel."

There was a long drawn out silence in the room, and Royce continued speaking even though it looked like neither his father nor grandfather were listening. "I know what you're getting ready to say. But just because I didn't experience it, doesn't mean I don't understand it. I don't have to get my head cut off to know it will kill me."

Royce and everyone in the room waited tensely for either Jimmy or James Sr. to say something. The men looked at each other hotly. If eyes threw daggers, both men would be dead.

Hesitantly, James Sr. replied, "The children seem to have better judgment than the parents in this case. You're right. We didn't come all this way to argue. We came so we could be included in your lives. We want to be a part of your family, and we want you to be part of ours. I'm tired and I . . . we want peace. Your mother and I are willing to try." James Sr. stood up and held out a hand to his son. "What if we start over again, and I'll hold my opinions to myself if you can do the same?"

Jimmy looked at his father's hand. "All right, I'm agreeable. No more fighting." Jimmy shook his father's hand and went back to his seat.

"Thank you, thank you. Oh my, I feel so much better." MaryBeth clapped her thin hands together and looked at her husband with a genuine smile on her face. "Now I want to do what we really came for. We have something for our grandchildren."

Chrystal looked at Royce and hunched her shoulders in question. *What now? They probably have some expensive-ass gift for Royce, who's not even their grandson. Becky will probably pull a scarf or some shit out of that purse for me.*

MaryBeth fumbled in her big Louis Vuitton purse for a moment. Finally, she pulled out an envelope with Chrystal's name on it.

"Chrystal, since you are the first born grandchild, this is for you." She handed Chrystal a cream-colored envelope. "Your grandfather and I thought long and hard about this and we hope you can use this." She took another envelope from her purse and handed it to Royce. "Royce and Jessica, our wedding gift to you both. Please enjoy."

"I know this doesn't make up for all the years we've been out of your lives." James Sr. looked at Chrystal and Royce expectantly. "But we want to show you that you both have been in our hearts and minds."

Jimmy and Bryan looked on at the scene unfolding in front of them. Bryan had a pleased look on his face, but Jimmy's mouth was drawn tight. He looked as if he was ready to make some caustic remark at any moment.

Chrystal's hand shook slightly as she opened her envelope. She pulled out a folded piece of parchment and read aloud to the room.

"The bearer of this letter, Chrystal Mattock, is entitled to her choice of a new automobile (make and model her choice) or fifty thousand dollars cash. Any combination of vehicle and/or cash is at her discretion to make." Chrystal's hands shook even more as she read. Tears sprang to her eyes as she looked at her grandparents. "I . . . I don't know what to say. This is overwhelming. Thank you both so much. I'm . . . I mean, I don't . . . Thank you. This is just what I need." She gave them both a big hug.

"You are more than welcome," said MaryBeth as she wiped tears from her eyes with a handkerchief she pulled from her purse. "Now, Royce, you and Jessica open yours, please."

Royce gave the envelope to Jessica, who opened it and pulled out another thick piece of paper.

Jessica looked at Royce briefly as she read out loud. "The bearers of this letter, Royce and Jessica Mattock, being newly married, have been granted a second honeymoon of their destination choice or twenty-five thousand dollars cash. Any vacation and/or cash combination is at their discretion to make." Jessica teared up and her voice caught as she gave her grandparents-in-law a big hug. "Thank you. I don't know what to say either. This is just wonderful. Thank you both so much."

Bryan clapped his hands and gave a little shout. "This is more than great. This is fantastic. You both are so generous. Jim, isn't this just wonderful?"

"Yes, yes, it is. I never would have expected this from you all. But it is indeed a pleasant surprise." Jimmy looked at his father with a tight skeptical smile on his face. His words totally belied his facial expression.

"Thank you, Grandmother." Royce gave his grandmother another big hug. "Grandfather, you shouldn't have, but thank you. You're both too generous."

"Now, we can sit back and talk like a real family. I don't know when I've felt such joy. I'm so glad we made this trip." MaryBeth continued to smile as she sipped on her water.

Chrystal was so surprised she was left speechless. *I can't believe they gave me so much. Not even Daddy has done this for me. I just wonder what I'll have to do to repay them. Nothing comes without strings attached. I bet theirs are gonna feel like steel cables, but I'm gonna take this big-ass check and party.*

James Sr. leaned back in his seat and crossed one leg over the other. He turned to his son and a crafty look crossed his face.

"Well, son, how's your wife? Jackie, isn't it?"

MaryBeth gave her husband a scathing look. "James let's not talk about that. Let's just enjoy our children."

"That's all right, Mother." Jimmy looked at the stricken expression on Bryan's face. "Jackie and I have been divorced for more than ten years. I'm sure Teresa told you that since you're in constant contact with her. It's no secret. Jackie still lives here in Atlanta and she's doing fine. We saw each other at Royce's wedding. But she lives her life, and Bryan and I live ours."

"I didn't mean to make anyone uncomfortable. I was just asking a question. Yes, Teresa did mention that you and Jackie weren't together, but meeting Bryan here today was a bit of a surprise." James Sr. looked in Bryan's direction. "So . . . you and Bryan have been together for how long?"

"James, that's enough." MaryBeth sat up straighter in her seat. "Why are you trying to be so difficult? James is a grown man and so is Bryan. I'm sure, like any couple, they're together because they love each other. Leave it at that."

Whew! Tell him, Becky! Chrystal couldn't help but smile to herself. *I never would have thought my nervous little grandmother could talk shit, but she got it going on.*

Chapter Twelve

Thursday evening, June 15th - Ms. Sylvi's House

Jackie couldn't believe the story Chrystal was telling them. It was blowing her mind, and it was a good thing she was already sitting down, or she would have fallen down in laughter. If it hadn't been for Nancy bringing up Jimmy's parents before Royce's wedding, she would never have thought of them at all. They definitely weren't fans of hers; in fact, she hadn't seen or thought about them in years.

"So Jimmy's mother said that she wanted to be included in her son's family?" Asked Jackie shaking her head. "I never knew the woman could put together three words. It's hard to imagine she held a conversation. What about that awful father of his? What did he say?"

"Jimmy's parents came to town unexpectedly and started showering gifts on you and Royce?" asked Ms. Sylvi as she moved around her immaculate kitchen wiping down an already clean countertop.

"Lord, those people are unbelievable. You haven't heard from or seen them since you were about twelve. And even then, they didn't act like they liked anybody. Including their only son, Jimmy." Jackie snorted as she took another sip from her iced tea.

"Yeah, we were blown away. I kept looking at Royce, and he kept looking at Jessica. It was too funny." Chrystal picked up her iced tea and took a drink. "Royce and them were just getting over the gift Daddy gave them, when bam! Here come Grandmother Becky pulling envelopes out of her big-ass Louis Vuitton bag."

"Grandmother Becky? Who the hell is that? I thought James Sr. was married to a MaryBeth." Jackie continued to shake her head at Chrystal. She wanted so badly to laugh out loud, but she held it in.

Chrystal laughingly said, "Grandfather James got all upset when Grandmother looked ill. So I guess he forgot himself and hugged her and called her Becky. It was kind of cute in a way. But she was giving out just as good as Grandfather was. She wasn't taking no shit from him."

Jackie looked at Ms. Sylvi. "Do you believe this? Those people came all the way from Denver to hand out money like it's Christmas candy. What in the world! I knew they were wealthy, but why now, after all these years? Just trying to buy my children's love. I wonder what strings are attached to that money?"

"I don't care if they are trying to buy my love. I got a little love for them now that I got fifty in my bank account. I'll sell them a little more if they got more money."

Ms. Sylvi and Jackie laughed hysterically at Chrystal's reaction.

"I wish I could have been a fly on that wall. I bet Jimmy was about to piss his pants when he found out they were in town. What did Bryan do? I bet he was just crying and holding on to Jimmy like a baby." Jackie continued to smirk as she thought about how Bryan was caught again.

Chrystal leaned back in her chair and continued. "Well, I kind of felt sorry for Bryan. Before Grandfather got there, Bryan was really having a fit. He looked like he was so embarrassed to be caught like that."

"I bet," said Jackie. "Believe me. He's been caught before. He ought to be used to it by now. Anyway, what did they say about Jimmy and Bryan's little relationship?"

"Oh my Lord, Jackie. You need to stop. You know the Lord don't like ugly," said Ms. Sylvi as she laughed along with Jackie.

"Grandfather tried to start some more stuff, but Grandmother Becky checked him. She said Daddy and Bryan are grown men, and obviously they love each other, so leave it alone. I thought I would die laughing."

Chrystal turned her head at a sound coming from the hallway. "Uh, I think I hear my little demons. I'm gonna go get them."

Jackie motioned to her mother to sit down. "Mama, sit down and stop all that cleaning. This kitchen can't possibly get any cleaner. I can't believe Jimmy's folks did what they did. They must be ready to die or something."

Ms. Sylvi took a seat at the table and huffed. "You can't never get a kitchen too clean. But you right about Jimmy's folks. That is way too generous. I guess they're trying to make up for all the years of neglecting Chrystal and Royce."

"I know I shouldn't feel this way, but I kind of wish Jimmy and Bryan had gotten what they deserved."

"Jackie you can't mean that. I certainly don't approve of that kind of relationship, but if they love each other, then just leave it alone. You don't have to have anything to do with them and their relationship." Ms. Sylvi picked at a spot on the placemat and had a faraway look in her eyes. "Besides, everybody deserves to have some love in their lives. It's so lonely otherwise."

"You're right, and you and I both know just how lonely it can get."

Chrystal came back to the kitchen with Jade in her arms, leading Jewell and Oro.

"Okay, you guys sit here a minute while I finish visiting. I have one more workday tomorrow, and then Mommy will stay here with you guys. Thanks again for keeping them here while I finish up working, Grandma." Chrystal adjusted a sleepy Jade in her lap and directed Jewell and Oro to seats around the table.

"You're welcome, baby. It only makes sense. You'll be moving in here, so they might as well stay here until you finish.

"So, Chrystal, what are you thinking about doing with your newfound blessing?" Jackie turned a smiling face to Jewell as she pulled on her curly ponytail.

"Well, since they already deposited fifty thousand dollars in my bank account, I'm just overwhelmed with looking at the balance. I've never seen that much money in my life, and it all belongs to me. I just want to watch it for a while." Chrystal laughed happily and Oro laughed along with her, just because his mother was happy.

"I can understand that," said a smiling Jackie. "But seriously, if you want some unasked for advice, I think you should save some of the money and get a really nice used SUV so you can transport the kids easier."

"That's exactly what I was thinking. And thank you for the advice." Chrystal thought for a moment. She had been rocking Jade gently in her arms and the baby was asleep.

"Give me that baby, Chrystal. You look like you got more on your mind. I don't want you to accidently drop her." Ms. Sylvi reached out her arms for Jade as Chrystal stood up and took Jade to her.

"You're always right, Grandma. I do have something else I want to talk to you two about. I wish Aunt Nancy was here too. I want you all to be included. But I guess I can talk to her later."

"This sounds so serious, baby. What is it?" Jackie pulled Jewell closer to her as Oro came around the table and started playing with a necklace around Jackie's neck.

Chrystal went over to the counter and leaned against it. She blushed, but taking a big breath, she made an announcement. "Jade's father is coming to town tomorrow, and I want you all to meet him." Chrystal blushed even more and fanned her face with a dishtowel.

Jackie looked at Ms. Sylvi, who couldn't have looked more surprised if a bomb had exploded in the center of the kitchen. They both started talking at the same time. But Jackie won out and asked her question louder than Ms. Sylvi. "Who is this young man, Chrystal? What's his name?"

Chrystal wrung the dishtowel in her hands as she answered. "His name is Tyler Jamison and he's a musician, and he plays an acoustic guitar, and he's really talented and he travels a lot, but he's playing here tomorrow and I thought you might want to meet him you know, but you don't have to if you don't want to." Chrystal was so nervous she ran the entire statement together into one long sentence.

Jackie looked at Chrystal with tears in her eyes and said, "I think that's wonderful, and thank you for wanting to share with us. I would be happy to meet him. I can tell this wasn't easy for you to even say, so I feel honored that you're finally willing to trust us with this."

Jackie turned to her mother. "I know I talked all over you, Mama, but I was excited and couldn't help myself. You can go ahead."

Chrystal looked at her grandmother and waited. She was still nervous, but she needed to hear what her grandmother had to say. If it was negative, she didn't know how she would feel.

"Thank you, baby, for trusting us enough to share him with us. I can't wait to meet your young man. And he plays the guitar too. He must be very special, very special indeed."

Chrystal visibly relaxed against the countertop.

"Thanks, Grandmama. Thank you both. I'm still deciding on the details, but I think I want to bring him here. Is that all right with you, Mama? I mean, I thought it would be easier if everybody just comes over here."

Chrystal looked back and forth between her mother and grandmother. Jewell and Oro had slid down to the floor and were happily playing with a toy. It was quiet for a long moment.

"That's fine with me if it's fine with Ms. Sylvi. Anything you want to do is just fine with me."

Thursday night, June 15ᵗʰ - Jimmy and Bryan's house

Jimmy Mattock sat at his desk in his office. The visit from his parents had shaken his world. So many things he'd planned and tediously put together, now seemed to be rapidly unraveling. His father, who Jimmy had hated all of his life, appeared to be accessible, like a real decent person. *After all these years and the horrible way he has always treated Mother, Teresa, and me, Father now seems to have a conscience.* He stared at one of the sedate-looking portraits on the wall.

"Jim, what are you up to?" Bryan cautiously entered the room, nursing a glass of wine.

"I'm just thinking about Mother and Father's visit. I spoke with them a little while ago. They were still recuperating from their travels and the long night."

Bryan moved over to a comfortable club chair and sat down. He crossed his legs and sipped at his drink.

Jimmy leaned his elbows upon his desk and steepled his fingers under his chin. "I knew they were getting older, of course, but Mother looked so frail. I guess she looked like all the life had been sucked out of her body. I felt such compassion for her."

"And that surprised you?"

"Yes . . . yes it did. I'm confused by my feelings. I thought I left them back in Denver. My feelings, that is. I've always prided myself on thinking logically, without emotion. Now it

206

appears that I don't know myself as well as I thought. I want to believe they both have changed for the better."

Bryan went over to Jimmy and hesitantly rubbed his shoulder. Finally, he spoke what was on his mind. "Jim, your parents aren't the only ones who needed to change for the better, but I'm happy they appear to have done that."

Jimmy turned his head to look up at Bryan. He asked, "And exactly what do you mean by that?"

Bryan hesitated in answering again. He went back around to the front of the desk and looked directly at Jimmy. "I mean, you're not the perfect son, brother, or father. You have behaviors that border on manic. You act without compassion, especially if you think someone has wronged you. You fixate on the negative, or what you perceive as being negative, and try to destroy it. You, my husband, are not God, and you are not always right. But you rush into things with a vengeance that's terrifying." Bryan stopped and hunched his shoulders.

Jimmy stared at him and said, "Go the hell on. You seem to be on a roll. Get it all out."

"This can't be news to you, Jim. I've said these same words to you before. You want things your way, in your surreal timeframe, the way only you think it should go, and damn anybody else. You hurt the people closest to you, and you just don't seem to care. That's what I find the most distressing. You don't seem to care about who you damage in the end."

Jimmy glowered at Bryan. He saw a sheen of tears in Bryan's eyes. "So what do you propose I do about these so-called faults of mine? What's your formula to transform me into a nice person?" Jimmy made air quotes as he said the word nice. *Can he possibly be right? Is that how he really sees me, or is he just saying shit to make me angry? But those look like real tears in his eyes.*

"For starters, you can stop being so damn smug every time I say something that you don't like. The air quotes weren't necessary. You intentionally try to hurt me with your words, and all I'm trying to do is help you, to help us."

Bryan moved back to his seat. He had a faraway look in his eyes. "You know when I first met you, I guess when we first ran into each other, I knew you were the one. I saw a shy young man who seemed out of his element."

Jimmy laughed, interrupting Bryan. "You're right about that. I had no idea what I was doing. I remember some skinny little guy trying to pick me up. I didn't know I was gay, but he did." He laughed again, but this was not a happy chuckle. It was painful and bordered on a disturbing sadness.

Bryan hung his head and continued, as if Jimmy hadn't laughed that deep, soul-shredding sound. "I loved a sweet young man who was so passionate about science and technology. I wanted to smack him every time he said something about quantum physics or whatever. I had no idea where we were going, but I knew I wanted to get on that ride and take it to the end." Bryan went over to the tall windows overlooking a beautiful side yard. "That young man had dreams that he was going to be the president of some big tech company, inventing some grand new thing-a-ma-jig that everyone would want."

Jimmy joined Bryan at the window. "Yes, I remember that young man also. He had great ideas, but no way to bring them to fruition. I also remember another young man who gave him every penny he had inherited from his grandmother. I haven't forgotten any of that. I know I act like I have sometimes, but I haven't forgotten what you did for me or what you mean to me."

"Let it go then." Bryan looked at Jimmy.

"What the hell are you talking about? I'm not doing anything," replied Jimmy as he went back to his desk and searched through some papers there.

"This thing with Jackie and Eric. Let it go before you're lost to me. Before you hate yourself more than you think you hate Jackie."

Jimmy grunted. "What thing? What are you talking about? I don't understand what you think you know. I don't have a thing to do with Jackie and Eric." Jimmy searched frantically through the papers on his desk. *Shut up, just shut up. You can't possibly know about that.*

"Remember the other day, when you went to the store and forgot to take your cell phone with you? I heard it ringing on the bathroom counter where you left it. I wasn't trying to snoop in your business, but I answered the call, thinking it might be something important."

"I know you didn't do that. You know how I feel about people touching what's mine." Jimmy looked at Bryan, who had a dismayed frown on his face.

"Well, yes, I do know how you feel about that, but like I said, I thought it might be something important. And it turned out to be very important. It seems that a person, calling himself Duck, can't go through with the job. You know the job that involves Jackie and Eric having an accident."

Jimmy stormed over to the window and took Bryan by the arm. "What are you saying?"

Bryan shook off Jimmy's hand and continued. He took a piece of folded paper out of his pocket. "I'm saying, quote, 'Tell the man that we bout to catch a case for some bullshit and taking it low. We gonna be deep for a minute and can't do that job. If you want, I can hook you up with some of my peeps, but that's up to you.' End quote. I wrote it down so I wouldn't forget."

That damn fool. I knew I shouldn't have trusted that idiot, thought Jimmy. To Bryan, he said, "It's not what you think. I was just …"

Bryan slowly folded the piece of paper and put it back in his pocket. He looked at Jimmy with such sadness that Jimmy couldn't go on with his statement. "Stop, Jim. It's exactly what I'm thinking. And it's so much more horrible than I would have ever believed you capable of. I shouldn't ask why, because I know you'll lie to me, like you have for the last how many years. But why, Jim?"

Jimmy moved over to the club chair Bryan had vacated. He shook his head in denial and rubbed his hand over his face, smoothing an already smooth moustache. "I don't know."

"Yes, you do. You know, but you want to continue to lie to me and yourself. For once, after almost forty years, please at least be true to yourself." Bryan kneeled in front of Jimmy and took both of his hands in his.

Jimmy gave a shake of his head and made a sound between a laugh and a sob. After a few minutes, he said, "I never had a girlfriend growing up. Not that I wanted one, but I went to this private school where the other boys talked about girls a lot. I told you how awkward I was."

"Okay, I see. So what did you think about that?" Bryan kept his voice low and intently looked at Jimmy.

"I was jealous of how easily they took for granted that the girls were there just for their pleasure. My father, he told me over and over what my duty was. Family first. What he really meant was he was first and then me. Girls, women, they only served one purpose. They were there to have children, preferably sons, and that was all they were useful for. They weren't there to cherish or to love."

Jimmy quieted for a moment and looked out the window. Bryan didn't say anything. He waited patiently for Jimmy to continue.

"Somehow, I knew his thinking was flawed. I couldn't bring myself to do what he was telling me. My first defiance was going to the school of my choice, studying what I wanted to study. My second was ignoring any girl who looked in my direction. All I kept hearing was my father's voice, telling me what they were good for. I didn't want that. I hated him and anything he told me I must do. I knew he was wrong. I knew it wasn't right, what he constantly drummed into my head."

Bryan released Jimmy's hands and pulled up another club chair directly in front of Jimmy. "But you wanted what the other boys had? How easily the other boys got girls and how it came naturally to them. Is that what you're saying?"

"Yes. It was like a love-hate thing. I found women attractive, but I was afraid. I knew they found me attractive also. I wasn't used to compliments and flowery words. I didn't know how to talk to them, and I certainly didn't know what to do with them sexually. I was afraid I would be like my father. So I pushed them away. Then you bumped into me. You were so

211

flamboyant and dramatic. I was like, I can't believe this guy."
Jimmy chuckled at the memory.

"Well, I always had style. That's just me." Bryan grinned at
the memory.

"You were so easy to talk to. I felt like I didn't have to
pretend. I could be me. You didn't pressure me to be someone
I wasn't comfortable with. You understood me without me
having to tell you a bunch of lies. It was great to have a real
friend. And then you became so much more."

"Go on. I'm listening. You have my full attention."

"Well, you know how it went from there. It was wonderful. I
still thought of women though. I was still attracted to them. And
then my horrid father made his crazy demands. He was going
to cut me off without a dime if I didn't get married and produce
a child. I owed you and needed a way to pay you back, so I did
what I had to do. Hence, the Jackie project."

"Yes, I do know how it went from there. I hated every
moment of that distasteful and hurtful lifestyle." Bryan screwed
his eyes closed.

"It was difficult," Jimmy said as he captured Bryan's hand in
his. "But some of it was so good. It wasn't all bad. I mean, I
came to care about Jackie. And then Chrystal came along and
then Royce. It made me feel like I did better than my father
demanded. I beat him at his own game, so to speak. I felt like
I had you, Jackie, and the children. You all were mine to do
with as I chose."

"You can't live in two worlds, Jim. Nor can you have it all,"
said Bryan as he stood up and went back to the window. He
had a distant look on his face. "We're not puppets that you
manipulate to your purposes by pulling a string. We're real

people with real emotions. The things you've done have repercussions. It's never a happy ending."

"Wait. Don't be angry. Me wanting Jackie never took anything away from what we have. It was just . . . I don't know. It was like I could have it all. I thought I had it all."

"Did it ever occur to you what you were doing to me or to Jackie? I know I was hurting. I was ashamed. I had to live a lie that didn't fit, no matter what I told myself. Did . . . did you intentionally let Jackie catch us that day?"

Jimmy guiltily hung his head. "I knew it needed to end. The lie we were all living. But I never meant to hurt you. Then, Jackie was so upset. Like you said, I didn't think that far ahead. No, I didn't think how you or she would feel."

"I see," said Bryan with shining tears in his eyes.

"Well, that's something because I still don't see. I thought I had it all figured out. It was so clear to me. Crystal clear. Get rid of Jackie, then you and I go on with our lives. But I . . . I underestimated how miserable the whole thing made me feel."

"I know. I remember. You weren't yourself for a long time. But I thought you'd gotten over it. Why now? Why go back to that dark place?"

"At Royce's wedding," Jimmy visibly shook as he hesitated, then finally went on. "I saw Jackie and she looked beautiful. She looked as if I had never been in her life. As if I . . . I hadn't meant a thing to her. And then later, when all hell broke loose, I knew I hadn't meant much to her. She had gone on with her life. She had another man who loved her, and she actually despised me."

"Jim, don't. She had to move on. It's what you wanted."

213

Jimmy continued as if Bryan hadn't spoken. "I was so angry. I saw red. All I could think about was how she fucking left me. How she didn't need me. I wanted to hurt her and hurt that damn Eric too. Because she chose that muscle-head over me."

Bryan came back to the chair Jimmy was sitting in. He pulled Jimmy up from his seat. "Please, for your sake, for all our sakes," he said, "let it go. Live in the here and now. Appreciate the fact that God has given you another chance. For once, do the right thing. Hurting Jackie and Eric won't take away the anger, the hurt. It will only make it so much worse. Leave them alone and concentrate on us. On Chrystal and Royce. On your grandchildren. Learn to be happy with what you have. And please, forget about what you don't."

Chapter Thirteen

Thursday night, June 15th - Chrystal's house

C hrystal dragged her feet up the driveway of the small rental she shared with her housemate, Chantrelle. She had just made it to the stop in time to catch the last bus from her grandmother's house. It was almost ten o'clock, and she was tired. But she was in a good mood. The talk with her mother and grandmother had gone so well. She could hardly wait for them to meet Tyler. *It's gonna be good. I just know it. Plus, I can't wait to get my new, used SUV. No more buses and trains. Yay!*

She noticed Chantrelle's car was missing from the driveway. *She must still be over her mom's house. At least I don't have to answer any more questions. I can get some rest. Tomorrow is the last day at the nursing home, but the first day of a new beginning.* As she unlocked the door, she heard someone call her name.

From around the corner of her house, Nikki and Smoke slunk into view.

"Hey, Chrystal, we need to talk," said a grinning Smoke. He was pulling a reluctant Nikki by the arm.

"What the fuck you two low-life's want? I ain't got nothing to say to either one of you." Chrystal hurriedly went through the kitchen door. She tried to close it, but Smoke stuck his oversized foot in the door before she could shove it closed.

"Please, let's go. We don't need to be here. Let's just go." Nikki pleaded with Smoke, but he grabbed her arm and flung her into the kitchen.

"Shut up, Nik! I done told you. Don't let me have to show yo stupid ass again." Smoke stomped into Chrystal's kitchen and turned around and locked the kitchen door. He stared at Chrystal.

Chrystal had her cell phone in one hand and stood back from Smoke and Nikki. "Y'all got two minutes before I call the police. What you want?"

"You ain't got to be that way, bitch. I said we needed to talk. That's all. You acting all crazy just like yo nutty cousin here."

Chrystal noticed Nikki had a big bruise on her cheek. "So you beating up on Nikki now. That's all you and your sleazy friends know how to do. Y'all just go around beating up on innocent women. That sure do make you some big-time men."

"Chrystal don't make him madder. He just wants to ask you sumthin, then we'll leave. Okay?" Nikki looked from Smoke to Chrystal. She pleaded with her eyes for Chrystal to understand.

"You better listen to yo cousin. I just came by to get what's mine. You and yo trifling ways done cost me some money. I had to get up off ten stacks cause of you. I'm gonna give you one chance. I just want my money, or I'm gonna have to take it

216

in ass." Smoke laughed crazily, like it was the funniest thing he ever said.

"Look, I told you. I don't know anything about your money. All I did was what Nikki here told me. I didn't look in the package, and I sure as hell didn't take nothing from it."

Chrystal silently prayed Smoke would just disappear. *I don't know how in hell I let Nikki talk me into messing with his crazy ass.*

"So I guess you got a problem then. How you gonna pay me back?"

"What is wrong with you, man? I told you. I don't have anything to do with your missing money. Maybe you need to ask Nikki here. She's the one who gave me the package. What you keep asking me for? I don't know nothing about it."

Chrystal had enough. The look on Nikki's face told her the answer to the missing money. Nikki had taken the money and was trying to make it look like Chrystal had stolen it. She didn't know why her cousin was doing this, but she knew nothing good was going to come from it.

"Chrystal, please," said Nikki, "can I talk to you for a minute? Let's go to your bedroom. I need to use your bathroom too."

"Look here, don't be trying to pull no shit. You go to that bathroom and come right back. I'm gonna be waiting right here in this damn chair. But don't make me wait too long," Smoke said, still grinning at Nikki and Chrystal. He sat down at the small table as if he was at home. He scratched in his nasty hair and looked at his fingernails for dirt.

"Don't you be nosing around in my kitchen either. I still got my finger on 911," Chrystal told Smoke as she led Nikki down the hall. She dragged Nikki through her bedroom and into the small bathroom, where she locked the door. "That stank asshole. I hate him. Why do you let that negro treat you like this?" Chrystal folded her arms across her chest and waited for Nikki to answer.

Nikki gently touched the bruise under her eye. She hung her head and answered. "I wish I'd never met Smoke, but it's too late now. I ain't got your nerves. I just can't stand up to him. I try, but now . . ." Nikki spoke so low and soft that Chrystal could barely hear her.

"What? What are you trying to say?"

Nikki didn't answer. Instead, she rocked back and forth.

"Well it don't matter now," Chrystal told her. "But why did you take that money? I know I didn't do nothing, but what you said. You must have done it."

"Yeah, I took it, but you got to understand. I was high and feeling crazy. So I don't know." Nikki covered her face with her hands and sat down on the toilet.

Chrystal turned on the faucet and leaned on the sink for support. "Nik, what's going on? Why'd you do that? You must have known he was going to blame me."

Nikki slowly looked up at Chrystal. "Yeah, that's why I did it. You got everything. You're smart and got a slamming body. You got a great family, you're beautiful, and everybody want you, including Smoke. I ain't got nothing worth nothing. All Smoke did was talk about you day and night. I wanted to make you look bad. I wanted Smoke to be mad at you. I wanted to be the one he turned to."

Chrystal looked down at Nikki. *Damn! She is so messed up. I can't imagine having so little self-respect that you'd be wanting Smoke.*

"Look, I'm trying to understand. We've been girls for a long time, but I'm not taking the blame for this. What did you do with the money?"

"I still got the money. I ain't that stupid, but if Smoke find out I took it, he'll beat me to death." Nikki started crying as she rocked back and forth on the toilet.

"Okay, let me think. I don't know why I'm even trying to help your stupid ass. You set me up, and for stupid shit. You know how fucked up my life has been. I got three babies by three different guys and not one of them in sight. How the hell do you think I got it going on, huh?"

"I'm sorry, okay? I didn't think it would end up like this. I just wanted to shine like you, for once. All I did was end up being used and left at the curb like week-old garbage. I know you won't believe it, but I love you. You my girl. You all I got." Nikki shuddered as big liquid drops of misery fell from her eyes.

"Okay, you just a mess, but I'm still gonna try and fix this. Let me think a minute." Chrystal looked in the bathroom mirror at her reflection. Suddenly an idea formed in her mind. "How about I tell Smoke I'm going to ask my father for the money and can give it to him tomorrow? That way, you give me the money and I'll give it back to him. Do you think that'll work?"

"Thank you, yeah, I think that'll work. Girl, I don't know how to repay you—"

"You bitches been in there long enough, you hear me? Come on out of there." Smoke banged on the door harder and harder. "Get your asses out here. It don't take that long to piss."

"We're coming, psycho. And get away from my damn door!" yelled Chrystal.

To Nikki, Chrystal whispered, "Come on. Let's see if we can do this. And the best way to repay me is to get that piece of shit, Smoke, out of your life for once and all!"

Friday morning, 1:30 am - Chrystal's house

Thank you, Lord, for your help. That crazy Smoke worked my last nerve. But all we have to do is meet up tomorrow and exchange the money. I still don't understand what he meant though. He was talking like he knew Daddy.

Chrystal replayed the conversation in her mind.

"So you gonna ask that crazy daddy of yours for the money. Well, that's cool. He owe me too. I can deal with that." Smoke scratched his head again. "But don't be playing no games. I ain't got time for shit like that."

Nikki had finally spoken up. She whined as she pulled on Smoke's sleeve. "So that'll make everything even, right? We can go on with our business, okay?"

"Sure, just as long as missy here do what she say. I'm tired of messing around with her and her daddy anyway."

Chrystal was anxious to get them out of her house. "Yeah, whatever. I'm still not admitting to losing your money, but if it will get your stank ass out of my life, I'll do it. You'll get your money tomorrow at four, and then stay the hell away from me and mine. I don't ever want to see or talk to either one of you again."

Not only was Chrystal mad at Smoke, but she was so disappointed in Nikki that she could cry. *I know I shouldn't feel betrayed because Nikki ain't never had my back, but I never would have thought she would set me up like this. And like a fool, I'm still trying to help her. And that damn Smoke! I wonder exactly what he was saying about daddy. It seems like something is going on that I need to know about.*

Chrystal came back to the present and forgot about Nikki and Smoke as her cell phone rang. It was Tyler.

"Hey, babe. I know it's late, but I wanted to hear your voice before you fell asleep."

"Hi, Tyler. How's it going?" Chrystal was happy to finally talk to him. She needed him to cheer her up after the Smoke and Nikki mess.

Tyler sounded drowsy, but he came alert when Chrystal answered him. "I'm doing great now," he said. "Just hearing your voice gets me in a good mood. I can't wait to see you tomorrow. Or I guess I should say later today."

"Well, about that. I hope you won't be angry, but there's been a change in the plans."

Chrystal heard a sharp intake of breath from Tyler.

"Oh? Please don't tell me you're not coming. Please, Chrystal, please meet me." Tyler's breathing became harsher as he waited for Chrystal's reply.

"No, it's not that, but I told my mother and grandmother about you. They want to meet you. So I told them I'd bring you over as soon as you get here."

"Chrystal, don't tease me like that. I just about had a heart attack. Sure, I'd love to meet them. I've been waiting for this chance for years."

"I know, and I'm sorry I made it sound like I wasn't going to meet you. But you kind of deserve it after your last no-show. You better be here, or that's the last time I believe anything you say."

"Don't worry. I'll be there. In fact, my plane leaves Austin at three Atlanta time. I should be touching down at the airport about five. Then it's straight to your place. I don't have to be at the club until nine. So we good, right?"

"Yeah, babe, we good. Now I can go to sleep knowing my man is on the way."

"Goodnight, baby, and I love you. See you later."

"Night, sweetie. See you later."

Chrystal clicked off her phone and turned over in bed. *Okay, Lord, I still need you. I want everything to go right tomorrow. Let Smoke get his money and get out of my life, and let Nikki get away from him too. And Lord, please, if Tyler is the one for me, let it be for me and him to be happy together. Please. Lord, let everything go right for a change. Amen.*

Chapter Fourteen

C hrystal had promised to meet Nikki at the train station at three thirty. She was running a bit early, so she waited at the bottom of the escalator for her. It was her last day at the nursing center where she worked. It had been bittersweet, but she was glad it was over.

Man, I didn't think my co-workers would have chipped in to give me a gift. And cash too. I got three hundred and fifty dollars. But I hope everything goes right with Smoke. If it does, then . . .

"Chrystal, wake up, girl. I could have been a crackhead and you wouldn't have noticed," said Nikki as she snuck up behind Chrystal's back, laughing.

"Why you sneaking up on people? I thought you'd be coming down the escalator. Where you been, coming from that way?" Chrystal looked at Nikki and shook her head. She wanted desperately to have this ridiculous situation with Smoke over and done with. *I hope this bitch ain't up to some more shit.*

223

Nikki laughed again and took Chrystal by the arm. "I was downtown for a minute. I didn't have it on me. I had to get it from my secret place."

"Oh, really? Well, hand it over so we can get this done with. And why you looking too happy? You ain't been hitting that stuff again? I told you before you need to lay off that juice. That's what got you into so much trouble."

"I know, but I felt like celebrating since we about to settle this. I just needed a little bit to settle my nerves. That's all, okay? And here's the package. You can count it if you want."

"Let's get on the train and get settled, and then I'll see. Believe me, I'll make sure it's right. Come on, let's catch this train to Smoke's place."

Chrystal and Nikki made the trip to Smoke's house in relative silence. He lived in a renovated loft off Boulevard, and it would take about ten minutes from the train station uptown to make it there. While they rode, Chrystal counted the money as quickly and unobtrusively as possible.

"Okay, it's all here, and we can get off at this stop. I just want to get him this package and get the hell out of there. Do you understand?"

Nikki had dozed off as they rode.

"Bitch, wake up!" shouted Chrystal. What's wrong with you? Get your fat ass together so we can get this taken care of."

"I hear you, bitch. Stop that yelling. I ain't deaf. Where we at anyway? This ain't the right stop. We can go to the next stop and be right at his place."

"Just follow me and keep it quiet. We got time. I don't want everybody all up in our business."

Chrystal and Nikki exited the train three streets over from Smoke's house. They walked for another five minutes before they came to Boulevard.

"Okay, when we get there, just let me do the talking, Nik. Don't you say nothing. Your ass so doped up. You need to get yourself together. Stop hanging with that psycho and get a real job."

"Sure, that's easy for you to say. I ain't got peoples to give me money every time I boo-hoo over a pinky cut. I ain't got no skills either. What kind of good job you think I can get with just a high school diploma? Huh? Tell me if you got all the answers."

Nikki looked away from Chrystal as they walked down the street. Her shoulders had dropped and she hung her head as she started to cry.

Chrystal watched Nikki struggle to hold back tears. Chrystal didn't want to feel sorry for her, but she did. Nikki was as much a victim as she was. The difference was Chrystal no longer wanted to be victimized and was doing something about it. Nikki still lived in the city of denial, blaming everyone else for her bad choices and the failures in her life.

"Look, Nik, when we get out of this, I promise I'll help you get back on your feet." *Why in the hell did I say that? I don't want to have anything to do with her. Oh Lord, why're you making me say this?*

Sniffling and wiping snot, Nikki answered, "Really? You mean that? After everything I did to you? You're willing to help me? I don't know what to say. Why would you do this for me?"

"I don't know why either, but I mean it. Let's just get this over with, and then we'll see how I can help you."

225

"I'm sorry I got you involved with Smoke though," said Nikki. "He really is a piece of mess. And he ain't even cute. But he hooked me up so many times. I felt like, you know, like I owed him."

"Well, I don't owe him nothing. When this is over, I don't ever want to hear his name again. That's my one condition, Nikki. I help you and you stay away from Smoke. Deal?"

Chrystal held her hand out to Nikki. She waited as Nikki looked up and down the street. They were literally standing on Smoke's doorstep.

"What? You're gonna leave me hanging?" Chrystal held her hand out for a moment longer. Just as she was dropping it, Nikki reached out.

"Deal," Nikki said. "Thank you. I really mean it. Thank you."

Chrystal and Nikki rung the bell and banged on the door until a nosy neighbor stuck his head out to see what was going on. They both gave him the side eye until he finally closed his door with a bang.

At last, Smoke made his way to open the door. "Well, you bitches finally got here. I was just about to call the whole thing off." Smoke moved back and let them into the loft.

"What the hell? You know you heard us beating on this damn door. We got your money, and I want a receipt too." Chrystal looked around the large space. It was filled with stank-looking clothes all over the floor. Half-eaten plates of food and empty liquor bottles littered nearly every surface.

Nikki held her nose as she asked Smoke in a sarcastic voice, "What's that nasty smell? It smells like chitlins and old dirty feet."

226

Chrystal wanted to laugh, but she didn't have time for it. She wanted a receipt from Smoke just to mess with him, and then she wanted to get the hell out of his stank house.

"What do you mean? My place don't stink. And why you need a receipt? We ain't at the grocery store. You two talk a whole lot of bullshit."

Chrystal shook her head at Smoke and pulled the package full of money out of her big bag. "I want you to acknowledge that I gave you the ten thousand dollars you said you lost. I want you to write paid in full across the bottom and sign your government name, Calvin Dotson. Is that clear enough for you?"

"Come on, Smoke, we got things to do. Let's do this so we can go." Nikki stared at Smoke for a long moment.

Smoke stared back as if he couldn't believe Nikki was standing up to him. "You must have smoked too many rocks, Nik. Who you think you talking to?" Smoke looked from Nikki to Chrystal. "I swear, I ain't never gonna mess with you two crazy-ass bitches again. Give me a piece of paper so I can write your damn note. You just as crazy as yo old man. Always wanting us to beat up anybody who look at you twice. It's a good thing me and Duck ain't got time to hit your mama and her boyfriend. I'm tired of all that bullshit."

Chrystal was handing Smoke a piece of paper and pen from her bag when his last comments stopped her short. "What the hell you talking about? Who did you beat up, and what about my mama?"

Nikki edged towards the front door. "Come on, Chrystal, let's go. He just talking trash."

"Wait a minute, Nikki. I want to hear what he got to say." Chrystal watched Smoke as he took the paper and pen and wrote something. "What do you know about my mama?"

Smoke handed the piece of paper back to Chrystal. He had a smug look on his face as he answered her. "Yo crazy-ass daddy wanted that foreign guy to disappear out of his precious baby's life. Remember about three years ago? We made it happen. So now he pissed at yo mama, so he wanted her and her new boyfriend to have a little accident. But we ain't got time for shit like that no more."

"You lying! My daddy would never do that. He would never hire you and Duck to hurt my mother." Chrystal didn't want to believe what Smoke was telling her. But she had gone to her father about Omar, and right after that, Omar had disappeared. She was so distraught at the time that she never bothered to ask her father what happened. But to hurt her mother, that was just too damn much.

"Come on, Chrystal. Let's go. We did what we came to do. Let's go." Nikki pulled on Chrystal's arm while Smoke looked at them both and laughed like a crazy man.

Chrystal sat quietly on the train ride home.

Nikki was still apologizing as she tried to get Chrystal's attention. "I'm so sorry. What do I have to do to make this up to you? I swear I never meant to hurt you. Your daddy said it was to protect you, and I wanted to help."

Nikki wiped at her eyes. "Listen please. I want you to understand why I did what I did. When your daddy first came to me asking about sketchy folks to do shady shit, I turned him on to Smoke and Duck. I knew you was in trouble and I wanted to help. You my girl. I didn't want you to be in trouble. So your daddy gave me five bills to keep my mouth shut. Girl, for real, I just wanted to help you. But I didn't know nothing about him asking Smoke them to hit your mama. You know I'd never do anything to hurt my family. Girl we family. I swear I didn't know nothing about that."

"Shut up, Nikki. I don't want to hear anything else from you. I'm so mad right now that I want to whip your stupid ass." Tears gathered in Chrystal's eyes, scarlet tears of frustration and disappointment. She'd always thought her father had her back. But this was too much; this was the ultimate betrayal. How could he want to hurt her mother? All these years, and she had blamed her mother for her sorry life, thinking her father was the one who was misunderstood and ill used by her mother.

And to think she had lain down with that piece of shit Smoke to get a couple of dollars here and there. In her bones she knew it was wrong to be kept by Smoke, but that was over a year ago when she had nobody she thought to look out for her. Tyler was in and out of her life, so she had let Smoke use her as he did. True she didn't know all the shit Smoke was involved in but that didn't take away the bitter taste in her mouth.

Bile rose in her throat. How could she have been so blind, so naive as to trust Nikki and believe anything Smoke said. The past hour had finally opened her eyes. *It's way past time for me to get myself together. I'm the only one who can control my life, and damn if I'm going to let Daddy or anybody else control me anymore.*

Friday afternoon, 5:45pm - Chrystal's house

Chrystal had just emerged from her shower. She had washed and scrubbed herself over and over, trying to get the smell of Smoke's house off her skin. She was still drying off when her cell phone rang.

"Hello. Are you finally on the ground?" Chrystal walked into her closet. There were only about three outfits left there. The rest of her things were at her grandmother's house.

"Not only am I on the ground, but I'm on my way to your house. I set up a rental car, and it was waiting here at the airport for me. I didn't want anything to slow me down. I should be there in about half an hour." Tyler sounded excited and happy. It made Chrystal happy to hear him this way.

"Okay, I'll be ready when you get here. And babe, I love you. I really love you. Bye."

"Bye, Chrystal, and I really love you too."

Chrystal was trying to get in a good mood. She was determined that last horrific scene with Smoke and Nikki would not bring her down. Tyler was coming and her eyes were wide open. From now on she was taking control of her life. The days of letting people like Smoke and Duck use her were over. That was the old Chrystal, who let Nikki convince her the love of money was more important than self-respect. That Chrystal was dead and buried, and it was about time.

Friday evening, 6:30pm - Chrystal and Tyler

Chrystal couldn't stop hugging and kissing Tyler after she let him into her small living room. She had turned away from looking out the window when he surprised her and knocked on her door. She was overjoyed to finally see him in person after more than two months. He looked like her Tyler, but more so. He was still just as tall but had put on a few pounds in all the right places. He was wearing a light gray t-shirt and dark jeans. She couldn't wait to run her fingers through his thick, kinky head of hair.

He practically swept her off her feet in the big hug he gave her. He couldn't stop hugging and kissing her either. He was so excited; he took big breaths trying to calm himself. "Babe, I can't believe I'm finally here. It's been so long since I've held you in my arms. You look amazing! Here, just let me look at you."

Chrystal stood back and let Tyler look her over. She wore a sky-blue silk blouse and a dark-blue denim skirt. Chunky sandals completed the outfit. Her natural dark hair swirled around her face, framing it beautifully. From the way Tyler looked at her, he liked what he saw.

"You're beautiful as always. I've missed you so much. I'm sorry it took me so long to get here," said Tyler. "I have something for you." He dropped to his knees in the small living room and pulled a tiny box from his pocket. He took a ring from the box and held it out to Chrystal.

"If you'll have me, I promise to never leave you alone again. I promise to be a good father to Jade and to Jewell and Oro. I promise to love and respect you. I promise to put no one and nothing before you. What do you say?" Tyler waited on the floor as Chrystal looked at him with golden tears in her eyes. He fidgeted as Chrystal took her time answering.

"I should tell your ass no just for putting me through so much shit, but I don't have time for all that drama. So yes, yes! I want to be with you forever. I'm so happy right now I could cry. And I'm just glad you're here. I didn't know. I never thought you would ask me to marry you. I'm just, I don't know what I am. But yes, I will marry you."

Tyler stood up and hugged Chrystal to him. He kissed her again and looked at her with love radiating from his smile.

"I want to stay here and just look at my ring, and it's a big-ass diamond sitting right dead center too. It fits me exactly right. But we got to get moving. The kids are over my grandmother's house along with my mother, my aunt, and my grandmother. Everybody's waiting to meet you. Come on. We can talk as we ride."

"I want to stay here and look at you with nothing on but the ring. I guess I'll just have to wait though. We can celebrate later tonight after I finish at the club." Tyler gave Chrystal a mischievous grin and hugged her even tighter.

Chrystal was overjoyed with Tyler's proposal, but she knew she had to tell him everything that had gone on earlier with Nikki and Smoke. She hesitantly started talking as they rode to Ms. Sylvi's house. She finally finished and was silent after she told Tyler about the awful afternoon she'd had. It had been a difficult story to tell. She told him most of the truth about Smoke and Nikki, but she left out the part about her intimate involvement with Smoke. She didn't want him to know she had been so foolish as to let Smoke use her as he had.

"So this Smoke person is not only a drug dealer, but he and his crew hurt people for money?"

Tyler gripped the steering wheel of the rental car and jerked the car out of the lane before righting it. "Man, I don't know what to say. I mean, I'm so mad at these people, this

Smoke guy and your cousin too. I want to go upside his head. But I should've been there for you. I let you get hurt by these low-life people. I should've been in your life the right way."

"Well, yeah. But you had no way of knowing. I wasn't exactly honest about some of this. I kind of didn't want you to know I'd been that stupid. I can forgive you for that, if you can forgive me for holding back the truth."

Tyler nodded his head in answer to Chrystal's statement. "I love you babe and nobody's gonna come between us. I'm here for you now, so don't worry."

Chrystal rubbed Tyler's hand as he gripped the steering wheel. "Okay, we got this, but still to think my father was behind a plan to hurt my mother just makes me sick. I don't want to believe Smoke, but what he said about Oro's father is way too many facts for him not to be telling the truth. I don't want to believe it, but I have to. My father is a bigger psychopath than everybody thought. I guess my mother was right when she said he was pure evil." They were almost at Ms. Sylvi's house. Chrystal started silently crying.

Tyler looked over and saw Chrystal trying to hide the tears. "Oh, babe, what's wrong? Don't cry. You said they weren't going to do the job, so don't worry about your mother."

"I know, but it's just been so ridiculous. I'm so tired of all this. I just want a normal family, a normal life. Why does all this stuff keep happening to me?"

Chrystal tried to wipe her eyes with her hands, but the tears fell too fast. She finally found some paper napkins in her bag and dried her eyes.

"Look, we're here at your grandmother's house. Let's get those beautiful eyes of yours dry. You don't want to upset them with all this. I want to meet them without all this overshadowing everything. Let's go in and try to have a nice time. We'll take care of this later. I promise you I'll take care of it. I won't let you down."

"You're right. I know it will only make things worse if I let them know all this has happened. Give me a second, and I'll be okay. But I'm talking to my father as soon as possible. He's got a lot of explaining to do."

Chrystal held true to her promise and as soon as she had a moment to herself she called her father Jimmy. She was in the ladies' room of the club where Tyler was performing. She couldn't wait until later to confront her him. After they left her grandmother's house, she was feeling so much better. Everything had gone so well with them all. Jade went to her daddy like she had just seen him. And Jewell and Oro hugged him and gave him lots of sloppy kisses. Her mother, aunt, and grandmother seemed impressed with Tyler. It made her so happy that they were so accepting of him. She and Tyler had even announced their engagement, showing off her ring, and her grandmother had cried tears of joy.

Everything was going well, so now she was ready to get the truth from Jimmy and no one or nothing was going to stop her from getting it.

Chapter Fifteen

Friday night, 9:30pm - Jimmy and Bryan's house

Jimmy had gone into his kitchen to refill the ice bucket when his cell phone rang. He pulled it from his pocket and was surprised when he saw that it was Chrystal. He had left Bryan in the family room with Jimmy's parents. His father was deep in a bottle of Scotch and his mother was drowning in vodka and tonic. They had eaten at Jimmy's favorite steakhouse. The food and wine were excellent, and his father hadn't complained once. It had been a very nice visit so far.

Jimmy felt things were finally going well after the hurtful conversation he'd had with Bryan the day before. He was still reeling from the directions his emotional state had taken. He'd admitted to much more than he ever thought he would have. But it had been a cleansing that was long overdue. It had brought him and Bryan much closer together.

"Hi, baby. How's my little girl?" Jimmy fumbled with the ice bucket and Chrystal's comment almost made him drop the whole thing to the floor.

"How could you try to pay Duck and Smoke to hurt Mama? I can't believe how evil you are."

Jimmy stumbled to the kitchen island and sat down. "What? What are you talking about? I haven't hurt your mother."

Chrystal shouted into the phone, "Don't play with me! Smoke told me the whole story. Even how you paid them to get rid of Omar. That I understand, but you wanting to hurt Mama, I can never forgive you for that."

Why in the hell did she talk to Smoke? I should have known that fool would mess up everything. "Baby, I would never hurt your mother. You know that. This is all a big misunderstanding. I don't know what Smoke told you, but it's not the truth. You have to believe me." Jimmy leaned on the dazzling white countertop and dropped his head into his hand.

"If you don't know what Smoke said, how can you know it's a lie? Huh? Tell me that if you can." Chrystal dropped her voice. "Just tell the truth, Daddy. For once in your freaking life, tell me the truth"

"Chrystal, let's not have this talk over the phone. Are you at home? Come over and we can talk about it in person. Your grandparents are here now, and I need to get back to them." Jimmy rubbed his hand over his closed eyes. He lowered his head, rubbing his forehead over and over. He suddenly had the worst headache he'd ever felt. *How has everything gone so wrong? Now Chrystal hates me too. I've got to salvage this somehow.*

"No, Daddy. I want to talk about this now. Smoke said you've been working with them for years. Paying them to hurt people you don't approve of. I know I went to you for help with Omar, but not once did I think you would hurt somebody. And now you paid them to hurt Mama and Eric. Just because it all came out about their relationship. I can't believe you could be this evil, this hateful. Mama was right. You're crazy and dangerous too."

"Baby, please listen. I was angry at your mother. I . . . I messed up. I acted without thinking, and I'm sorry. I wasn't going to go through with it. You have to believe me. I was wrong. You saw my father. You know how difficult it was for me growing up with him. I just lost it, I guess. I'm sorry. Come over and we'll talk. Okay?"

Jimmy stopped rubbing his forehead and opened his eyes. He finally noticed Bryan standing in the open doorway. He had come into the kitchen wondering what was taking Jimmy so long, and he had a stunned look on his face. Jimmy knew Bryan had heard a good bit of his side of the conversation.

"I'm here with my friend and as soon as he finishes playing at this club, we'll come over."

"All right, that's fine. We'll be here. And who is this friend you're talking about?" Jimmy motioned to Bryan to come forward.

"I'll tell you all about him later. And Daddy, you better be ready to prove to me that all this mess with Mama is over. I won't accept anything less."

Chrystal clicked off and Jimmy looked at his phone as if it was a live and deadly thing. He slowly put his phone back in his pocket.

"Was that Chrystal?" Bryan picked up the ice bucket, which Jimmy had apparently forgotten. He moved to the refrigerator to fill it with ice.

"Yes. Apparently, she has been talking to Smoke and he told her all about his dealings with me. She's not happy with me at the moment. I have a killer of a headache now."

"From what I heard from your side of the conversation; I can understand why your head's hurting. Is she coming over?" Bryan brought the filled ice bucket back to the kitchen island. He sat on a stool beside Jimmy.

Jimmy hesitated in answering. He looked around his spacious kitchen. He wondered at how easily everything was unraveling. How all his carefully laid plans were disappearing like mist in sunlight. "She has a friend coming with her. She said a 'him' would be accompanying her. I only pray it's not that Smoke." Jimmy made a choked noise in the back of his throat.

"Oh, Jim, it's going to be all right. Just tell her the truth. Beg her forgiveness and be open to what she needs to heal from this betrayal." Bryan rubbed Jimmy's shoulder but Jimmy pulled away from his touch and stood up.

"Betrayal! Everything I did, I did for her. That terrible Omar person was trying to take my grandson. I couldn't let that happen. And if I could have found that first piece of shit that impregnated my baby, I would have had them whip his ass too."

"What do you mean? What has Omar to do with this? And are you talking about the boy from high school that Chrystal was involved with?" Bryan had a stunned look on his face.

"Yes, that boy was the first one to break my baby's heart. By the time Chrystal came to me, he was out of the scene. She wouldn't even mention Jewell's sperm donor. So I let him go.

But that Omar person, who I never wanted in her life to begin with, had to go."

"So you paid these same people to hunt Omar down and get rid of him?"

"It was the only way to stop him from breaking my baby's heart. They didn't kill him. They just made it clear he needed to go back to where he came from." Jimmy slowly picked up the ice bucket and moved to leave the kitchen. He had a faraway look on his face.

"Oh, Jim. You didn't?"

"Well, I guess you finally get what you wanted. Everything I did for Chrystal is coming to roost on my head. She hates me now. I'm about to lose my baby's love. She'll never forgive me now." Jimmy chuckled, a dark and manic sound.

"Jim, stop. You made mistakes, but I never wished for you to be hurt. I only wanted you to do the right things for Chrystal. Hurting other people is not the answer. You know that. Stop trying to make yourself the victim in all this. You started something that was wrong to begin with."

"I don't want to talk about it anymore. I'm going back into the family room to spend time with my mother and father. Chrystal will be here soon. I'll just have to wait and see what piece of trash she brings home this time."

Friday night, 2:15am - Jimmy and Bryan's house

Jimmy's parents had finally said goodnight a little past midnight, after an uneventful but pleasant evening. It was after two in the morning, but Bryan and Jimmy weren't speaking to each other. They both sat silently in the family room, deep within their own thoughts. They had been this way for hours, occasionally glancing at each other.

When the doorbell rang, Jimmy looked up from contemplating his fingernails. He set his tumbler of whiskey on the side table. Bryan continued to stare at the wall.

"I guess it's showtime," said Jimmy.

"Really? Is this how you think about a very serious situation? Is everything a game to you?" Bryan gave Jimmy a pitying look before he turned back to studying the paint on the wall.

Jimmy chuckled and offered Bryan an irritated shake of his head. "I have to think about it this way, or otherwise I might explode. I do know this is not a game and believe me; I know what's at stake."

Jimmy slowly moved to the front door. He could see Chrystal and a young man standing on his doorstep. *At least it's not that shithead Smoke. Thank you, Lord, for that.* Jimmy hesitantly opened the door. "Come in, baby. Who's this young man at my door at this late hour?"

Jimmy tried to hug Chrystal but she pushed back and grabbed Tyler's hand instead. "Daddy, this is Tyler, my fiancé and Jade's dad." Chrystal glared at Jimmy waiting for his answer. "I see you still want to play games. We're not here just for a little friendly chat."

"Well, I'm happy to meet you anyway Tyler. Chrystal said she was bringing a special friend, but I didn't realize just how special. Come in, and welcome to my home." Jimmy stood back and allowed Tyler to usher Chrystal into the house. *Well, at least he looks like a regular black guy and not that foreign trash she was messing with. It could be so much worse.*

Bryan came down the hallway to greet them. "Chrystal, sweetheart, you're a sight for sore eyes. And who is this young man?" Bryan smiled warmly at Chrystal as he reached out to hug her. He held her tightly to his chest as she hugged him back.

"Well, I see Bryan gets a hug, but I don't?" Jimmy looked on at the scene unfolding in his foyer. He couldn't help sounding spiteful as all three people stared openly at him.

Bryan ignored Jimmy in favor of reaching out to hug Tyler. "You must be the special someone Chrystal mentioned. I'm Bryan, and it's such a pleasure meeting you."

"Thank you, sir. Yes, I'm Tyler, Chrystal's fiancé. It's nice to meet you too. Chrystal has told me so much about you, but nothing beats meeting someone in person." Tyler hugged Chrystal to him and smiled warmly at her as Jimmy gestured for them all to follow him down the hallway.

"Well, let's sit down and get to know each other better." Jimmy crossed his leg as he sat in his favorite chair in the family room. He looked to both Chrystal and Tyler as they took a seat on the sofa. "Bryan, why don't you get some refreshments. Or would you two like a nightcap?" He waved his hand and indicated the liquors on the bar.

Bryan stared at Jimmy. "Chrystal, Tyler, would you care for some water, or how about coffee? It's late, and from what I understand, you guys have a lot to talk about."

"Thanks, Bryan," said Chrystal. "I don't need anything. I just want to clear up all this stuff Daddy's been doing. Apparently he has a habit of lying and deceiving everybody. I thought I knew you, Daddy. I thought you really had my back, but all this stuff you've being doing behind my back is just too much."

Jimmy gave Bryan an ugly look before he turned his attention to Chrystal. "Baby, wait a minute. It's not what you think. I was trying to help you. I only wanted what was best for you and Oro. You came to me for help, and that's just what I did. I helped you to rid yourself of that horrible man who wanted to take your baby boy from us."

Chrystal jumped up. Tyler tried to pull her back down to the sofa, but she clinched her fists and shouted at Jimmy as tears fell from her eyes. "You know damn well I'm not talking about Omar. Although you did that without me knowing what you were planning. I'm talking about Mama and Eric. I'm talking about you paying Smoke and Duck to hurt them. I'm talking about you lying and doing so much wrong that I can never believe anything you say again. I can never forgive you for what you've tried to do. I believed in you. I fought against everybody who said you were evil. I defended you against my own mother. I turned away from her, because of you. I loved . . ."

Chrystal slowed to a stop and big tears of pain and sadness rained down her soft cheeks.

Tyler gathered her into his arms and hugged her tight. "It's okay, babe. I'm here. It's going to be all right. Everything's going to be all right," said Tyler as he sat Chrystal back down.

Bryan stared at Jimmy as Tyler tried to console Chrystal. "Well Jim, what do you say to this? Your one and only daughter is distraught because you've betrayed her trust. You have lied, misled her, and broken her heart, you her father, who she trusted. What do you have to say to make this right?"

Jimmy snorted and shook his head. He rolled his eyes at Bryan. Jimmy was one word away from telling everyone to go to hell.

"Mr. Mattock," said Tyler, "Chrystal has told me how much she loves you and believe me I'm not trying to come between you two. But as you can see, Chrystal has been hurt so badly by all this that I had to agree with her. I think maybe she and you need a break from each other. Enough time to heal, if such a thing is possible. I think—"

"Look here, Tyson. I don't give a damn about what you think. You're in no position to agree or disagree with Chrystal. Apparently, you're new in the picture. Where have you been all this time? Jade is almost sixteen months old. My baby has been struggling all on her own with three children. One of whom is yours. This is the first time I've ever heard of you. So I don't think we need to hear anything from you!" Jimmy was seething. *How dare this little boy try to tell me what's best for my daughter.*

"Besides, Chrystal has leaned on my help all her life, and I've been totally involved with every one of her children. As a good father and grandfather, I believe I know what's best for them."

Chrystal wiped her eyes with the back of her hand. She nervously gripped Tyler's hand. "His name is Tyler, not Tyson." She turned to her fiancé. "But it's okay. You don't have to explain anything to him. Thank you for trying to make him understand. But I got this." Chrystal gave Tyler a small kiss on the cheek.

She looked to Bryan as she sat back down. "Bryan, thank you so much for always trying to calm Daddy down, but right now I want him to talk. I want him to come right on out and tell it all, and I want him to tell me exactly how he's going to make this right. I want action not just pretty words."

Chrystal switched her attention to Jimmy. "Daddy, you have hurt so many people. And you wanted to hurt so many more. Why should I believe anything you have to say? As they say, talk is cheap. So what are you going to do now?"

"Do? I don't know what you mean. I told you all that had been taken care of. Duck and Smoke are no longer working for me. So that's that." Jimmy looked at everyone in the room. He had a smile on his face but his insides were churning.

"I see. So you think that's good enough?" Chrystal shook her head as she stared at her father.

"Of course. Your precious mother and her homophobic boyfriend are safe from me. I said I was sorry. So that's that." Jimmy was silently praying that Chrystal would drop the whole thing. He continued to smile as he stood up and moved to the liquor cabinet to refill his drink. "I need a little shot to soothe my throat. Anyone else want a drink?"

"Mr. Mattock, I feel you're not listening to Chrystal. She's asking you for your plan to make this situation better. She's not a child, and you owe her the respect of listening to what she has to say." Tyler hugged Chrystal closer to him and kissed her cheek.

"As I told you, Terry, you've barely been in Chrystal's life enough to offer your deluded advice. I suggest you keep your damn mouth closed. By the way, why haven't you been paying child support for Jade? By my count, you owe Chrystal a considerable amount of back support." Jimmy smiled at Tyler as he sat down with his drink.

244

"Daddy! You just can't stop, can you? You can't bullshit your way out of this with all your crazy talk to Tyler. The point is you've done something so horrible there's only one thing you can do to make it right." Chrystal went over to Jimmy. She took the glass of whiskey from his hand and set it on a side table. She pulled him reluctantly into a standing position and looked up into his eyes.

"I demand that you, right now, come with me to grandmother's house. Mama and Aunt Nancy are spending the night. I want you to tell them what you planned to do to them. I want you to tell them how horribly wrong you've been and beg them for their forgiveness. I want you, for once and for all, to do the right thing. You owe Mama that much."

"You must be out of your fucking mind! I will do no such thing. I don't owe your damn mother anything. You're just as crazy as she is if you believe I would even consider doing that."

Chrystal jerked back as if Jimmy had hit her. In fact, his words hurt much more than any physical pain ever could.

Bryan hurried to intervene between Jimmy and Chrystal. "Jim, Chrystal's right. You need to do this, not only for their sake, but for yours also. This is an opportunity to finally put all this to rest. Do this, please. If I ever meant anything to you, please do this."

Jimmy looked at both Chrystal and Bryan and chuckled. He shook his head, side to side in denial.

"I'm sorry, Bryan, but apparently Daddy doesn't care about anyone but himself. Even you don't carry enough weight to stop him from being such an evil monster."

Chrystal addressed her father. "Okay, so that's how you want to play. I should have done this a long time ago, but from now on, me and the kids can do without your kind of love and support. I can't trust you, and you don't want to do right. Please don't try to contact me anymore. Treat me just like you did when I was fourteen and I called you. Remember how you just ignored my calls and went on about your life. It's time I go about mine. Besides you have your son, Royce, to manipulate. Oh, my bad, he's really not your flesh and blood son, is he? Anyway, he'll just have to do."

Jimmy stared at Chrystal. Hesitantly, he reached out to pull her back to him, but she turned away again.

Bryan gasped and visibly shook. "Oh no! Chrystal, you don't mean that. Please, Jim, tell her you'll do as she asks. Please, Jim."

"Shut up Bryan. I'm my own man. I will not be blackmailed by my daughter. If that's how Chrystal wants to act, then fine. I've done all I will do. I am not going to Ms. Sylvi's house. I am not going to tell Jackie that I'm sorry. I am not apologizing for something that didn't happen."

Bryan was openly crying as he looked to Chrystal and Tyler and back at Jimmy. "I don't know what to say. I believed there was still a chance for us, Jim. But you don't even have enough love in your heart to try to be decent. I can't believe, after all these years, that you would be this way. I love you still, but I can't stay with you. This is the last straw. This is—"

"Daddy, you're just going to let Bryan leave? I can't believe it. So this is how it ends then? You're one big piece of shit to do this to him. I don't want —"

"Chrystal, stop. Don't talk to your father that way. He's still your father even though he's so horribly wrong." Bryan hugged Chrystal as tears danced in her eyes. "Let me pack a small bag. I don't trust myself to drive, so please wait for me. I'll get out of your way Jim. I don't believe I have anything left to say."

Defeated, Bryan left the room as Jimmy picked up his glass and took a big gulp. Jimmy's eyes followed Bryan out the door. He looked to Chrystal and shook his head.

"See what your selfish demands have done. You've upset him until he's ready to leave me too. If you want to act like a spoiled child, then do that. But don't come begging me to forgive you. Because I won't."

"No, Daddy, I won't come begging you for anything. When we walk out this door, that's it. Tell Bryan we'll be waiting for him in the car. I don't have anything left to say to you either."

Tyler and Chrystal turned and walked out of the room. The stillness that took over Jimmy scared him. He stared at the liquor in his glass. Across from him, a portrait of a man with a horn stared back at him, and the man seemed to point his instrument directly at Jimmy's head. Jimmy looked at the painting and saluted. "So you blame me too?"

Bryan stuck his head in the room, looking for Chrystal and Tyler.

"If you're looking for those traitors, they're waiting for you outside." Jimmy moved to the bar and poured himself another shot of whiskey.

Bryan clutched his small bag and started to say something, but Jimmy cut him off. "If you're leaving, then leave. Don't waste my time standing there sniveling.

Bryan recoiled as if shot. He looked at Jimmy and sadly shook his head. "I'm sorry for you, Jim. You've driven everybody away. I hope you're happy, but I'm really sorry for you."

Chapter Sixteen

Saturday, June 17th, 8:00am - Ms. Sylvi's house

" Come in, come in. I didn't expect to see y'all this early. But anytime is a good time." Ms. Sylvi stood back from the glass front door and welcomed Chrystal, Tyler, and Bryan into her home.

"Thanks, Grandma. I'm sorry to bring all this to your door this early, but I felt like I had to." Chrystal hugged her grandmother and then sat down on the sofa.

"Lord! What's wrong? I see something on Bryan's face, and it don't look good. Please don't tell me you and Tyler are breaking things off." Ms. Sylvi wrung her hands together as she faced Tyler.

"No, ma'am, I have no intention of breaking up with Chrystal. I love your granddaughter, and nothing will ever keep me from her side again. But Chrystal has something she wants to tell you guys." Tyler sat down beside Chrystal and held her hand.

"Actually, I need to tell Mama because it definitely affects her, but I want to tell it once so you all hear it together."

249

Ms. Sylvi looked from Chrystal to Bryan. "Well, let me get your mama and auntie. I believe the babies are still asleep so I'll just check on them and be right back."

"Chrystal, again I just want to say how sorry I am about Jim. I never would believe he would be this stubborn. After all these years and he's still . . ." Bryan trailed off as he looked at the floor. There were tears in his eyes and he sighed as he sat in a nearby chair. He fingered a huge potted plant sitting in the corner, as he looked forlornly at the leaves.

From where Tyler was sitting he could see out the glass front door. "Babe, is that your brother and sister-in-law getting out of that car?"

"Yeah, let me get the door. I see he got my text to meet us here this morning."

"Hi Sis, what's going on?" Royce hugged Chrystal and stepped aside to let Jessica do the same. "Hey man, you must be Tyler?" Royce reached out and shook Tyler's hand. "Chrystal told me all about you. She said you guys were engaged. Congratulations."

"Thanks, and this must be your wife. It's great to finally meet all of you guys. I wish it was for a better reason, but at least we're finally getting a chance to get to know each other." Tyler shook Jessica's hand as he led her into the room.

"Yeah, I know, right? Bryan, how you holding up? When Chrystal called me last night, I couldn't believe the stuff had hit the fan liked that. I'm sorry. I know dad can be stubborn but I never thought he would do this to you."

Bryan hugged Jessica and mumbled, "hello sweetheart."

He gave Royce a sturdy handshake and finally answered. "I'm sorry Jim's acting this way too. But I can't live with

250

someone who treats his love ones with so much disrespect. It's breaking my heart in two, but I'll live. I just hope you all can forgive him one day."

"Don't worry about it, it's not just us, but you too, that daddy really needs to ask for forgiveness." Chrystal looked Bryan in the eyes as she said, "he has done so much wrong. I don't even want to call him my father."

Bryan turned sad eyes to Chrystal. He couldn't tell her no, all he could do was lower his head.

Chrystal, Tyler, Ms. Sylvi said you guys have some news or something to tell us. But first, I'm so glad to see you all again. I didn't know Royce and Jessica were here too. Welcome. Even you Bryan." Jackie was drying her hands as she came from the kitchen. "We just finished breakfast and was talking about our girl's cruise. What's wrong? You all look like somebody died."

Nancy and Ms. Sylvi both came from the back bedrooms. "Good morning guys. Bryan too. What's going on? Why is everybody here this early? If the look on everyone's face is any indication, then I probably don't want to hear it." Nancy took a seat beside Jackie as Ms. Sylvi sat in her favorite chair.

Chrystal still stood in the middle of the floor. "Are the kids still asleep?" She twisted the engagement ring on her finger that Tyler had given her. She didn't want to really talk about what she came for. "I figured they would be full of energy by this time."

"Well they were about five thirty this morning. I fed them and watched some cartoons with them. I guess all that jumping around tired them out. Jade fell asleep in my lap. Jewell and Oro followed not too long afterwards. But I know you didn't come this early and with Bryan and everybody to discuss that. What's really going on?"

Jackie tried to smile as she looked from Chrystal to Tyler. She sat up straighter in her chair, bracing herself for whatever was to come.

"No Mama, we didn't come this early to talk about that. I really don't know how to tell you. I'm ashamed about my part in it as well as daddy's."

Nancy glared at Bryan and asked, "what does Jimmy have to do with anything? I thought we had put all that behind us. Don't tell me that snake is up to something else."

Chrystal spoke up again still fingering her ring finger. Please, don't look at Bryan like that. He had nothing to do with this. In fact he tried his best to stop daddy, but you can see it didn't go well. That's why he's here with us now. I'm going to try and tell you all everything that went on. Like I said, I have done some things that I am ashamed of, but please let me get the whole story out before you say anything."

For the next half hour, Chrystal told her family everything that had occurred from the disastrous situation with Omar, Oro's father, down to the drug dealing criminals, Smoke and Duck. She had told Royce some of the story the night before, but even he didn't know the full extent of their father's treacherous behavior.

Chrystal mentioned Nikki's part in getting Jimmy in contact with Smoke and Duck to get Omar out of her life. She told them how she found out from Smoke how Jimmy had been using them to hurt people, and how Jackie and Eric were on his hit list. She concluded with her plea to Jimmy to come clean, but instead it ended up with Bryan leaving Jimmy because of his horrible actions.

Chrystal had tears in her eyes as she finished. "Okay, now you can say whatever you have to say."

Jackie had stood up during the time it took for Chrystal to finish her story. She now paced back and forth from the front door to the sofa. "This is totally blowing my mind. In all my dealings with Jimmy, I never would imagine he could be this despicable. This horrible. He is just . . . I don't know what to say. I can't think. Bryan, I'm sorry for you. I . . ."

"Sit down before you walk a groove in the floor." Nancy tried to grab onto Jackie's arm as she made a turn from the sofa. "For some reason this doesn't surprise me. In my heart, I've always distrusted him. He's one of those disgusting two-faced kind of men. They laugh with you, all the while they have a knife ready to slip between your ribs."

Ms. Sylvi finally raised her head from where she had hung it on her chest while listening to Chrystal. "My Lord, my Lord. You mean he was really going to pay these criminals to hurt Jackie and Eric, just because his feelings where hurt? Never in my life would I believe he would do that. Satan is alive and working. Jimmy, my Lord, what an evil man."

"I'm so sorry. I never meant for any of this to happen. I believed daddy when he said he wanted to help me. All these years, he hid his real self from me. I loved him and I trusted him. You got to believe me. I never knew he would do the things he has. I never meant, I just, I don't know . . ." Chrystal buried her face in her hands and let Tyler pull her to his side.

Royce looked to his mother and saw the sadness taking over her face. "Mom, I'm so sorry. I feel like I should have known.

Dad was always carrying on about one thing or another to do with you, but I never thought he would go this far. When Chrystal told me he had put Bryan out and refusing to come clean about all of this; I was astonished. I'm so sorry."

"It's gonna be all right. Royce, you couldn't have known. You don't have that type of abilities. And, Chrystal don't cry baby. You didn't do this either. Your father has always been a manipulator. He's the evilest bastard in the world. It's in his DNA apparently. You're just as much a victim as the rest of us. You did what any young girl and woman would have. You love your father and look up to him. Don't ever blame yourself for loving someone. It's just that he has so much hate in his heart. So much anger. It's scary what that can do to a person."

Quiet took over the room as each party thought to themselves. Every face held a look of tension, sorrow, and pity. Jackie went to Bryan's side and took his hand in hers.

"I have to apologize to you. For more years than I want to admit to, I have blamed you for Jimmy's behavior. I blamed you for Jimmy's lack of love towards me. I blamed you for my failed marriage and in some ways I blamed you for making me feel less of a woman."

"Stop, you don't have to apologize to me. Believe me, I never wanted to live the way Jim thought we should. When I met Jim in college, he was such an innocent boy. He was shy and standoffish. But he had been brainwashed by his father to believe a certain way. To act like this macho man. He was hurting so badly. It was hard to get him to love himself or anybody else."

Bryan stopped and dropped his head again. "Unfortunately you happened upon him when he needed a woman to appease his father. I was so jealous of you. You got to live openly with

Jim, while all I got was to be kept in the closet. You had his children and he could openly show you his love. And believe it or not, he still loves you. Of course I can understand if his actions makes all this sound like a lie."

Bryan slowly looked around the room at all the faces. Each face held a look that ranged from pity to disbelieve. It made his insides churn. He continued with his truth, even though he only wanted to run and hide.

"It was a terrible way to live, and I hated every day that I was forced out of his life. But now, what he has done is beyond redemption. I never knew he had planned to do you, and Eric harm. I found out by accident just the other day. Believe me I would have put a stop to it if I had known. I have kept quiet and buried my head in the sand over a lot of things Jim did, but even I can't make up an excuse that's good enough for me to convince you, to forgive him. In fact, for once I don't believe I can forgive him."

Epilogue

Saturday, June 17ᵗʰ, 10:00am - Jimmy's home

James Jimmy Mattock the second, sat in his favorite leather chair. The chair that was so soft and buttery that it molded itself to Jimmy's buttocks. He continued to drink his whiskey from a ten ounce water glass. He had long ago substituted it for the little snifter that held only a couple of ounces. He had never gone to bed, nor had he had any solid food since way before the others left his home hours ago.

"Good riddance to you too," he slurred. He glared at the portrait on the wall. "So what you keep looking at me for? I'm a man. I will not be intimidated by you, Bryan, Chrystal, whoever. Jackie, damn you to hell! You're just a skank that I needed to play a part. You don't scare me!"

He yelled this last sentence as if waiting for the man in the portrait to jump off the wall and challenge him.

"They think they can tell me what to do. I do what I want. My own damn father can't tell me what to do. They think they won. Well they got another think coming, cause I don't care. I don't give a fuck about any of them. They can all rot in a deep grave. It's all Jackie's fault. That bitch. I never should have married her. She corrupted my baby girl. She did this. She made me do this."

He continued to rant at all the people he blamed for this accursed place he found himself in. He cursed his father and his people and his people's people. He called Jackie every foul name he could think of and then made up a few. For Bryan, he held a special bitterness as he called him traitor, turncoat, son-of-a-bitch, whore and anything else that flew through his mind.

Jimmy drained his glass again. He stumbled to the liquor bottle sitting on the cabinet. It was empty and there didn't seem to be another bottle handy. He looked at it as if he couldn't believe it. "I'll be damned. You run out on me too. You just as worthless as they are."

He pitched the empty bottle towards a trash can beside his chair. He missed and laughed hysterically when the bottle bounced and rolled towards the fireplace. As the laughter turned to ugly crying, he slid to the floor. He lay in a heap on his expensive Burmese rug. A pain unlike any he had ever felt before, ripped through his chest. Even still he raged against the unfairness of it all.

"I don't give a fuck. I don't need none of y'all. You'll come begging me to take your sorry asses back and I'm just gonna laugh in your face." He continued to cry from the excruciating pain stabbing behind his ribs, but he shouted even louder, "I'd rather die on this damn rug, than ever have one of you fuckers in my house again."

As the gentleman in the portrait on the wall looked on in silent judgement and condemnation; James Jimmy Mattock the second, slowly rolled to his back and closed his eyes. A lone crystal clear tear escaped his closed lid and gently slid down his cheek, for the last time.

Who Commanded?

I saw dazzling crystal clear light
Emptied from a cloudless sapphire sky
From that same sky now ashen, rain
And I wondered, who commanded?

I saw liquid more precious than gold
Shower down over all the earth
All nature was thoroughly nourished
And I wondered, who commanded?

I felt frozen flecks of wonderment
Glide by my now cooling cheek
More diverse than the blades of grasses
And I wondered, who commanded?

Amazingly, now came sizzling lightning
Lashing daggers beyond my reasoning
Followed by sound so bold and fearsome
Again I wondered, who commanded?

Now a peaceful breeze sailed by my brow
Soothing the strange fear from my face
Heralding a majestic grandly power
Without a doubt I knew, who commanded!

The story that started it all

Now available on Amazon

The Color Of Your

Tears

The Color of Your Tears
A novel by Barbara Combs Williams

When their son Royce came along, Jimmy completely forgot about their daughter Chrystal. Jackie remembered a little three year old Chrystal looking at her as she fed baby Royce, saying; "daddy loves him more, he don't piggy-back ride me no more." And Chrystal would cry big golden teardrops and Jackie's heart would break, because she knew it was true.

Maybe it was because Chrystal was conceived in desperation that made her so volatile, so unstable. Chrystal was so fussy as a baby that only Jimmy could handle her. She cried for whatever she felt she didn't have at the time. Nothing Jackie did for her was good enough.

Or was it because she wanted so badly to have a baby, thinking it would take away all the troubles in her marriage? She had done everything in her power to make a baby. And she was successful.

Royce on the other hand was conceived in joy and love. Royce was a good baby. A simple silly face would make him giggle and coo. She had never been in a better place in her life than when she carried Royce. It brought Jimmy back home and he rubbed her back and stomach for her. He did everything he could to live up to his vows.

About the Author

Barbara Combs Williams is a Georgia native. She is unapologetically old school and southern grown.

She lives in the country with her husband of over forty years. She enjoys growing flowers and watching the hummingbirds poke their beaks in the blossoms. She hopes everyone can identify with her writing, and if you haven't yet, just wait; you will.

Chrystal Clear is the second novel of the Mattock family saga. See *The Color of Your Tears*, the first novel that introduced us to Chrystal's mother, Jackie.

Other books by the Author
Soul Catcher, A Simple Maiden's Tales
Leighanne Abigail Hortense Packracker and Her Magical Growing Shoes, a children's story

Please see Barbara's website at:
www.BarbaraCombsWilliams.com

A Remember Too Design
©2020